LEGENDS OF THE
LOST CAUSES

BRAD MCLELLAND & LOUIS SYLVESTER

SQUARE
FISH

HENRY HOLT AND COMPANY

NEW YORK

SQUARE FISH

An imprint of Macmillan Publishing Group, LLC
175 Fifth Avenue, New York, NY 10010
mackids.com

Square Fish and the Square Fish logo are trademarks of Macmillan and
are used by Henry Holt and Company under license from Macmillan.

Our books may be purchased in bulk for promotional, educational, or business use. Please
contact your local bookseller or the Macmillan Corporate and Premium Sales Department at
(800) 221-7945 ext. 5442 or by email at MacmillanSpecialMarkets@macmillan.com.

Library of Congress Control Number: 2017945043

ISBN 978-1-250-29427-2 (paperback) / ISBN 978-1-250-12433-3 (ebook)

Originally published in the United States by Henry Holt and Company
First Square Fish edition, 2019
Book designed by Liz Dresner
Square Fish logo designed by Filomena Tuosto

10 9 8 7 6 5 4 3 2 1

AR: 5.3 / LEXILE: 760L

PART 1

THE HOME FOR LOST CAUSES

OCTOBER 1855

CHAPTER 1
BAD WHISKEY

Keech Blackwood splashed up from the cold waters of the Third Fork River and blinked at the bright autumn sun. Sam was standing on the bank, holding the prized musket stick and hooting laughter.

"I finally got you!" Sam shouted. "I finally put you down!" Overcome by his victory, the boy bounced on one foot and started a champion's dance.

They had been awake since first light, exploring the lush northwestern Missouri hills. Sometime after setting out, Sam had spotted a plump cottontail, his favorite animal, and Keech had cooked up the idea of tracking the critter and snare-trapping it for practice.

They set the rabbit snare using a couple of oak branches, a bent-over sapling, and a strand of dogbane for the noose. After waiting a whole precious hour for the animal to reappear, Sam lost all patience and offered a second suggestion: a game of Grab the Musket.

The boys had wandered down to the river searching for a long stick. Keech found a strong lacebark limb half-buried in the frosty mud. He washed the limb in the river, and then both boys stripped off their shirts and boots and squared off on the dark riverbank soil.

Pa Abner had taught them Grab the Musket a few years earlier. The rules were simple. Both contestants took a firm grip on the stick and then squared their shoulders and dug their feet into the ground. Keech would yell "Pull!" and they would wrestle to yank the stick free. When they had first learned the game, Sam was an imposing competitor. But now that Keech was two months shy of fourteen, and had grown much taller than his toothpick brother, he could pull the musket out of Sam's grip every time.

Except today.

Sam had managed something new. When Keech pulled, the smaller boy stepped forward and pushed. Keech rocked off balance. Sam pivoted his heel and twisted his body to the left, and before Keech could figure out what was happening, the rascal yanked hard on the stick.

Keech released the musket as his feet slid out. For a weightless moment he felt disconnected from the world, like a bird in flight. Then he flopped into the chill waters of the Third Fork.

The moment he lifted his head from the river, Keech spotted a man on horseback with his hat pulled low, gazing down at them from atop the wooded hill.

"Sam, pause your prancing."

"Can't do," bellowed Sam. "The victory's too sweet!" His champion's dance continued.

The Third Fork River was wide and shallow at this edge, rising only to Keech's waist, the riverbed beneath his bare feet paved with smooth stones. He pulled a wet curtain of dark hair out of his eyes and focused across the open. The sun hadn't deceived him. There was a man on the hill, dressed in a long, black overcoat and mounted on a chestnut stallion.

"Hey, I mean it. We're being watched."

Sam turned to look. As if on cue, the man in the black overcoat called down, "Mornin', pilgrims!" and doffed his hat. His voice sounded wrong, as though speaking pleasantries was new to him. "Don't dash off, as I mean ya no harm!" The man dismounted, gathered his reins, and began to walk down the hill, the chestnut stallion in tow.

Sam held out the lacebark limb. "Here." Keech grabbed it and Sam helped him out of the river.

"Let's get back in our shirts and boots," Keech said. "If he means us ill, we may need to run."

Sam regarded the stranger with a frown. The narrow scar on the left side of Sam's face paled even whiter than usual, as it did whenever he got nervous. "I'm the Rabbit, remember? I can run just as fast in bare feet."

"Put your boots on anyhow."

Both boys hurried to slip their muddy feet into their boots and put their shirts and coats on. Keech grabbed his bowler hat and kept his eyes locked on the man, who continued down the hill.

When the stranger was about twenty feet away, he dropped the reins and smiled, revealing a mouth full of gaps. Now that he was close, Keech could see that the man's black overcoat was threadbare, riddled with holes in the elbows. He wore his trousers tucked into tall black boots and carried a heavy revolver on his hip, a Colt Dragoon with a glinting black barrel. Keech had never seen a real Dragoon before, but he recognized the revolver from a fine pencil drawing in one of Pa Abner's books.

"Quite a chill in the air this morn," the man said. He wore a long goatee pointed like a dagger at the end and greasy black hair drawn back into a ponytail. His left eye was yellowish and glazed over, surely blind.

Making sure his path to the trail was clear, Keech set his footing, ready to move in an instant should this man decide to get mean. He noticed Sam also steeling himself to run, just as Pa Abner had taught them to do if they ever encountered strangers with ill purpose. *Run first, live to tell*, Pa would always say, usually before their day's training began.

"Yessir, quite a chill," Keech replied. He fanned his wet bangs out of his eyes again and crammed his hat back on.

"This weather ain't so bad, I s'pose," the man said. "Could be worse. Farther north the brush rabbits have gnawed the sassafras sprouts down to nubs. Means a heavy snowfall comin' for those poor folk."

The stranger took a step closer. He reeked of pig slop, as though he hadn't taken a bath in weeks. "Why are you little pilgrims dippin' into icy rivers?"

Keech said, "We were playing war when my friend tripped me and I fell."

The man laughed—a slippery sound, full of bad air. "Ah, now I see why you was wrestlin' for that stick. You little pilgrims remember the Alamo! Which of you's Jim Bowie and who's got the awful job of playin' Santa Anna?"

"But we ain't playin' the Alamo," said Sam.

The man clicked his tongue. "A mighty shame you'd waste a chance to play Mr. Bowie. Can you name a more heroic figgur in all of history?"

"No, sir," said Keech, though he and Sam had both long ago agreed Davy Crockett was their favorite hero of the Alamo. "Sir, I do apologize, but we need to be getting home." He tapped Sam on the leg and they stepped away. A wind blustered and made every inch of Keech's damp skin bump with gooseflesh.

The man coughed into his fist. "Hold on there a tick, pilgrims."

Keech glanced back. "We must run off, sir. Time for chores." The boys increased their pace.

The stranger called after them. "But surely you pilgrims can tell me where I can find a man named Isaiah Raines?"

Keech was happy he'd never heard the name. "No, sir!" he called back.

The stranger said, "What about Abner Carson?"

The boys stopped in their tracks—that was their pa's name. Sam loosed a muffled gasp.

The man squinted at them, his yellow eye moist and dead.

"I was told down south somebody named Ab Carson might

know of Mr. Raines's where'bouts. You see, I got important business to conduct, so please tell me the way to Mr. Carson's doorstep. If he knows of Isaiah Raines, I sure would like to hear it."

Keech turned to face the dark man with the dead eye. "No disrespect, sir, but you're a stranger."

The man snorted surprise. "My apologies! I answer to 'Whiskey,' like the drink. Anyone who knows me calls me that."

"But we don't know you," said Keech.

Whiskey winked his good eye. "But ya do know Ab Carson. I can read that plain as dirt."

Sam leaned in close. "Reckon it's time to run?"

Keech whispered, "I have an idea."

He nodded to the stranger. "Yessir, Mr. Whiskey, I have heard the name. A few months back I went down to Farnham with my pa to buy a wagon. During our supper I heard a man at the next table say his name was just that, Ab Carson. He told a group of fellas he was traveling out west to seek the Fountain of Youth. I don't recall more since I was involved in that fat steak I was eating."

The man held up his hand. "Okay, pilgrim."

"I'm sorry your hunt's been for naught, Mr. Whiskey, but that's the lot of what I know. If you wish more, I'd suggest you go down to Farnham. It's about two days' ride." Keech turned and shoved at Sam. The boys started back into the woods.

Sam shot a backward glance at the figure. "That fella didn't believe a word of your nonsense story."

"Just keep moving. When he's out of sight, start running."

They were about to hurry off when Whiskey's gruff voice filled the air. "Hold up."

Again, both boys froze. The stranger picked up his reins and led his stallion closer. His free hand now hovered near his revolver.

"Keech, what do we do?" whispered Sam.

"Hush your tongue. If he goes for that gun, I'll clean his plow."

"But that's a Dragoon!"

"Quiet," Keech hissed.

Whiskey led his horse till he was roughly ten feet away. A vibrant wind rustled through the cottonwood trees, shaking branches and driving the man's stink right up Keech's nostrils. Whiskey said, "You heard the name of Abner Carson in the town of *Farmhan*?"

Keech considered changing his tale. There was a village called Farmhan up north, and sending this scoundrel up and down the state on a fruitless hunt seemed a worthwhile idea. But he worried that adding another layer of deception might bring the whole story tumbling down. "No, sir, Mr. Whiskey. I said I heard mention of Carson in *Farnham*. Down south."

The one-eyed man looked at Keech, then Sam, slowly tilting his head as though his single eye was staring through each of them. After a long, breathless moment, the man nodded.

"Farnham, then. I reckon I oughta let you pilgrims run along. I'd hate for ya to catch yer death of cold." On those words, Whiskey turned and led his horse back toward the river.

Keech and Sam didn't wait to watch the man depart. They ran into the woods, leaping over rocks and sliding down slopes, till the river was well behind. They allowed their pace to slacken only when they crested a final hill and saw the two-story farmhouse where they'd been raised.

They dashed across the property, the front yard camouflaged by heavy ranks of firethorn shrubs and weigela bushes. Sam slipped ahead, huffing, and as they approached the shakepole fence that bordered the yard, he hopped on one foot and smacked the painted sign that hung above the gate. Keech followed suit. It was always good luck to slap the sign on your way to the house. It was their beacon in the harsh frontier, a symbol of family, a symbol of strength. The sign read:

CARSON'S HOME
FOR LOST CAUSES

PROTECT US, ST. JUDE, FROM HARM

CHAPTER 2

THE GUARDIAN

Keech threw open the front door to find their brother Patrick waiting for them by the rumbling fireplace. The moment the small boy saw them, he jumped to his feet, bounded over to Keech, and squeezed his right leg in a bear hug.

"Keech! Sam! I've been waitin' all morning!" the boy yelled. His legs were uncovered, since he often forgot to wear any sort of trousers. In fact, his bare bottom was a common sight around the Home. At four years old, Patrick was the youngest of the five orphans. His blazing red hair stood straight out like a lion's mane, and smears of blackberry jelly stained his lips.

"Hey, flapjack," said Keech.

"I ate your biscuit while you was gone. Every last crumb."

"You better not have." Keech scooped up the half-naked boy in one arm and spun him around.

"Not yours. *Sam's*."

Sam gasped, and Keech snickered. "That's a good boy." He set

Patrick back down on the rug. "Now where's your undershorts? Your derriere's hanging out."

Patrick noticed his naked lower half. "Whoops."

"Scurry on upstairs and get dressed."

Patrick darted to the stairway and stopped. "Oh, I almost forgot. Granny Nell says she's gonna whip the both of ya for skippin' breakfast and mornin' chores." With a loud cackle, he then scrambled up the Home's spindle balusters.

Keech called after the boy, "You know you're not supposed to climb like that! Pa said you ain't no squirrel."

"I know I'm not!" Patrick hollered down. "I'm a monkey!"

As Keech hung his bowler hat on the front door rack, Sam frowned at the entrance to the kitchen. "If Granny's in a foul way, maybe we should head back out."

"And put an extra nail in our coffin? Best we just take our punishment."

No sooner did the words come out of his mouth than a voice rang out from the kitchen. "If you two so much as think about running off again, you'll be whitewashing shutters all the way to next Christmas! Now get your skinny hinds in here!"

Granny Nell was sitting at the kitchen table, sharpening a butcher's knife on a long whetstone. Stacked behind her on the counter, dirty breakfast plates awaited the daily chore of washdown and rinse-off. When she turned to inspect the boys, the blue ribbon holding back her silver hair came untied, dropping ringlets around her wrinkled face. Granny huffed a breath to move the hair out of her eyes. "First things first," she said. "Who is the culprit who left his Holy Bible sitting in the stairwell?"

Sam's eyes widened.

Granny Nell adjusted the black wool shawl around her shoulders. "Samuel, we may live in a home built square in the center of nowhere, but that does not mean you can act like a heathen. You are twelve years old and can use a bookshelf like the rest of us civilized folk."

"Yes'm."

She pointed to the bookshelf in the sitting room. "I placed your Bible there. Take care not to leave it underfoot. It'd be a terrible thing to murder an old woman with the Good Book."

Keech snickered—a dangerous mistake. Granny Nell turned her sharp, owl-like gaze upon him. "Do I hear laughter, Mr. Blackwood? From the boy who dragged poor Sam all over the countryside without his breakfast?"

Keech dropped his head. "We were tracking rabbits is all."

"Oh, tracking, were ya? Then tell me, Lewis and Clark, what do your keen eyes see when you gaze at yonder empty table?"

"That we missed a fine breakfast," lamented Sam.

"And what else do you gather when you see that barnload of dirty dishes?"

Both boys groaned.

───※───

Granny Nell finished sharpening her butcher's knife as Keech and Sam soaped and dried the plates. She stood to replace the cutlery. Although the shoulders beneath her black shawl were frail and her back slightly bent, she moved with an energy that rivaled young Patrick. One time Keech had seen her pick up two unruly shoats under each arm and haul them, squealing and kicking, back to the pigpen from where they'd escaped.

"I want that table wiped down to a perfect shine," Granny said. She cracked her old knuckles, a sound that sent the shivers through Keech. "I wrapped up some biscuits and placed them in the crock by the back door. When your chores are done, you may eat them. I wouldn't delay, though. I suspect Little Eugena will be prowling about any moment."

"Yes'm," Sam said, clearly worried. Their orphan sister Eugena—always referred to as *Little* Eugena for her size—tended to harvest up any seconds that might be available after a meal. But Keech figured they were safe for now. After breakfast and chores, Little Eugena usually disappeared into the woods for an hour to play her brass bugle, an instrument that Pa Abner had given the girl for her eighth birthday. Little Eugena resolutely believed that her dreadful-sounding contraption had once belonged to the 41st Regiment of Redcoats at the Battle of the Oakwoods in 1812. She played the bugle the way she ate her meals, with the fervor of a lunatic.

Granny Nell planted kisses on their cheeks, and all at once Keech's shivers were gone. "I want to see your smiling faces at breakfast tomorrow," she said. "If you behave till then, I'll make sausage links."

"That sounds nice," Keech said, hating that he and Sam had hurt her feelings. Granny had lived a difficult life, the worst of it many years ago when her husband had died over in Big Timber, the town a few miles east of the orphanage. The man's death had apparently been awful; he had been a slow victim of the disease everyone in the region called the Withers.

Keech remembered all the campfire stories about the Withers, the dreadful outbreak in the winter of 1832, the disease that took half the people in the county. If you died of the Withers, it was told, you got buried in Bone Ridge, the massive graveyard located somewhere out in the western wilderness. Most of the people in these parts knew the spook stories about Bone Ridge, and the old saying that went along with it:

> *Beware the high ridge made of bone.*
> *All those who enter turn to stone.*
> *Should you be there in deepest night,*
> *in moon as dim as candlelight,*
> *you'll stand alone as ready prey,*
> *until your soul withers away.*

As Pa Abner had once told it, Granny Nell's husband—a blacksmith named Abraham—had died in her arms, whispering her name as he had taken his last breath. He was buried out there in the west, in the vast expanse of Bone Ridge alongside the others, the unspeakable number of lost souls, taken by the Withers.

"Mr. Blackwood!" Granny barked. Her severe tone gave him a jolt, and he almost dropped a plate on the floor.

"Yes'm?"

"I've never known you to be so untidy at dishes. What's got into you?"

Keech hesitated. He was unsure if he should keep the morning's events down by the river a secret or come right out and spill every detail. As the oldest of the orphans, he had long taken upon himself the role of guardian for the others, which meant facing things they could not yet handle. Sam was twelve, and had practiced all the same training as Keech, had excelled at the forest lessons and games with Pa, but his own confidence sometimes misguided him. Little Eugena was nine but weighed barely fifty pounds after a hearty meal. Patrick had just turned four a month ago. Robby was eleven but had a crooked hand that sometimes slowed him down. Keech felt like most of his duty at the Home was to keep the others safe. The last thing he wanted was to scare anyone with tales of one-eyed strangers.

Then again, keeping secrets was a surefire way to upset the whole house.

Keech said to Granny, "This morning, out by the river, Sam and I met a traveler."

"Oh?"

"Yes'm. He rode a chestnut horse and had a long goatee."

"Was it a farmer up from Big Timber?"

"No, ma'am. He wore a long black coat and smelled worse than any farmer by a long sight."

"Lord, child, he got close enough to smell?"

"That ain't the curious part," added Sam. "This fella had a bad eye, like a pirate only without a patch. And he wanted to know the where'bouts of a man named Raines."

Granny Nell staggered as if she had been pushed. "Boys, tell me, who was this man?"

"He said his name was Whiskey, like the drink," Keech said. "He asked if we knew of any Isaiah Raines, because they had business. When we told him we didn't know the name, he wanted to know where he could find Pa instead."

"But on no counts would Pa have any dealing with such a fella," Sam said. "So we sent him down a false trail. Told him we'd heard the name all right, but that he'd headed out west in search of the Fountain of Youth."

Granny Nell lowered her silver eyebrows. "You lied to this man?"

"It was Keech's fib!" Sam said, quickly passing any blame.

Keech recognized his imminent danger. Of all the terrible things a kid could do, Granny Nell despised a lie the most.

"I didn't lie to be spiteful," he said. "The man didn't seem right, is all."

Granny pondered and then said, "You boys should have told me this before I made you wash the dishes. I want you to run to Pa right this minute and tell him everything you heard."

The boys turned to go.

"And Keech?"

He stopped, his boots skidding on the hardwood floor.

"Tell Abner every word. Leave out nothing."

"Yes'm," he said.

He stepped out the back door, and Sam followed.

CHAPTER 3

PA ABNER'S SECRET

Pa Abner was sitting under the shady overhang of the woodshed, a scrap of wood that would soon be a chair leg resting on his lap. The straps of his suspenders hung loose off his white shirt, and a sheet of sanding paper had been tied by a narrow string to his right hand. A thick brown beard covered Pa's face, but he kept the top of his head shaved close. To Keech, his head always looked a little bit upside down.

Pa didn't rise when they approached. "Well, well, it's the Wolf and the Rabbit, back from their adventure," he said, and continued to brush at the chair leg. Keech noticed that Pa's hands were splotched with dried red and blue paints. Sometimes at the break of day, Pa Abner woke up cantankerous from bad dreams. He made himself feel better by painting pictures on old newspapers in his study.

Across the yard, their brother Robby was sitting on a tin pail inside the chicken coop, hammering away at the edges of a roosting bar that had come loose from its frame. He held the end of the bar in place with his left arm, the hand of that arm curled dramatically under and the fingers twisted, and pounded home a nail with Pa's claw hammer. In the pigpen behind the coop, the sound of the hammering disturbed Granny's sow and her little brood. They squealed at the noise till Robby yelled at them to hush.

Robby had come to the Home a couple years ago, right after Keech had turned eleven, and had promptly taken to Pa's lessons on woodworking. Though his crooked left hand caused him much frustration, Robby still could craft the finest toys for Patrick and Little Eugena.

Pa Abner's hand slid the sanding paper across the chair leg. With each stroke, the trusty pendant he always wore around his neck, a silver charm attached to a black leather cord, swung back and forth. The ornament was a tarnished fragment of sorts, old and mysterious and shaped like a jagged quarter moon, as though it had been broken from a larger piece. Grooved lines and swirls that meant nothing to Keech decorated the pendant. He suspected the etchings had meant something important before the pendant was shattered.

This strange charm was at the center of Keech's earliest memory. He'd been three years old and something terrible had happened to his real parents, but he couldn't remember what that terrible something was. His only memory was of Pa Abner shouting while holding him in the crook of his arm. A whirlwind of dust flew about, and there had been a dry heat on Keech's cheek, a heat so intense he'd been forced to hide his face against Pa's chest. His hot cheek had touched the charm. His next memory was of an unnatural chill, like the coldest ice on Earth, pulsing out of the silver pendant.

In the years since, Keech had uncovered very few details about that day, not even his parents' names. Pa Abner refused to speak about anything related to the past. All Keech knew was that Pa had saved his life.

The memory of the charm was most likely a confused dream. One afternoon a few years back, Pa had stripped for his weekly bath and left the pendant resting on his nightstand. Keech had touched the metal, expecting bolts of ice to pulse through his fingers. But there was nothing. The charm was simply a piece of tarnished silver.

Still, Keech liked to think it brought his family a little extra luck.

Pa's discerning gaze shifted back and forth from Keech to Sam. "Something's got you two all lathered up," he said.

Sam nodded. "Granny sent us out to tell you about the man—the traveler."

"What traveler?"

"A fella who wore a black overcoat and rode a chestnut horse," Keech said. "And he carried a Colt Dragoon on his right hip."

"A Dragoon, you say." Pa mulled it over. "That's a whoppin' hog leg for these parts."

Just beyond the eastern wood line, Little Eugena's bugle honked and tooted a frightening, painful noise. When the sound petered out, Sam said, "He needed a shave. Had a goatee, all sharp at the end like a porky-pine."

"And one of his eyes"—Keech grimaced at the thought—"was dead and colored like the guts of a smashed slug."

The pleasant grin on Pa Abner's face dropped away. "Which eye was dead?"

"The left one," the boys said in unison.

Pa Abner stood. Sawdust sprinkled off his lap.

A low breeze swirled over the ground, summoning a loud stink from the pigpen. The constant work of Robby's hammer pounded in Keech's ears. "He told us his name was Whiskey."

Every last shade of color drained from Pa's face.

"Whiskey like the drink," Sam added. "And he asked about you, Pa."

Without turning, Pa Abner called out, "Robby, son! That board is done. I need you to come here."

Dusting chicken debris off his breeches, Robby crawled out of the coop and walked over.

"I need you to go round up Little Eugena," Pa said to the boy. "Then head to the house and gather up Granny and Patty."

Robby frowned, but Keech had never known the boy to argue or disobey. "Yessir," he said, and headed off to the woods to find the bugle player.

Pa turned his attention back to Keech and Sam. "Who *exactly* did this man ask about?"

"First he asked if we knew a fella named Raines," Keech said. "He claimed to have business with him."

Pa Abner peered across the land, observing the stubby tree line beyond the stable, then the long gravel road leading up White

Elm Peak and east to Big Timber. He gazed at the wooded Low Hill to the north. He turned back to the boys.

"I take it you didn't send him back this way."

"We pointed him down to Farnham. Told him you were headed out west, in search of the Fountain of Youth."

"You should've heard Keech spin that yarn," Sam said. "He was brilliant, Pa."

Pa Abner patted Keech on the shoulder. "Good work." But his compliment sounded distant.

After a silence, Pa said, "Boys, I do know this man. But I always called him *Bad* Whiskey, and when I knew him, he rode with a most terrible gang. They called themselves the *Gita-Skog*, a name stolen from the Abenaki tribes up north. Means 'big snake' or some such. I'm proud you both recognized his rotten character when you laid eyes on him."

"Do you think he'll find out Keech was fooling?" Sam asked.

From the other side of Low Hill, a dark bird cawed and took high to the air. Pa Abner watched it bank away toward the tree line. It was the only bird in the sky, and Keech didn't like the look of its cruel solitude. Only things that bullied were left alone.

Sam rephrased his question. "Will Bad Whiskey find us, Pa?"

His eyes still trained on the bird, Pa Abner said, "Yes. In fact, if I'm not mistaken, I'd say Whiskey is already here."

They followed Pa's gaze to the top of Low Hill.

A chestnut stallion had appeared in the distance, its rider framed in a cascade of morning sun.

Pa Abner patted sawdust off his hands. "Boys, when this man

rides up, you are to say nothing. Not a word about the others, and not about yourselves. Understood?"

Both boys nodded.

Pa turned to Keech. "And don't speak your last name. Mention nothing about 'Blackwood.'"

Keech meant to nod again, but frowned instead. He wanted to ask why his name was so important, but the expression on Pa's face told him the time for questions had finished.

They stood in silence as the figure in black rambled his way down Low Hill. When the rider drew near the shakepole fence, he called out, "Hello, the house!"

Pa Abner said nothing. The one-eyed man continued forward, easing his stallion through the open gate and giving a slightly amused gander at the painted sign announcing the Home for Lost Causes.

As he approached, the sunlight pulled more features out of his horse—details Keech had missed back at the river. The first thing he noticed was that the animal's ribs were peeking out from beneath the heavy cinches of his saddle. The critter was terribly underfed, and ridden too hard. The second thing was the brand. Ownership brands were located on the left or right hip in these parts, but this brand was in the dead center of the stallion's forehead. A spiral of some kind, coiling to a dark point under the horse's bushy forelock. Keech thought the brand was intended to be a flower.

More specifically: a rose.

When the rider got within fifty feet, Pa Abner held up a warning hand. "That's close enough," he called out.

Bad Whiskey reined in his steed. His good eye skimmed first Keech, then Sam. He offered the devilish grin of one who keeps unwholesome secrets.

"Howdy, old friend," the ragged man said to Pa. He doffed his filthy black hat. "Been a dog's age."

"Bad Whiskey Nelson," Pa said with a low voice. "As I live and breathe."

Bad Whiskey lowered his reins to let his mangy horse stand free. "How long's it been?"

"Since 1845," Pa said. "You oughta remember that date well."

"That's right! Spring of forty-five. My, how a decade does burn."

Pa Abner kept a watchful eye on the man's trigger hand. "Your standing here tells me the Reverend's woken in the Palace," he said. "Some devils just don't know when to stay down."

Bad Whiskey laughed. "You know as well as I do some devils can't be *put* down."

Pa Abner took only the slightest notice of the comment. "My boys tell me you've been looking for Raines."

"Indeed. The tall one there"—Bad Whiskey gazed at Keech—"he told me a grand tale about the Fountain of Youth or some such. But as I was circlin' down to Farnham, I remembered yer all finished huntin' for fountains, so I turned my mule around. Good thing I did."

"Well, I've got unhappy news, Bad." Pa Abner frowned at Keech, as though he didn't wish to keep talking in their presence. "Isaiah Raines is dead. Been dead a long time."

"He looks mighty fit to me." Bad Whiskey chortled.

Keech and Sam exchanged a bewildered look.

Bad Whiskey noticed their confusion. "Raines, don't tell me you've been *lyin'* to these little pilgrims?" He clucked his tongue.

Keech took one defensive step toward Bad Whiskey. "Mister, watch what you say about my pa."

Pa turned on Keech with clenched teeth. "I told you not to speak a word."

"But Pa, he's calling you a liar!" Sam said.

The next command was sharper than glass. "Silence, boys. I won't say it again."

Bad Whiskey's chortle turned into long, raspy laughter. "I feel sorry for you little pilgrims. Havin' gone yer whole lives thinkin' this man is Abner Carson, when in fact he is someone worse than me!"

Keech looked again at Sam, his head whirling.

Bad Whiskey went on. "Smart way to hide, I reckon. Change yer name, raise orphans in the middle of nowheres. No one'd ever guess an Enforcer lurked among 'em."

"State your business and leave us in peace," said Pa.

"Peace?" Bad Whiskey cackled. "Peace is for good men, Raines. And you and me, we ain't good men." He pulled a slender cigarette from his shirt pocket and stuck it between his lips. "Now, send them little pilgrims away so we can speak open."

Keech saw the unease in Pa Abner's eyes, and his heart galloped. "Pa, I'm sorry! I didn't know he'd track us back here."

Pa Abner dismissed the apology with a wave. "It's not your fault," he said, dropping his voice so that Whiskey couldn't hear. "What's important is you do what I say. Take Sam and hurry back inside. Bar every door. Tell Granny to get the kids up to my bed-room. I won't let that cur take one step near the house, but just to be safe, tell her to get the rifle down from the mantel. Wait there with her and help keep the others safe." Pa Abner worried at the whiskers above his lip, then added, "If anyone other than me tries to get in that room, do your best to slow him down. There are six shots loaded in the rifle. Granny Nell will make each one count, but she'll need you to keep the others clear."

Keech wanted to say he understood, but he felt strangely light-headed.

Tears rimmed Sam's eyes. "Is Whiskey gonna shoot you, Pa?"

Pa Abner offered a meager smile. "I doubt it, son. I reckon if he wanted me shot, he would have already pulled. Now get inside."

Keech and Sam were turning when Pa stopped them. "And boys? Don't forget your training."

Bad Whiskey reined his bony stallion left and right, as though impatient. But he was still grinning when he shouted, "Hurry up, Raines! My charger ain't fond of chicken manure."

Back inside the house, the boys worked together to lower the lock bar, then Keech crossed to the fireplace. Granny Nell and the others were gathered at the small window that overlooked the backyard. Patrick stood behind Granny's skirt, clutching the wooden stick-and-ball Robby had carved for him. Robby stood next to Little Eugena, their faces glued to the dusty glass to get a glimpse of the dark stranger. Little Eugena raised her brass bugle to her lips. "I'll play Pa a battle hymn!" she crooned, but Robby grabbed the instrument before the racket could sound. "You'll do no such thing."

Mounted on steel hooks above the mantel was Pa's Model 39 Carbine rifle. Keech grabbed the rifle and then faced the orphans. "Everyone upstairs into Pa's room," he ordered.

Granny Nell gasped at the weapon. "Heavens mercy, Keech, what are you doing?"

"Pa said to—"

Before he could finish, Granny snatched the carbine out of his hands. She inspected the cylinder for ammunition, then thumbed back the hammer. Her small, wrinkled hands looked strong and healthy around the gun. "You are only to touch this during lessons!"

"That's right, Keech, *Granny* will handle the shootin'," scolded Little Eugena.

"Not now," Sam told the girl. "Pa said everyone should get upstairs."

Granny raised an eyebrow. "He said upstairs? Not to hide in the cellar?"

"Up to his room," Keech affirmed.

Granny Nell appeared to consider this option, then called out, "Okay, everyone, you heard your big brother. Upstairs." When the kids didn't move, she stomped her boot heel. "Hurry up now! March!" Patrick dropped his toy and began to bawl. "Patty, no time for tears," she said. "Follow Robby." As smoothly as a practiced soldier, she chucked the rifle to one hand and scooted the orphans ahead of her with the other. The kids moved in a tight cluster toward the stairwell.

As Patrick passed, Keech scooped up the stick-and-ball and handed it back. "Everything's all right, flapjack. Just do what Granny says."

"Don't hurt anybody!" Patrick said, his hair pasted to his cheeks by tears.

Keech turned to Sam. "Go on up. I'll be back."

"Where are you going?" Sam had grabbed his Holy Bible and was holding the book close to his chest.

"Outside. Pa may need me."

"But he said to help Granny protect the little'uns."

"Then you stay and keep watch. I'm going back out."

"Pa will whip your behind!"

Keech shook his head. "Doesn't feel right to make him stand alone. I'll stay out of sight unless he gets in trouble."

Sam opened the door for him. A frigid breeze circled in from the porch. "Once you're outside, I'll throw the latch."

Keech nodded quickly, grabbed his hat, and slipped out. Before the bar locked in place, Sam shouted through the door, "Be careful!"

Keech passed the stretch between the southern edge of the Home and the chicken coop without the stranger or Pa spotting him. He paused behind the coop to catch a quick breath, ignoring the snorts of displeasure from Granny's sow in the pigpen. Keeping low, Keech scurried the remaining distance to the narrow back door of the woodshed and hurried inside. He squatted behind the workbench and peeked through a wide crack in the shed's front door, which had been left partly open. From this vantage point he could now clearly see Pa and the man in black.

Keech was panting so hard he had to cover his mouth, but he could still hear Pa's voice, filled with anger.

"I don't know where it is," Pa was saying. "Haven't known for a long time. That's not my life anymore."

Bad Whiskey grunted. "You swore an oath, Raines. All of ya."

"The Enforcers are disbanded. I have nothing to do with Rose or that blasted Char Stone. I care only for my kids now."

"Yer kids? Who gives a hoot about them? The Char Stone is all that matters."

"That foul thing is cursed, Bad. You and I both know what comes from it. It never should have seen the light of day."

"Yer a bad bluffer, Raines. You know where it is."

"If I did, I'd never let the likes of you touch it."

"You know what the Reverend will do if ya don't surrender it."

"I *know* what the Reverend would do if he got his hands on the Stone. It's you who don't know. You're under the control of a scorpion, Bad Whiskey. One day soon you're bound to get the stinger."

Keech tried to make sense of what was being spoken. Who was this Reverend and what was a "char stone"? Pa Abner had never breathed a word about either of them.

Bad Whiskey ground his cigarette butt into the dirt. "Give me the Stone now, or tell me the name of the Enforcer who's got it. Does Horner have it? O'Brien?"

Pa answered, "Ride off my property now or leave in a box."

Bad Whiskey bared what few teeth he had left. "You think yer the patron saint of orphans? You think this house washes you clean of yer sins?" He pointed a dirt-stained finger at Pa Abner's face. "You still belong to Rose. Nothin' can free you from that bond. Not even that silly trinket." He pointed at Pa's pendant, which gleamed bright orange in the rising sun.

With a sweep of his hand, Bad Whiskey snatched his Dragoon from its holster and leveled the barrel at Pa. Keech steadied himself for the deadly gunshot. Instead, Bad Whiskey said, "The amulet shard. Take it off."

"I figured Rose would want this," Pa said. "He's too vulnerable without it." He tugged at the charm's leather cord. With a snap the pendant came free. Pa tossed it aside. The gleaming pendant clunked in the dirt.

Bad Whiskey took three strides and came face-to-face with Pa. He pressed the end of the Dragoon against Pa's gut. Whiskey grinned, and from where he hid, Keech could see the shabby man's pink tongue through the gaps of his putrid teeth.

"Now take me to the Stone, Enforcer. Else I put a hole in yer gut and drag yer bleedin' hide across this county."

He cocked the revolver.

From the corner of his eye, Keech saw a coiled rope hanging by a peg on the wall next to Pa's work lantern. It was the rawhide lariat Pa Abner used for his rope lessons. The past couple of years Keech had grown lightning fast and dead accurate with the lariat. He could put his horse, Felix, into a fast gallop and lasso the head of a cedar post at ten yards. The barrel of a Dragoon might be no different, if he worked fast.

Pivoting on one foot, Keech grabbed the coil. He remembered one of Pa's rules of survival from their wilderness training: *Hesitation means death.*

Drawing a deep breath, he prepared his feet at the woodshed door. He had no plan other than to charge across the yard and rope the revolver out of Whiskey's hands, but before he could take another step, Keech saw an amazing thing.

Pa Abner moved with the speed of a striking rattler. His left hand lunged for Bad Whiskey's revolver, and his fingers wrapped around the cylinder. At the same time, he sank his thumb into the space under the Dragoon's hammer.

Bad Whiskey pulled the trigger. Instead of firing, the hammer landed without a sound on Pa Abner's thumbnail. The one-eyed fiend barely managed to grunt before Pa planted his right fist into the man's nose. Black blood poured from his nostrils. The man stumbled back, stepped on the tails of his own coat, and toppled to the ground. As he fell he lost his hold on the Dragoon, leaving the revolver in Pa's hand. Pa deftly spun the weapon and aimed it at the scoundrel's head.

Keech was so surprised, he could barely breathe.

"Here's what you're going to do, Bad," Pa said. "You'll forget you found Abner Carson, and you'll set your sorry rear back on that saddle and ride away."

"I am the *Gita-Skog*!" Whiskey spat. "Don't you know what I can do?"

Pa Abner squared his aim between the man's eyes. "A member of the *Gita-Skog* would never let his sidearm be taken. You may fancy yourself a part of that depraved militia, but I'd wager you lick their boots every day, low dog that you are."

"How dare you!" Bad Whiskey yelled.

"Tarry one moment longer, I'll make you eat dust."

The outlaw burned with fury. "I got a thousand eyes, Raines! And every one of 'em is now trained on you!"

Pa Abner dipped the Dragoon and fired a shot. The revolver thundered, and a cloud of dust kicked up between Whiskey's boots. He jerked backward in surprise. "Bullets won't stop me, Enforcer! I'll come for ya!"

"Mount your mangy horse. Don't look back, Whiskey Nelson, or it'll be the true end of you. I swear it will." Pa Abner stepped over to the fallen silver charm and scooped it back out of the dirt. In his hand it appeared to reflect the sunlight all the more brightly.

At the sight of Pa retrieving the charm, Bad Whiskey turned tail and ran for his mount.

Keech slumped beside the woodshed, the coil of rope hanging useless by his side. Pa Abner's back was to him, but once the outlaw had ridden away and disappeared over Low Hill, Pa turned toward him.

"What are you doing out here?" Pa hollered. He stormed at Keech. "I told you to take the kids and hide in the bedroom."

"Granny and Sam are watching them," Keech mumbled. He'd meant to speak loudly and courageously, but the look of righteous fury on Pa's face made him wince, though he knew Pa would never hurt him.

Pa's chest heaved. "Why in the name of Saint Peter are you carrying a rope?"

Keech hoped a respectable answer would pop into his brain. All he could muster was, "When Whiskey pulled his Dragoon, I thought I could help."

"With a lariat? Son, we were standing clear over there." Pa

pointed back to where he and Bad Whiskey had scuffled. "If you had run out, Whiskey would have shot you lifeless! You can't just rush an armed man, and you sure can't lasso a sidearm out of his hands. I thought I taught you to think before acting."

Keech's head dropped. "I'm sorry."

Pa Abner tossed the Dragoon onto the workbench. "You're a brave boy, Keech. Brave as any man I've ever known. But I worry that bravery will get you hurt. If you can help a man in need, fine. But remember, if you're ever in danger, *be smart*. Weigh every decision with care. And for Pete's sake, remember your training. You can't help anyone if you're lying dead in the dirt."

"I understand, Pa. I'll do better."

"Come here." Pa Abner wrapped his arms around Keech and squeezed. "You're practically a man now. But I hope you're not too old for one of these."

Keech returned Pa's hug.

Pa Abner broke away from the embrace and stepped over to the workbench to examine Bad Whiskey's Dragoon. Narrow slices of sun stabbed through the rusty holes in the tin roof and flickered on the revolver's black barrel. Keech thought the weapon looked far less frightening up close. He still couldn't believe how skillfully Pa had removed the Dragoon from Whiskey's grip.

But Keech couldn't shake an unpleasant thought. He didn't know who his pa was anymore. The man he'd known to be kind and strong had once been someone else. Perhaps someone wicked.

Sunlight flashed on the silver charm, which Pa tied back

around his neck. The metal now looked dull and lifeless compared to the gleam it had captured in the yard.

"Son, I need you and Sam to do me a favor," Pa said, his face bleak with thought. "I need you to saddle up Felix and Minerva and ride to Big Timber."

Keech was surprised. "Just me and Sam?"

"It's not safe for me to leave the Home undefended."

"Pa, what's going on?"

Pa Abner gazed out again at the northern forest, at the verge of Low Hill where Bad Whiskey had disappeared. Dark clouds had begun to amass over the land. "Not here. Let's head to the house. I have something to give you. And I'm afraid it cannot wait a moment longer."

CHAPTER 4

A MESSAGE OF GRAVE IMPORTANCE

Patrick and Little Eugena were hollering at the back door when Keech and Pa stepped inside. The orphans clutched the man's legs.

"Pa, you broke that man's nose!" Patrick yelled.

"I don't suspect it broke," Little Eugena said.

"He fell right to the ground. That means Pa broke it."

"Nuh-uh. He tripped on his coat. That's why he fell."

"Granny," Pa Abner said, working to pry the kids off his legs. "A little help."

"Sam, Robby, you heard your pa," Granny Nell told the older boys. "Let's go." Working together, they herded Patrick and Little Eugena to the other side of the house. Along the way, Sam glanced back with a wounded face, a look intended to make Keech feel guilty for excluding him. Keech only shrugged.

Pa Abner led him to the study, the small room next to the kitchen where Pa enjoyed his private readings and painting sessions. It was the room where the orphans received their weekly lessons on the Native peoples, particularly the Osage, who had once inhabited the river lands south of the county. Having been close friends with important Osage leaders, Pa kept the study festooned with a veritable treasure trove of gifts and traded objects—a beaded vest of red, yellow, and blue; a pair of dress moccasins; a hand-carved box full of sumac leaves and dried tobacco for smoking. It was here, in this room, that Keech and Sam had first learned how to make Osage parfleches from rawhide and how to speak the names of all the sacred animals of the forest.

"Shut the door," Pa said, as he sat behind his red cedar desk, one of the many pieces of furniture he had built for the Home.

Keech bolted the door and took a seat. His eyes drifted to one of Pa's paintings, a colorful but dreary portrait of a tall, lonesome mountain of red stone, painted over an old, yellowed page of the *Daily Missouri Republican* newspaper. A few ominous numbers were scrawled in black across the bottom. The image of the red mountain always gave Keech the willies and made him wonder what bitter secrets Pa could have possibly dreamed to conjure such an eerie landscape.

Pa folded his hands on the desktop. "Son, do you remember the new telegraph office in town?"

Keech knew the office in Big Timber well. The telegraph was five months old there and only ran across the state to the towns that could afford it. In a couple of years, word had it, every message in the States would be dispatched by telegraph and a person would be able to send a letter all the way to New York City in a matter of minutes. The owner of the Big Timber office—a lively, white-haired gent named Frosty Potter—had promised Keech a part-time job as a telegraph clerk once the company expanded.

Pa Abner said, "I want you and Sam to ride to Frosty's office and deliver a telegram. This task is of utmost import, so you and Sam must act like serious men. No shenanigans, understand?"

Keech nodded.

Pa Abner drew the silver pendant from his shirt. A solemn look fell over his face. "Remember what I've always told you and Sam? If you look hard enough—"

Keech finished the old proverb for him: "You might find two ways to look at a thing."

Pa smiled. "Just so." He lifted a wooden chest from the floor, a strongbox of stained oak secured by a lock with a narrow, strange-looking slot for a keyhole.

He then turned, bent, and slid the pendant into the warded lock on the oak chest. The fit was perfect in the narrow slot, a keyhole that Keech realized Pa had fashioned specifically for the silver charm.

Pa Abner turned the pendant clockwise. The opening hinges made a loud popping noise—the sound of old secrets coming to life.

He opened the chest and reached inside.

What came out was a folded piece of paper, a document sealed with a fat dollop of stamped scarlet wax. The wax made the paper look threatening, as though blood itself had done the sealing. Pa handed the paper to Keech. When Keech turned it over, he could see the faintest impression of Pa's handwriting visible through the paper.

"This here is a letter that needs to be telegraphed to a man who lives in Sainte Genevieve," Pa said. "Do you know where that is?"

Keech shook his head.

"It's a good ways down the state. On the west bank of the Mississippi. Tell Frosty this message must go to an old friend named Noah Embry. Do you have that? *Noah Embry*. Memorize the name."

"Noah Embry," Keech repeated.

"That's right. In Sainte Genevieve. And make sure Frosty puts in all the stops. It's important this letter reads exactly as written. Say all that back."

"Mr. Potter is to wire the letter to Noah Embry of Sainte Genevieve."

"And what else?"

"He's to put in all the stops. Make the letter exact."

"Very good."

Keech examined the sealed paper. This note had something to do with Bad Whiskey's arrival; he was sure of it. Maybe something to do with Pa's old life as a man named Isaiah Raines.

"After the telegram is sent, I want you to stand and watch Frosty burn it." Pa leaned forward. "He is not to throw it away, but to burn it to ash. It's very important this letter be destroyed after it's sent. This world has many crows, Keech, and those crows can see far, and take what they see to dangerous places."

"Crows?"

"I don't want to say too much. But when you were hiding in the woodshed, I'm sure you heard Bad Whiskey speak of the Reverend, did you not? Tell the truth."

"Yessir," Keech said.

"This Reverend is a terrible man, Keech, and not what folks think. Neither are the crows that follow his men."

"Pa, does this all have to do with the . . ." Keech rooted through his memory for the proper name. "The Char Stone?"

Pa's face darkened. "Never mention the Stone again. Forget you ever heard of it."

"But what is it?"

"A cursed thing. But it's gone, never to be touched by another man."

"Gone where?"

Pa gritted his teeth. "Beyond reach. I have taken precautions. I'll say no more."

"What about Whiskey?" Keech was so full of questions he was almost bursting. "Why'd he call you Isaiah Raines? And what's an Enforcer?"

A small silence. "Someone I used to be, a long time ago. There were many of us, and we followed a man, an explorer. He called himself the Reverend Rose. He was a missionary, of a sort, and we were his disciples. We did everything he ordered."

"Bad things, Pa?"

Pa Abner's eyes cast down to his desk. "We had forgotten where we came from. We had forgotten our honor. Then one day things turned worse. Far worse. Six of us abandoned him, and scattered to the wind. The rest of his Enforcers, the ones who stayed loyal, changed their name. They now go by the *Gita-Skog*."

"And they're hunting you," Keech said.

Pa nodded. He seemed to be holding something back. "Someday, son, I swear to tell you everything. All I'll say now is, the day your real ma and pa died, Bad Whiskey Nelson was there."

Keech's mind churned with memories of screaming. Of dry, burning heat. A whirlwind of dust and terror.

"Did he kill them?" he asked.

Pa Abner heaved a sigh. "Just know Whiskey is only a messenger. Less than pig slop and doesn't deserve an ounce of the life given to him. He's not the one to be concerned about."

"Pa, did he kill my folks?"

Another silence. Then: "He was part of the gang that did, yes."

Keech didn't quite know how to feel about this news. All his years of wondering who had killed his parents, and one morning the very rattlesnake responsible comes riding up to his home.

"I wish you had just killed him," he said.

"Killing is never the answer, boy. Bad Whiskey is lower than dirt, but killing him wouldn't have solved anything."

Keech felt his face go red with shame. But it didn't change the fact that Bad Whiskey was now free to torment his family all over again.

"Keech. Son." Pa's solemn voice pulled him back into the moment. "The message on this telegram is of grave importance. Send it, and then have Frosty burn it."

Keech slid the paper into the chest pocket of his coat.

"Consider it done, Pa. But why does Sam have to go? Shouldn't one of us stay and help you guard the Home?"

"Remember—work as two, succeed as one. Sam is your left hand, and you are his right. God forbid there's trouble, but I want you to have backup in case."

So this excursion to Big Timber was no mere chore. It was a *mission*—his and Sam's very first, outside the forest training Pa had given them—and a mixture of excitement and fear rattled Keech's stomach at the thought of it.

Pa Abner put a hand on Keech's shoulder. "You've always been strong, son. You will accomplish great things. I can feel it. Now go fetch Sam. You two have a lot to do and little time to get it done."

CHAPTER 5
The Code Breakers

Keech rounded up Sam and then escaped the house without drawing too much attention.

"Where are we going?" Sam asked.

"Big Timber, to deliver a telegram."

"By ourselves?"

"I'll explain on the way," Keech told his brother. "We best hurry. If Little Eugena finds out what we're up to, she'll start a mutiny."

Still clutching his Holy Bible, Sam nodded.

Inside the stable, Felix and Minerva were grazing side by side on thick mounds of hay. The boys set to work saddling the ponies.

As they finished up, Pa stepped inside the stable, holding two small bundles. "Here's a couple of ham and egg sandwiches for the road. Granny's afraid you'll waste away if you don't eat something."

The boys tucked the lunches into their saddlebags. Sam had a difficult time fitting his bundle inside, as he had stuffed his Bible into the bag.

After the boys mounted up, Pa Abner asked Keech, "Remember everything I said?"

"Yessir."

"Good." Pa Abner then delved into his trouser pocket and pulled out a small leather purse, cinched at the mouth by a piece of yarn. "Here's thirty-one cents. Normally a message is a penny a word, but I'm giving you enough in case Frosty charges for each letter."

He handed over the purse. Keech let the pennies join the telegram in the chest pocket of his coat. Pa added, "If there's money left over, buy everyone a licorice wheel at Greely's."

"Yessir."

Pa looked at them with a sad smile. "I want you to know, I'm proud of you both. And I am truly sorry I brought this cursed man down upon us."

Keech found he could say nothing, and neither could Sam. It was troubling to see Pa so fretful over the sudden ghost of his past.

"Now, you two get on the road," Pa said. "I want you back in time for supper."

He slapped Felix on the hind, sending a cloud of dust flying from the animal's rear.

As the ponies crossed their way to Big Timber Road, a strange premonition sank over Keech. He felt that things would be changed before springtime's first bloom. He couldn't guess what might happen, but with Bad Whiskey's arrival and Pa Abner's peculiar behavior, he could sense the coming of something terrible. A vicious thunderstorm blowing straight in their direction.

❦

Less than half a mile down the road, Sam could not contain himself a moment longer.

"All right, what in blazes is going on?" he said.

"Don't you worry about it." Keech gazed off into the woods, pretending a deep study of the trees.

Sam leaned across Minerva and yanked Felix's reins out of Keech's hands. Startled, the big horse stumbled through a large puddle.

"Give those back!"

"Only after you spill the beans."

"They're not my beans to spill," Keech said. "They're Pa's."

"And Pa's back at the house, ain't he."

Keech was itching to tell the secret of Pa Abner's letter and figured Sam would find out soon enough. "All right. I reckon it won't hurt to show you."

He tugged the telegram out of his pocket and passed it to Sam.

Sam gave the paper a long look. He rotated the letter in the faint sunlight. "What's it say?"

"No idea," Keech said. "But Frosty Potter has to send it."

"To who?"

"Some fella named Noah Embry. Pa made me memorize the name."

"Who's that?"

"How am I supposed to know? Now give it back."

Sam ran his finger across the seal. "Let's break it open."

"The devil we are!" Keech tried to snatch the paper, but Sam held the letter out over the gravel, as if to drop it in one of the icy puddles that pocked the road.

"You grab after this letter, Blackwood, I'll send it to a watery grave."

Keech recoiled. "Pa said no shenanigans. He'll tan your hide."

"I'd say a gust of wind caught the paper out of your hand. Pa would ask why you was fooling round with it in the first place. His wrath would fall square on your shoulders."

Here they were, less than fifteen minutes down the path, and they were already in danger of failing their first mission.

Sam said, "Hear me out. We're gonna have to open it for Mr. Potter, right? Well, why not here and now?"

"But Pa said Mr. Potter was to burn it."

"Which is why we ought to go ahead and read it now, while we still can."

Keech pondered. On the one hand, Pa had sealed and locked away the message for a reason. But how could he object to the boys knowing the contents? Besides, Pa had hidden his fair share of information. You should guard secrets only from enemies, not family.

"Well?" Sam said.

"You're right. Let's have at it."

Sam snapped the seal. As the scarlet wax crumbled into the boy's lap, Keech felt a wave of guilt slam through his gut. Pa

Abner had warned them to act like serious men and not give in to horseplay.

As soon as Sam unfolded the paper, Keech leaned headlong over the space between them and yanked it back out of his hand.

"Hey!"

"Take it easy. I'll give it back."

Allowing Felix to set his own pace, Keech read the contents of the strange telegram aloud:

$$N \; E$$
$$39 \; 3{:}1.$$
$$52 \; 5{:}2.$$
$$26 \; 7{:}25.$$
$$40 \; 24{:}42.$$
$$A \; C$$

"Well, I'm up a stump," he said. "Pa said this note was to be sent word for word, but there ain't no words here at all. How can a pile of numbers and letters be of grave importance?"

"My guess, it's some kind of cipher," Sam said.

"Of course! A code." It did seem probable, given Pa's secrecy. "What do you reckon it means?" Keech asked.

"Well, I don't think the '*NE*' at the top is a real word at all. I think it's initials."

"For Noah Embry. That one's easy enough."

"And *AC* stands for Abner Carson."

"Right. But what about the rest?"

Sam shrugged. "Are you sure Pa didn't say anything else?"

"Only to make sure Mr. Potter put in all the stops." Keech pointed to the periods behind each line of numbers.

"So each group of numbers is a sentence."

"I reckon."

"But how can a whole sentence be said with only four or five numbers?" Sam asked.

Properly confused, the boys pushed the ponies on to Big Timber. Keech wrapped his reins around the saddle horn, freeing his hands so his finger could move over each line of numbers.

Soon the horses drew near Copperhead Rock, the enormous brown boulder that sat at the weedy verge of Big Timber Road. As the boys approached the rock, Keech noticed something about the telegram. He sat up straight on his saddle.

"Wait just a second."

"What is it?"

"The colons! I'll be blasted if it's not a message after all. Just the kind you've got to turn to a *book* to read."

"What book?"

Keech grinned.

"Confound it, Keech, what book?"

Keech pointed at Sam's saddlebag. "Reach back and open your pack, Sam. I'll show you what book."

Sam retrieved his Bible from the saddlebag and rested it across his lap. He kept the tattered strip of ribbon inside marked upon the book of John, chapter 3, verse 5: "Except a man be born of water and of the Spirit, he cannot enter into the kingdom of God." It was Sam's favorite passage in the Good Book because Pa Abner, having once owned the old Bible, had underlined the verse a long time ago and penciled a big star beside it, and whatever Pa liked and thought was important must be true and good, Sam always said.

"Okay, so what's my Bible got to do with anything?" Sam asked now.

"I can't believe I didn't see it right off," Keech said, holding up Pa's letter, "but all these numbers, they aren't gibberish at all. They're *verses*. That's what the colons mean. Pa's telling Embry to read certain passages from the Good Book."

"Well, I'm a regular beef-head!" Sam said. "How'd I miss that?"

"What threw us off was the first number in each row. They must stand for books in the Bible."

Sam nodded in excitement. He turned to his Bible's table of contents and began to search down the list of books. "So where Pa's note says 'thirty-nine,' that's Malachi, the thirty-ninth book, the last book in the Old Testament. Fifty-two is First Thessalonians, see. The twenty-sixth book is Ezekiel, the prophet's book, and the fortieth is Matthew, the first gospel in the New Testament."

"I guess I didn't know Pa knew so much about the Bible. So what do the verses say?" Keech called out the numbers marked in the telegram: *39 3:1.*

Sam flipped to the proper page. "This first one is Malachi 3, verse 1. It says, 'Behold, I will send my messenger, and he shall prepare the way before me: and the Lord, whom ye seek, shall suddenly come to his temple, even the messenger of the covenant, whom ye delight in: behold, he shall come, saith the Lord of hosts.'"

"What's that supposed to mean?" Keech asked.

"Maybe nothing, unless we keep reading the verses. What's next?"

Keech read off the numbers and Sam flipped through the Bible again to locate the next book. "This second passage is First Thessalonians 5, verse 2. It says, 'For yourselves know perfectly that the day of the Lord so cometh as a thief in the night.'"

"That's about the Second Coming," Keech said.

Sam's fingers flew across the yellowed pages. When he got to Pa Abner's third passage, he hesitated. "Okay, this one is worrisome."

"What does it say?"

"It's from Ezekiel 7, verse 25. 'Destruction cometh; and they shall seek peace, and there shall be none.' Sounds like a war."

Keech had long supposed the Bible was meant to offer comfort, not stir intense apprehension.

Sam raced to find the last verse, the passage labeled *40 24:42* in the note. After he found the passage, he said, "Matthew. Chapter 24, verse 42. In this one Jesus himself spoke the words."

"Do you think that matters any to breaking the code?"

"Maybe."

"Go ahead. Read it."

"'Watch therefore: for ye know not what hour your Lord doth come.'" Sam rested the Bible on his lap. "That's it. All the passages."

The more Keech thought about it, the more the verses sounded like a warning. "'Behold, I will send my messenger,'" he told Sam. "That could be referring to Bad Whiskey. Earlier, when Pa gave me the letter, that's what he called Whiskey: a messenger. He said Whiskey wasn't the man to be concerned about, but another fella pulling Whiskey's strings."

Sam shivered a little. "The second verse, the one that talks about the Lord coming back like a thief, could mean Whiskey might be paying another visit."

"Or the string-puller. Whiskey did keep talking about a reverend like he was in charge."

"But what kind of reverend would give a mongrel like Whiskey the time of day?"

Keech shrugged. "Then there's the third line. 'Destruction cometh; and they shall seek peace, and there shall be none.'"

"Whatever that means, it sure don't sound good."

Keech remembered Bad Whiskey's warning that Pa turn over some kind of object—the Char Stone—or face destruction.

After a silence, Sam said, "A reverend and a messenger. Sounds downright scary."

Keech nodded. "'Watch therefore: for ye know not what hour your Lord doth come.' Sam, I think after what happened earlier, Pa Abner's trying to warn this fella Embry of some sort of attack."

"I believe that, too."

The boys swapped a gloomy look. All around, the lanky trees rocked in the wind. Keech couldn't help remembering all the endless hours of training in the deep woods, the lessons on tracking, course plotting, engaging enemies hand to hand. For years he and Sam had both considered Pa's training to be nothing more than pleasant adventures. But now, the purpose of his training seemed to be preparation for coming destruction.

"Maybe we ought to get this letter sent," Sam said. The scar on his cheek—the result of a tomahawk wound earned during a training game a few summers back—gleamed a nervous white.

"I think you're right." Keech looked again at the sky, which had turned the color of moldy clay. "With those clouds rolling in, we'll want to hustle to get home before dark."

"Do you really think Pa's in danger?" Sam asked.

"After what he did in the yard, I think Bad Whiskey's the one who needs to worry. Still, we ought to be there to help. Let's get this letter on the wire."

Clucking at the horses in unison, they drove on to Big Timber. As they traveled, Keech returned his gaze to the fretful sky. He didn't like the way the clouds were deepening, bunching together like the scales of a great armadillo.

But that wasn't the most worrisome part.

A lone black bird was drifting high above. The bird made no sound, only traced a steady course above the road. As if watching.

This world has many crows, Pa had warned, *and those crows can see far, and take what they see to dangerous places.*

Keech kicked his heels, urging Felix to quicken his pace.

CHAPTER 6

THE PEG-LEG BANDIT

After nearly an hour of riding, the boys topped a hill and saw the big weathered sign announcing:

**WELCOME TO BIG TIMBER
A FREE TOWN FOR ONE AND ALL
SLAVERS NOT WELCOME!
POP. 405**

"Big Timber," Sam said with relish.

As they started toward the final bend, Main Street and its tall buildings appeared before them. To the north stood the town's drugstore and barbershop, followed by the depressing front porch of Leonard's Mortuary. On the south side, Shady's Fruit Market burrowed inside the shadow of the lofty red building known as Greely's General Goods. A few steps farther stood Potter's Telegraph & Transport. Townsfolk traipsed up and down the wooden sidewalks.

"Let's get to Potter's," Keech said.

No sooner did they round the final curve than a terrible shriek whistled up the street, as though it was coming from the heart of the settlement.

"What in Sam Hill? Sounded like a screeching boar!" Sam gasped.

"That was no boar." Keech reined Felix to a careful stride. "It was a woman screaming."

Another furious shout echoed from the same direction.

All along Main Street, Big Timber residents went scurrying in panic. They sidestepped the muddy potholes in the street and disappeared into buildings for cover.

"What's happening?"

"A scuffle somewhere," Keech said, studying Main Street. "Keep your eyes open."

Moving toward Potter's, the boys passed a stock wagon parked outside Greely's. The wagon was piled high with feed sacks and digging tools, and looked as if it had been recently abandoned.

Keech was so focused on finding the source of the noise that he steered Felix right into one of Main Street's potholes. The pony's leg sank into mud, and he kicked with a surprised bluster. The world tilted and Keech toppled back over the gelding's rear. He landed with a painful thud on the wet gravel.

"Keech!" Sam exclaimed.

Keech shook mud off his hands. "I'm all right," he mumbled, feeling like a fool. This was the second time today he'd taken a tumble. He hopped to his feet and thwacked his head on a square-head shovel sticking out of the stock wagon.

Sam couldn't hold back a snicker. "Who taught you to sit on a horse—a drunken sailor?"

Keech rubbed his head. "You best keep this to yourself."

Sam reared back to laugh again, but a cracking gunshot roared across the town and the boy froze in his saddle.

At once, Pa Abner's lessons kicked in. Keech secured cover by ducking behind the wagon. "Sam, you're a sitting goose!" he shouted. "Find cover. Get out of the road!"

Sam bounded off Minerva, his boots splashing in a shallow puddle. As he hurried to join Keech, a second gunshot cracked down the street, followed by a third.

"Where's it coming from?" hollered Sam.

A fourth report echoed past.

"It's coming from Potter's Telegraph," Keech said.

He searched for a better hiding spot. In his mind he could hear Pa Abner speak one of his rules of survival: *If trouble stirs, get out of the immediate danger zone.*

"We have to get these ponies off the street. Keep your head low and follow me."

The boys peeked around the wagon's edge, saw that the way was clear toward Potter's, and bolted back into the middle of Main. When they reached the ponies, Keech patted Felix's nose, hoping to calm the skittish horse. Then he snatched up the reins and led him behind the wagon. Sam followed with Minerva.

"The feed sacks on this wagon should stop any lead balls," Sam said.

The door to Mr. Potter's office burst open and townsfolk

scampered out into the street. As they fled, one man yelled, "He's reloadin'! Every man for hisself!"

Another man squealed, "He's shot up the telegraph!"

A woman hollered, "Frosty's still inside! Frosty's still inside!"

Hearing that the telegraph had been destroyed filled Keech with dismay. But the fact that Mr. Potter was facing danger disturbed him more. Frosty Potter was a genial man, and the thought of his getting shot made Keech dizzy with concern.

Back up the street, the door to the sheriff's office burst open. A pair of lawmen rushed out, their Colt revolvers drawn. At the same time, Mr. Potter appeared in his doorway, the color of his face almost matching his snow-white hair. He made no attempt to flee, only called out something indiscernible to the approaching lawmen.

One of the officers, a broad, mustached fella Keech recognized as Sheriff Bose Turner, settled his large tan hat squarely on his head, whispered something to the other man, and continued marching down the dirt road toward Mr. Potter.

The other man, a skinny deputy with legs too long for his body, broke into a swift jog toward the dreary overhang of Leonard's Mortuary. He positioned himself behind an empty casket propped against the porch rail, giving himself a vantage point in case he had to back up Sheriff Turner with gunfire.

The sheriff paused a few steps from where Keech and Sam huddled behind the wagon. He considered the boys with almost casual interest. "Howdy, fellas. Keep your heads low," he said. Then he turned his full attention to Mr. Potter.

"Frosty, don't move; I'll get you out of this," Turner said. He took a step toward the telegraph office.

Mr. Potter's words were loud and clear: "Don't come any closer, Bose! He'll shoot!"

Something flickered in Mr. Potter's doorway. A ghostly face hovered in the dark interior. In the figure's right hand, the man held a small, black-barreled pocket revolver less than two inches from Mr. Potter's skull.

Sheriff Turner dropped to one knee and steadied his Colt. Behind the casket, Turner's deputy leveled his own pistol at the telegraph office. Turner yelled, "Drop your weapon, you mangy sodsucker!"

The ghostly man made no move to surrender. His voice sounded behind Mr. Potter's frozen form. "Back away, Sher'ff! Else I kill 'im dead."

Keech's mind reeled with scenarios, various situations that could help Mr. Potter out of his scrape. He could make a mad dash down the street, drawing attention and allowing the sheriff to flank the gunman. But Pa's voice spoke bluntly in his head: *You can't help anyone if you're lying dead in the dirt.*

He decided they should hold their ground at the wagon. For now.

Turner shouted again at the pale outlaw. "Come on out and we'll work this through. But leave the clerk unharmed."

"Master says I can kill any man I want!" The outlaw sounded sickly, as though on the verge of a coughing fit, yet there was a confidence in his simple words that chilled Keech.

The assailant shoved Mr. Potter out the door and the clerk

stumbled onto Main Street. The bandit reached out and coiled his arm around Mr. Potter's throat.

The first thing Keech noticed about the brute, other than his pale features, was the odd shuffle of his body. The man had a peculiar right leg. It tapered to the ground like a fat pencil and was built entirely of wood. The point of the leg, the place where the foot should be, stabbed deep into the gravel.

"That fella's got a peg leg!" Sam whispered.

The gunman wore no hat or kerchief, and the long, greasy strings of his brown hair fell into tangled piles on his shoulders. His clothes were filthy and torn, as though he'd been rolling in a pig stall. When Keech glanced at Turner, he noticed the sheriff's face had drawn up in a curious expression.

Turner called out, "Tommy Claymore? Is that you?"

The peg-leg bandit grinned, exposing toothless black gums. "Not no more, Sher'ff! The *Master* decides my name now."

A shifting pile of clouds cast a shadow over the street. Keech's eyes slid from the pale man to the object sticking out of the stock wagon: the shovel that had knocked him on the head after his tumble off Felix.

Keech grabbed the handle and pulled the shovel off the wagon. He clutched the tool against his chest.

From his cover behind the casket, the deputy yelled, "You got no way out! Let Potter walk safe or this coffin I'm standing behind will be your own!"

Steady as a rock, Sheriff Turner said, "Deputy Ballard's right, Claymore. Surrender!"

The outlaw answered, "I ain't afeared of yer threats, Sher'ff."

Keech turned to his brother. "Sam, I need you to make a distraction. If you ran for Greely's, do you think you could scuttle inside without getting shot?"

"No way! He'd cut me down in two steps."

"But Sam, think about it. Sheriff Turner's got the man's full attention. You could make Greely's front door before he even turned to look. And he's holding his iron in the right hand, so you've got the advantage of his blind side when he turns."

"What about you?" asked Sam. "If I stick my neck out, what are you gonna do?"

Keech held up the square-head shovel and smiled. "I'll need a wagonload of good luck, but I think I can get close enough to use this."

Sam looked skeptical. "But what if the sheriff and his deputy spook up and ruin your plan?"

"It'll work," Keech said, and then put a hand on his partner's shoulder. "Ready?"

The boy nodded, though Keech could feel him shaking.

"Steady, Sam. On the count of three, run like a devil."

Sam took a deep breath, his eyes focused on Greely's General Goods.

Keech started counting.

"One."

Sam chocked his foot against the wagon wheel, pivoting his body to run.

"Remember, Sam, you're the Rabbit. Two."

In the street, the bandit muttered, "I do as my Master commands," and moved the revolver to Mr. Potter's temple.

"THREE!"

Sam charged for the storefront, his boots carving chunks in the Main Street dust.

The next few seconds took on the hazy features of a dark dream, each second lightning fast, but also impossibly slow. The bandit, preparing to fire at Mr. Potter, spotted Sam dashing across the street. Surprise engulfed his ghoulish face. He moved his iron away from Mr. Potter's temple and centered the revolver on Sam's retreating figure.

At the same time, the sheriff bellowed, "What're you doing, kid?"

Thrown off by Turner's booming voice, the bandit hesitated. This offered Sam enough time to wrench open the door at Greely's General Goods and dive inside. The bandit shifted his iron to fire at Sheriff Turner. As he moved, he dropped the arm around Mr. Potter's neck. The clerk seized the opportunity to drop into a crouch.

Sheriff Turner saw the opening his aim had demanded, and he squeezed the trigger. A deafening gunshot filled the street, and with perfect precision a lead ball slammed into the bandit's right shoulder. The man reeled sideways. The startled telegraph clerk bounced back up, shoved his attacker, and ran.

While all this happened, Keech had been on the move. He raced around the side of the wagon, holding the shovel like an ax, and charged toward the bandit.

Even as he staggered back from the shoulder wound, the pale man spotted Keech approaching and snarled. The hand holding the revolver began to swing toward its new target.

Realizing there was no time to bean the outlaw in the head, Keech made the split-second decision to alter his plan. Never slowing, he twisted his body, hauled the shovel back, and threw it as hard as he could. The tool twisted through the air.

The shovel's head connected with the bandit's skull with a loud *thonk*. The outlaw flew backward, the tip of his wooden leg pointing straight up. He landed hard on his back, and the revolver skittered free.

Sheriff Turner rushed over, holding his revolver on the bandit, and scooped up the outlaw's weapon. Then he turned to look at Keech.

Keech expected to be scolded, but Turner said, "That was one bully of a throw, Mr. Blackwood."

Keech grinned. "Thanks."

Sam emerged from Greely's General Goods. "I can't believe that plan worked!" he said, rejoining them on Main Street.

Sheriff Turner stood over the half-conscious outlaw, his features fixed in unsettled thought. All around Big Timber, the townsfolk emerged, peeking out windows and tiptoeing onto porches.

Keech and Sam waited by Mr. Potter as Sheriff Turner and Deputy Ballard placed iron handcuffs around the gunman's wrists. As they worked, a shaken Mr. Potter explained his story, recounting the moments when the peg-leg bandit walked into the office and started shooting the telegraph machine.

"Did he say anything before he started shooting?" Turner asked.

Mr. Potter looked too frazzled to think straight. "Nothing that made sense. He just kept hollering that his master wanted no messages sent."

Turner scratched at his chin. "I've been hearing reports like these of late. Travelers telling strange tales about a gang of outlaws, a band of vicious killers taking down communications all across the Territories. For what purpose, I ain't certain. All I know is these travelers talk of unnatural things these men can do."

Sam gestured to the cuffed outlaw at their feet. "Sheriff, you called this man by a name before, when he had Mr. Potter choked."

"I didn't recognize him till he stepped out, but when I saw the wooden leg, I knew him to be Tommy Claymore," Turner said.

Deputy Ballard rubbed his cheek. "Why do I know that name?"

"Because I reckon you read the report, Jake," Turner said. "Four months ago, I traveled upstate to Athens, in Gentry County. While I was there, a young fella caused a ruckus in the town saloon, turned over tables, and cussed up a storm. Had a peg leg, he did, and limped about the whole room. The owner knew him and said, 'Tommy Claymore, I've done had enough!' The one-legged fella pulled a sidearm and started shooting. I had no choice but to put him down. Two shots straight to the heart."

Sure enough, Keech saw a pair of black, ragged holes in the moaning outlaw's chest, peeking like small eyes through his torn shirt. "What are you saying, Sheriff?"

"I'm saying, this fella here, he's the same rapscallion I killed deader than a doornail up in Gentry County this past summer."

Keech and Sam exchanged a look of surprised dread.

⌒

As the lawmen hauled Tommy Claymore off to jail, the boys attempted to help Mr. Potter put his shattered telegraph back into some kind of working condition. The effort took the better part of the day, till a distressed Mr. Potter declared the machine beyond repair.

"What about Pa's letter?" Sam asked.

"You can leave it, if you like," Mr. Potter offered. "As soon as a new machine arrives, I'll send it on through. Free of charge, of course. If it weren't for you two, I'd be a limp rooster."

"That's mighty nice," Keech said, "but Pa Abner would want us to wait."

After parting ways with Mr. Potter, Keech and Sam sat on their ponies at the edge of town, munching on Granny's sandwiches and watching autumn's early darkness descend.

"Keech, I can't shake a terrible feeling," Sam said.

"Like what?"

"Like that fella didn't have a soul."

Keech thought about it. Though he hated to address the idea, Sam was onto something. "But how can that be?"

"I ain't sure. The book of Genesis says God huffed his life into man's nose, and the man got his soul that way. It don't say anything about a wicked dead man keeping a soul to live."

Keech directed his attention to the ground. Talk of souls and such made him feel uncomfortable.

"Maybe the sheriff aimed wrong," Sam mused. "Maybe he never killed him in the first place."

"You heard him. Two bullets to the heart. No man could survive that."

A furious wind charged up the road and spooked the ponies. Keech brushed away his sandwich crumbs and stuffed Granny's cloth into his pocket.

"Let's ride on home," he said. "We have to explain why the telegram wasn't sent."

"But not why it's been opened, right? You don't mean to tell that part."

"We can't lie, Sam."

"But we won't sit for a week!"

"Then we won't sit. We can't lie." Keech glanced back at Greely's General Goods, sad that the business had closed a couple hours ago. "Too bad for the others. No licorice wheels tonight."

"Yeah, too bad. I wanted one."

"Me too," Keech said, and whipped Felix's reins.

As they traveled home, Sam couldn't take his eyes off the gloomy woods. The whip-poor-wills chanted in the long thicket, making the darkness and quiet all around them deeper.

"I think I'd rather hear Little Eugena's bugle than them whip-poor-wills," Sam said. "Sing me a trail song, Keech."

"What do you want to hear?"

"'Ol' Lonesome Joe.' I love that one."

So Keech sang "Ol' Lonesome Joe," a song Pa Abner had taught him one day while fishing. When he got to the chorus, he sang it loud and true, to make Sam feel better:

Ol' Lonesome Joe, come ride next to me.
Let's roll, ol' Joe, to the Alamo Tree.
Lonesome in the heart, lonesome as can be.
You won't be so lonesome at the Alamo Tree,
When you sit next to me, when you sit next to me.

Before they knew it, the miles had disappeared. Copperhead Rock loomed ahead, which meant the ponies would soon be cresting White Elm Peak. You could always catch the grandest view of the Home from atop the peak.

But when the ponies reached the top, something else captured Keech's sight.

A dozen men sat on horses, holding torches and surrounding the front yard. One of the horses was a chestnut stallion. And the rider of the horse wore black.

Bad Whiskey Nelson had returned.

CHAPTER 7
THE WHISPERING CROW

S piny fear clawed at Keech's skin. It filled his mouth with a
sour tang, like a bite from an unripe persimmon.

A memory of Pa Abner's training in the wild flashed
through his mind. A warm night in the early spring. Pa had shaken
Keech gently awake. During the night, a small pygmy rattlesnake
had curled up under Keech's blanket. Pa had carefully removed
the blanket and placed it beside them. The sight of the rattler
coiled in the crook of his legs had sent Keech's heart racing beyond
any fear he'd ever felt. His first instinct had been to spring up
from the ground and run before the rattler sank its fangs into his
thigh. But Pa had held him in place with a firm hand on his shoulder and whispered over and over again: *Stay in the moment, Keech.
Accept the danger. Doubt sparks panic, and panic sparks death.* After a
time, Keech relaxed. *Now, son, remove the danger,* Pa had said. After
a seemingly eternal process of maneuvering his hand down his
thigh, Keech had scooped up the comfortable, unsuspecting snake,
as gently as a feather grazing a pebble, and tossed the critter aside.

Remembering the lesson, Keech took a deep breath to calm himself.

Sam gripped his shoulder in a panic. "What do we do?"

"We need to get off this hill," Keech said.

"And go where?"

"Back to Copperhead Rock to hide the horses."

After moving down to the far side of Copperhead Rock, the boys led the ponies a few paces into the forest so they would be invisible from the road. They tethered the mounts to a large pignut hickory, the same tree where Keech had once carved the head and face of his favorite animal, a wolf, into the bark. The horses fretted against the tree, unhappy to be so close to home and yet not properly stalled. Keech patted their muzzles and whispered for them to be patient.

"What now?" Sam asked.

"Let's sneak back over the peak, follow one of our trails. Pa will need our help."

Sam nodded.

As they hurried over White Elm Peak and plunged into the trees, a fragment of moon cut through the clouds. Sam muttered, "They're surrounding the house!"

"We better punch the breeze, then."

Over the years they had explored every inch of the orphanage territory. They had spent countless hours in the woods with Pa. They knew how to move without snapping a twig or disturbing a nesting bird. They knew which paths offered the best cover and which paths would get them to the bottom of White Elm Peak the fastest.

They ran the switchback in silence, letting the moon guide them.

As soon as they were closer, the boys crouched behind one of the sagging weigela bushes that flanked the front yard. They paused on their haunches not fifteen feet from one of the torch-wielding outlaws. The brute was one of eight men surrounding the front door. They formed a semicircle in the front yard, while the rest of the invaders had disappeared around the back.

There was no light inside, and Keech wondered if Pa had cleared everyone out. Then he noticed the faintest blush of light flickering in the second-floor window and realized Pa hadn't had a chance to hide the family in the woods. He'd probably sent the kids and Granny Nell upstairs to take cover.

Sam pointed through the bush at the nearest bandit. The man wore a thick leather coat buttoned tight against the wind, and a heavy Pocket Revolver on his right hip. His hat brim was wide, casting smoky darkness across his face. His torch reeked of pungent tar, and shadows danced across the uneven dirt.

"That man is just like Tommy!" Sam whispered.

"Quiet," Keech mouthed, but Sam was right. The brute was as pale as a corpse, another moving dead man like Tommy Claymore. *I can't shake a terrible feeling*, Sam had said back in Big Timber. *Like that fella didn't have a soul.*

Near the man in the leather coat stood a towering fat man with a craggy beard and a mouth that dripped black tobacco juice. A flash of metal glinted on the plump man's face. A gold loop. It hung from the center of his nostrils, reminding Keech of a newspaper cartoon drawing he'd once seen of a big Jersey bull wearing a thick ring in its nose.

Most of the desperadoes possessed the same pasty flesh as Claymore. Even the bull-man with the nose hoop had the look of the recent dead upon him.

Keech tapped Sam on his boot and the boys crawled on their hands and knees behind the clusters of weigela and firethorn, careful not to upset a single leaf or branch. They stopped when their line of sight fell even with Bad Whiskey, who stood bathed in the dancing light of his goons' torches.

The outlaw's black overcoat rippled in the cold zephyr. He coughed onto the back of his gloved hand, and Keech's fists tightened when he caught a glimpse of the dead left eye.

A high-pitched whistle sounded from the opposite side of the Home. "That's the signal, boys," Bad Whiskey said. "The others are in place round back."

Sam grabbed Keech's arm in desperation. Keech raised his palms, both facing downward, and lowered them slowly: the hand gesture for *Stay calm*.

Bad Whiskey shouted at the Home's front door. "Isaiah Raines, come on out!"

The house remained quiet.

"Judgment has come, Raines! Face it like a man!"

The bitter wind howled across the property, then came to a stark rest, as if the world itself had stopped to catch a breath. The last hint of moonlight hid its face behind the dark clouds.

The front door of the Home for Lost Causes opened.

Pa Abner stepped out onto the porch. He was holding his

Model 39 Carbine rifle. He planted his boots shoulder-width on the porch boards. Keech recognized Pa's silence. He was taking a moment to size up each of the invaders crowding the yard.

At the edge of the half circle, the nose-ring monster—Keech could only think of him now as *Bull*—placed his hand upon his sidearm. The other desperadoes did the same, fingers inching toward their lead chuckers, but moving slowly to avoid any violent misunderstandings.

Pa Abner locked eyes on Bad Whiskey. "I made it clear you were to stay away."

Bad Whiskey shifted his weight. He fanned back his overcoat, revealing a holstered Navy revolver. "Reverend's orders. I don't leave Missouri without the Char Stone."

Pa ignored his remark. "I see you found a new hand cannon. Smaller than the Dragoon I took."

"The Dragoon ya *stole*. I'll be wantin' that back. I brought me a fistful of thralls. You don't stand a chance."

Pa Abner grimaced. "Did the Reverend raise them?"

"Nope. *I* command the *Tsi'noo* now."

"I see. You've borrowed the Prime. Your soul's sunk deeper into rot than ever, Bad Whiskey. I reckon you don't even *have* a soul anymore. I have a mind to put you down right here. You know full well I can."

Bad Whiskey grinned, his smile all gaps and rotten teeth. "You think you can outdraw me?"

"A wobbling toddler could outdraw you, Bad."

"Maybe yer faster, maybe you ain't. But we both know burnin' powder on me won't make a lick of diff'rence."

"Would this?" Pa lifted his left hand. Tied across his palm was the silver pendant. The orange light from the gang's torches reflected in the metal and made it look as if Pa held a flame.

The grin withered on Whiskey's face. He glanced at his banditos, as if seeking reassurance. They all backed away at least five steps.

Pa Abner seized the opportunity. "These mongrels see your fear, Bad. Get off my land or I'll send you to your doom."

Keech threw a hopeful glance at Sam. But his brother was gazing at something else in the yard and didn't notice. His mouth had gone slack with disbelief.

A monstrous crow had landed on Bad Whiskey's shoulder.

It was twice as big as any crow Keech had ever seen. Its beak was unnaturally long, like the jagged end of a scythe, and it moved its malformed head back and forth, as if examining the situation. The creature stood on a pair of whopping talons more suited for a bald eagle. But the frightful part was not the size or shape of the thing, but the way it leaned its massive body toward the outlaw's ear.

Keech rubbed his eyes, not believing his own sight.

"Is that crow *whispering* to Whiskey?" Sam mumbled.

Bad Whiskey took another five steps back. Then he began to speak. Not to himself or his gang, but to the bird perched upon his shoulder.

Around him the torches burned, sending tar-scented vapors into the night sky.

"The Reverend sends a message," Bad Whiskey told Pa. "He says surrender all the sacred objects and give up the hidin' places of the Enforcers."

As he spoke, the giant crow turned to look at Pa. It screamed a loud *Ack!* and Whiskey smiled, his courage renewed. His dead eye sparked yellow in the torchlight as the flames sliced in the wind, each flicker causing his foul features to pale and then darken, like a demon's heartbeat.

"Reverend says comply, or none escape this night alive."

Pa Abner raised his left hand, the silver gleaming like a bright candle on his palm as if the charm itself were glowing. "Ride out this minute or I'll lay you low."

Bad Whiskey sighed impatiently. "Raines, this needn't get ugly. Give me the sacred objects or I'll *compel* ya."

The anger that flashed across Pa's face convinced Keech that those words would be the outlaw's last. He was sure Pa was about to lunge for the one-eyed villain and beat in his ugly face.

Instead, Pa jumped back into the house and slammed the door. The move was so unexpected, the desperadoes didn't know what to do.

A deafening squawk split the night as the crow released Bad Whiskey's shoulder. It took mad flight across the yard, its wings lashing the air, and swooped down the center of the front porch. Keech heard the sound of slashing as the crow's talons scored lines into the planks. He tried to keep the crow in sight, but the creature charged up at the porch's edge, spiraled high into the October sky, and vanished into the darkness.

Bad Whiskey tilted his head. "Very well," he muttered. "Violence, then."

He peeled off one glove, brought his fingers to his mouth, and blew a shrill whistle.

CHAPTER 8

THE SIEGE

From their hiding spot behind the bushes, Keech and Sam witnessed three of the pale-fleshed triggermen scramble for the Home's front door. They spoke no words and Bad Whiskey issued no orders. The time for talk was done.

The trio of dead men—Bad Whiskey had called his followers *thralls*—kicked at the door, but found it securely blocked. One of them plucked a stone off the ground and tossed it at the sitting room window. The pane shattered with a terrible crash, but the shards fell outward. Pa Abner had nailed boards inside, across the windows. While Keech and Sam had been away, Pa had been preparing the house for a siege.

Bad Whiskey pointed at Bull.

The massive thrall stepped over to the porch, hunkered down, and hurled his entire weight at the front door. The house shook with the impact, but the door held secure.

Bull shook his head. "It's barred," he said to Whiskey.

"Of course it's barred. Try again."

Bull stampeded the door a second time. The torchlight in the yard revealed jagged cracks up and down the wood, but the door refused to budge. The thrall slumped on the porch, disappointed.

Bad Whiskey addressed the walking corpse wearing the leather coat. "Rance, get over there. Shoot yer way in."

The leather-coated man joined Bull on the porch and pulled his revolver. The harsh crack of gunfire exploded. After a few shots, the door began to splinter. Large pieces of timber burst and cracked, clouding the yard with sawdust and smoke.

"They're gonna murder them!" Sam bawled in Keech's ear.

The thrall known as Rance stopped to reload.

Bull slammed his boot against the bullet-riddled door. The entry shuddered. A new cloud of dust erupted into the air.

"Nearly there," the thrall grunted. He kicked again. This time the barricade shattered. The door swung wide, revealing darkness within.

Bad Whiskey pointed to a timid-looking thrall in a tattered brown coat. "You there, Copper."

The creature looked surprised to see his trail boss call on him. In the torchlight his flesh looked leprous. "N-n-name's *Cooper*," he stammered.

"I don't give a continental what yer fool name is. Get inside and fetch my prisoner."

Cooper stepped obediently across the yard. He edged past Bull and Rance and drew a small flintlock pistol. He pointed the weapon straight ahead and took a modest step over the threshold.

Something inside the house flashed bright white. A gunshot rang out.

Cooper grabbed his chest, took a step back, and collapsed on the porch. Keech couldn't see clearly what had happened, but he believed Pa Abner had just shot the fella straight through the heart.

Bad Whiskey guffawed. "A fine shot, Raines! But you know lead can't stop the *Tsi'noo.*"

To answer Whiskey's remark, Cooper sat straight up. He looked confused, perhaps a little scared, and pushed a finger into the fresh bullet hole, as if hoping to touch his own heart. "That smarted somethin' awful!" he shouted. Other thralls chuckled in the yard. Cooper climbed back to his feet.

Keech couldn't form a single clear thought. Their pa had prepared them for so much. They had spent years in the woods, training for any sort of danger, wild animals, savage blizzards. But not for men who stood up after being shot square in the heart.

Cooper stepped again toward the door. This time Pa Abner's hand flashed into view, the pendant tied across his palm. He slapped the glowing charm across the thrall's cheek.

A shudder ran down the dead man's body as if he'd been struck by lightning. Bull and Rance dived off the porch as Cooper collapsed in a heap, almost exactly where he'd landed before. The thrall shrieked an unspeakable noise and his face and neck took on the color of a midnight river. A black dust billowed from the creature's mouth. There was a final groan, and then Cooper lay still, a lifeless corpse.

Petrifying horror seized Keech's bones. Then he understood what he had just witnessed, and his dread turned to hope. The pendant! The second Pa Abner had touched Cooper with the silver, the sinister hold upon the animated body had shattered.

"Fill that house with lead!" Bad Whiskey screamed.

The outlaws opened fire. Wood splintered as bullets tore into the Home. The thralls emptied their revolvers, reloaded, then emptied again. Whiskey joined in, firing into the open doorway, screaming obscenities, and stomping his boots with glee.

"We have to help," Keech said.

"But if we break cover, we're goners!"

Bad Whiskey's men charged the house and poured in through the battered entrance, stepping over the still body of Cooper. A second later, more bright gunfire lit the front porch. Men shrieked inside the house. Black powder smoke, made visible only by the torchlight, spilled from the door.

Then there was silence.

A skinny, ghost-white outlaw emerged from the house. The man wore a fancy frock coat, blackened by dirt and ripped along the sleeves. In the crook of one arm he carried a long rifled musket, the end of its barrel seeping a thin fog. Clumps of gray hair hung like spiderwebs off his speckled, hatless head. Upon seeing the man, Keech couldn't help thinking back to his readings on sailors and pirates and the scurvy sickness they suffered from when they didn't eat fruit for months at sea.

Scurvy grinned, revealing bloodred gums and broken teeth.

"We got 'im, Master," the creature said. "That ol' punchbug put up quite the fuss. Ended five on the stairs before we managed to get *this* free."

Keech felt his throat tighten when the thrall held up a glimmering object. It was Pa's charm, glowing like a firefly, partially wrapped in a scrap of cloth. Scurvy was careful to keep the object off his own flesh. He tossed it across the front yard, where it landed at Bad Whiskey's feet.

From a distance, Keech could hear the sound of a wounded pup howling. Slowly he worked out that the wailing was coming from the Home. It was not a pup, but his siblings trapped inside, crying.

"They're gonna kill everybody!" Sam insisted. "We have to help them!"

Keech had no idea what to do. One stubborn thought played in his mind: *Destruction cometh; and they shall seek peace, and there shall be none.* The passage clouded any attempt to form a plan.

Then he remembered. Pa Abner had tossed Whiskey's Dragoon onto the workbench in the woodshed. If the revolver was still there, maybe there was some way he could use it to even the odds, or at least slow the dead men down.

He whispered to Sam, "I have a plan. I'll circle around the property to the south and get the Dragoon Pa took earlier. You head around to the back door; see if there's some way to slip inside. I'll start shooting in the air, cause a ruckus, and draw Bad Whiskey's men toward me. When I do, find Granny Nell and the others and lead them out to safety."

Sam's eyes brimmed with tears. "Protect us, Saint Jude, from harm," he muttered. Without another word, he slipped away on silent feet.

Keech watched him disappear through the dark brush and then shifted his weight, ready to dash back through the trees.

One of the henchmen stepped out of the house. He waved a hand as though shooing a pesky fly. "Dixon's bringin' him out," the thrall said.

"Raines better be alive or I'll have yer life," Bad Whiskey said.

"He is, mostly," the gunman answered. "A bit shot up."

A bearded leatherneck emerged from the Home, dragging the wounded Pa Abner. The thrall flung him to the ground at Whiskey's feet. Pa's beard was wet with blood. He looked as if he should be dead.

Keech knew he couldn't wait a moment more. He made his way quickly along a well-worn path that skirted the southern perimeter of the property. As he scampered behind the waist-high brush, he heard Bad Whiskey growl at Pa.

"Reverend Rose'll be happy to see this."

Glancing back through the bushes, Keech saw the outlaw snatch the pendant's leather cord and lift the blazing silver from the dirt.

He reached the woodshed and slipped inside. As his eyes adjusted to the dark, he fumbled around Pa's workbench. He ran his hand across the raw wood and drew a painful sliver in his palm, but the revolver was nowhere to be found.

He kept searching. Pa's lantern could be of use—he could rig a mean explosion with it—but it too was out of sight. A chunk of tree bark lay in the dirt, a leftover from one of Pa's projects. But that was just plain foolish. There was no way he could make an effective distraction with a piece of dumb bark. He needed something with teeth.

Keech turned his attention to Pa's toolbox. His fingers fell upon the handle of Pa's scratching awl. The tip was sharp enough to stab through pure oak. He stuffed the awl into his coat pocket and kept rummaging.

Gunfire ruptured the night again—three distinct shots from an elevated position—but this time the volley wasn't coming from the dead men and their pistols. This gunfire sounded familiar. Keech paused to listen. A fourth shot rang out, the crack of a Model 39 Carbine. The shots were coming from Pa's Colt rifle.

Keech guessed that Granny Nell must be firing at the desperadoes. If anyone could defend the Home besides Pa, it was Granny. She was the toughest old woman this side of the Mississippi.

Keech spotted a blunt object resting on Pa's sanding stool: the claw hammer that Robby had been using earlier that day. He hefted the iron to test its weight. He took a practice swing and turned the tool over so when the hammer swung, the iron claw would lead. If he banged it against the side of the woodshed, the ruckus would surely make Bad Whiskey and his devils come running.

There was no more time for uncertainty. The hammer would have to serve. Sam was waiting on a distraction so he could get into the house and save the others. It was time to act, even if it meant Keech would die.

The Carbine boomed twice more—then fell silent. Granny had used her six shots and was most likely reloading.

The hammer snug in his grip, Keech pushed open the shed door and stepped outside.

What he saw nearly made his heart stop.

Orange fire had erupted inside the Home. Flames devoured the drawn curtains hanging over the back windows. Inside, Keech could see monstrous silhouettes, the shadows of Bad Whiskey's thralls, stomping around the ground floor with destructive purpose, touching their torches to the furniture, the walls, anything that would take a flame.

"No!" Keech shrieked.

Clenching the hammer, he screamed with raw animal fury and ran.

CHAPTER 9
SMOKE AND ASH

Keech rounded the corner of the burning house and leaped into the center of the thralls, swinging Pa's hammer with reckless strength. He aimed the iron claw at the exposed head of a dastardly rotter in brown, tattered clothes. The thrall turned, shock writ across his features. Keech brought down the hammer, but the brute managed to raise his arm. The claw sank into the wretch's forearm. Keech expected the man to scream, but he barely opened his mouth. At least the man flinched and in the process dropped his rifled musket. The thrall dragged Keech to the ground with him.

Keech scrambled to pull the claw hammer loose, but the curved iron held firm in the man's forearm. The other outlaws were sluggish to move, perhaps shocked to discover another person lurking outside the Home.

From where he lay in the dirt, Pa Abner groaned in anguish. "No, son. No."

Keech yanked, but the hammer refused to pry loose. With his free hand, the outlaw beneath him slammed a meaty fist into his left ear. Ringing pain charged through his head like a nest of wasps.

The monster he thought of as Bull grabbed him by the shoulders and yanked him up. Keech tried to squirm free, but the thrall had pinned his arms behind his back.

Bad Whiskey stepped over to contemplate Keech. "Why, it's Jim Bowie, here to defend the Alamo!"

Wrenching one arm free from Bull's grasp, Keech scrabbled into his coat pocket and found the scratching awl. He pulled it free and with all his strength thrust the glinting tip deep into Bull's arm. Like the first thrall, the outlaw flinched slightly, but he seemed unperturbed.

"Enough, boy!" Bad Whiskey yelled. He swiped the back of his hand across Keech's cheek. Bull released his grip, and Keech felt as if he was falling from a cliff through shade and firelight.

A spangled darkness clouded his brain. When his vision at last cleared, Keech labored to lift his head, only to see flames devouring the Home for Lost Causes. His eyes filled with hopeless tears. A few feet away, Pa Abner struggled to rise.

The last of the desperadoes stepped out of the burning house. He was holding a black revolver. He held it up to his boss and said, "Lookit what I found, Master."

Squinting up from where he lay on the ground, Keech saw it was the Colt Dragoon.

Bad Whiskey accepted the weapon with glee.

"I *told* you I'd be gettin' that back," he crooned at Pa. He then turned with a grin to watch the fire spread.

Sweltering heat pressed against Keech, as if he were lying at the mouth of an oven. The whitewashed walls of the Home peeled, blackened. Frames and shutters cracked as the fire consumed everything.

Thick smoke billowed through the door and for one second, Keech caught a glimpse of Sam. He was standing inside the house, his face lit orange by nearby flames.

Sam lifted his hand, quickly moved his fingers to toss three quick signals at him: *Escape. Hide. Run to Big Timber.*

A desperate plea telling Keech to save himself.

The flames kicked up and a wooden beam splintered and crashed across the doorway, sealing off the Home. All sight of Sam was lost. His brother was trapped and doomed to die alongside the rest of his family.

All because of Keech's plan.

The remaining number of Bad Whiskey's gang stood side by side, torches in hand, and watched the fire. Their horses chomped and shuffled at the shakepole fence, worried by the wall of heat. The heavy thrall, Bull, casually pulled the awl from his arm and tossed it aside. He made no move to tend his injury.

Keech watched Bad Whiskey hand the silver shard back to Scurvy, who pocketed the pendant, again careful not to touch the glowing metal. Despite his care, it was obvious the charm was causing the thrall considerable distress.

Bad Whiskey stepped over to Pa Abner. The outlaw smiled at the sight of the man brought low. "Sit up, Raines."

"You leave him alone!" Keech yelled. He tried to rise to his knees and scurry to Pa, but Rance approached and held him down with a boot.

Pa moved at a defeated pace. He straightened his legs and pushed himself up on his hip. He clasped his hands together and lifted his eyes, looking like a man deep in prayer. "You didn't have to murder my family."

Bad Whiskey looked amused. "*Family*, he says."

A cough racked Pa Abner. Beads of blood painted his lips. "There was no need."

Bad Whiskey tilted his head, his face inches from Pa's. "Here's yer deal, Raines: Tell me where to find the Char Stone. And give me the location of the other Enforcers. You tell me those two things and I spare this boy's life."

Pa Abner shook his head. "I don't know about the others."

"Don't tease me. Horner, O'Brien, Jeffreys. Where are they?"

"I don't know," Pa said. "We parted ways forever."

Bad Whiskey laid his gloved hands on Pa's head. "I believe ya 'bout the other Enforcers. But I'd wager you do know where the Stone is."

"I don't. I swear."

Whiskey removed his hat, revealing a head of slicked-back hair. In some places the hair had fallen out in clumps, revealing yellowish patches of scalp beneath. He waved the brim of the hat beneath his pointed goatee. "That fire has sure turned this property to a furnace!" he sang, and wafted his overcoat. He turned and looked at the bearded thrall who had removed Pa Abner from the Home. "Dixon, what were the terms I just now offered?"

The creature named Dixon looked dumbstruck. "I think ya said, 'Tell me where to find the Stone and I'll spare the boy's life.'"

"Yes, I thought so. Too bad. You had yer chance, Raines."

Bad Whiskey raised his Dragoon.

Pa held up his hands in desperation. "I don't know the Stone's whereabouts, Whiskey! I'm not lying! After the shoot-out at the Blackwood place, I had it hidden! It's lost. Even from me."

Keech flinched at the mention of his last name. He had never heard Pa mention a shoot-out. Especially not one at the home of his mother and father, before he was orphaned.

"Hid even from you?"

"My mind was clouded. I remember nothing. I swear!"

Bad Whiskey shrugged. "That's a cryin' shame." He thumbed back the hammer.

Pa screamed, "Wait, Whiskey! A sullied place. A place of death. I don't remember details, but even now I can feel its wickedness pulling at me from the west."

"A place of death. To the west. Interesting." Bad Whiskey hesitated, his mouth twisting up to a smile. "Perhaps a boneyard? Or the site of a terr'ble battle?"

Pa wavered, his face full of despair. "It's a feeling of death and desolation pulling at my heart. That's all I know."

"Give me the name of the nearest bone orchard to the west. Speak or it'll be the end of Jim Bowie."

Keech looked into Bad Whiskey's good eye. He saw death behind it.

Frantically, Keech reached into his coat and drew forth the telegram. "Wait!" He held it out as a desperate distraction. "What if I gave you a secret letter?"

"Keech, don't!" Pa bellowed.

Lowering the Dragoon, Bad Whiskey accepted the telegram.

He unfolded it and quickly read over the stack of numbers listed down the paper. He shook his head in frustration. "This ain't nothin' but gibberish." Nevertheless, he stuffed the page into the pocket of his overcoat and then raised the Dragoon toward Keech again.

"Good-bye, pilgrim."

Despite his wounds, Pa jumped to his feet and lunged. He wrapped his hands around Bad Whiskey's throat.

Keech pushed up to his own feet. The other desperadoes had turned their attention to Pa and Bad Whiskey. Two of them struggled to pry Pa's fingers off their boss's throat, but Pa's grip was immovable.

"Run!" Pa shouted.

For a second Keech's eyes locked on Pa's, and the piercing gaze of his father revealed the ghosts of future memories they would never share. In some way, Keech had always known this moment would come, but he had hoped it wouldn't come till Pa was very old and lying in his quiet bed.

Keech turned to run and found Rance blocking his path with a rifled musket. Without thinking, he grabbed the rifle. Just that morning he had faced Sam on the banks of the Third Fork and they had played this very game.

He tugged on the rifle and Rance pulled back. The thrall was strong and his weight threatened to yank Keech off his feet. So he moved exactly as his brother had moved that morning. He pivoted on his inner foot and twisted his hip. Then, before his opponent could adjust, Keech yanked hard on the musket.

The weapon tore free. Rance's feet slid out and he tumbled backward, landing on his haunches.

Keech spun in time to see the gaunt Scurvy descend upon him. There was no time to aim and fire, so he swung the musket. The long barrel smashed across the thrall's head, driving him to the ground. A flash of orange light caught Keech's eye. Pa's charm, dangling from Scurvy's pocket. Keech dropped the musket and grabbed the cord. The pendant ripped free of the pocket. A chill burst up his hand.

Grunting, Keech spun on his heel and bolted for the white elm trunks, risking a backward glance to see if Pa had managed to strangle Whiskey. The thralls tugged at Pa, but he refused to let go. As he passed the tree line, Keech saw the outlaws yank Pa Abner away and push him to his knees.

Bad Whiskey pressed his Dragoon against Pa's chest.

Keech heard three words:

"So long, Enforcer."

A shot echoed across the night.

The gunshot hollowed Keech's soul. He drew a long breath to howl, but stopped himself before the scream could fly. If he was to survive, he had to stay sharp, remember his lessons.

In the distance he could hear the one-eyed murderer shout curses at his leathernecks. "Get the shard, you fools! The Reverend'll have our heads!"

Away from the burning house, the world was raven black. Keech found one of the trails he and Sam had cut the summer before and stumbled through the brush. He slung the charm over his neck and tucked it inside his shirt.

At last he made the gully and dragged himself into the shallow riverbed. His boots filled with toe-numbing water. The desperadoes were just behind him, beating the branches, calling out with mocking voices. As they stomped to the bank, one of them muttered, "He's close. I can feel it." Their torches cast eerie spindles of gold over the water.

At the riverbank, Keech stretched himself flat, submerging his body, allowing only his face to break the water's surface. The cold was bracing, but bearable, much like the river's bite earlier that morning. The worst of the cold seemed to be coming from the silver charm, which radiated an otherworldly chill upon his chest, as it did when he was a toddler in Pa's arms.

Seconds later, the thralls appeared only a few steps away. "The shard is near," one of them grumbled. Keech spotted a thorny bush slowly drifting in the water. He moved the bush over his body and face. Mercifully, the moon remained hidden behind heavy clouds, bathing him in near pitch darkness.

Through the bush he saw Scurvy, standing so close he could have touched his boot. Keech held his breath.

One of the thralls, the scoundrel named Dixon, hissed, "Anything?"

Scurvy paused, his speckled white scalp tilted toward the water. "Can't tell." The thrall's black eyes skimmed over the trickling surface. "Show yerself, chickabiddy. You can't hide."

A few yards away, a second voice called out, "There's tracks over yonder."

"But he's close!" Scurvy spat.

"Forget him. The Master calls," Dixon shouted.

"We can't leave," Scurvy said, running the toe of his boot over a submerged river rock. The boot grazed the thorny bush and threatened to knock it out of Keech's grasp.

"You fool," the second voice said. "His tracks are *yonder*!"

"The kid's long gone," Dixon said. "Master wants us to report back."

Grumbling, Scurvy backed away from the water. He turned his gaze once more to the riverbank, scowled, then stomped away into the woods.

Keech waited, unwilling to emerge into a trap. Time refused to pass. Every sound was the crack of a boot or the splash of a killer. He waited till he could no longer feel his arms and legs. Only when he realized his body was no longer cold, but instead sleepy, did Keech decide he needed to escape the water.

He bumbled across the gully, slipping on dead feet, and crawled up the bank. The ground was stone-hard, but his wet hands and soaked sleeves turned the dirt to mud. He struggled to his knees, wrapped his arms around an elm trunk, and pulled himself to his feet. After a few minutes, his blood thawed enough for him to risk taking a step.

He didn't get far before collapsing again, this time into a thick veil of unconsciousness. For hours he found himself fading in and out, wondering if the terrible night was just a dream. When he finally gained enough strength to stay awake, Keech judged the day's first light would arrive soon, maybe in less than an hour.

Shivering, he stumbled back toward the Home. Along the way he pulled Pa's pendant out of his shirt and clutched the metal close to his chest, the way Patrick used to grasp his toys.

When Keech emerged from the trees, he saw that Bad Whiskey's fire had turned the Home to a smoldering mountain of wood, a terrible heap that crackled and collapsed into itself. Even after hours of cold night, legions of bright red sparks and embers still sputtered in the air. Keech shuffled closer, barely feeling himself move. Heat from the ruin washed over him, driving back the river chill. Thick white smoke rose into the early morning sky. He dropped to his knees.

Bad Whiskey and his gang had ridden away, taking the bodies of their own dead with them. They had taken Pa Abner as well. The place where he'd fallen was a dark crimson, but Pa's body was gone.

Keech watched as the heavy streams of smoke circled the air. He remembered his final glimpse of Sam, standing in the center of the flaming Home, beseeching him to run and hide. Even as he faced death, Sam had thought only of the welfare of his brother. Sam had once laughed and played with the wildest vigor. He had cherished all life, from the foxes in the woodland to the tadpoles in the puddles. He had been Keech's best friend and brother.

And now he was gone. Forever.

Keech stood and brushed off his knees. Slipping Pa's charm into his coat pocket, he stared in silence at the smoke and the ash. He didn't cry, though destruction had come.

He was alone now. But he wasn't scared. For the first time in his life, Keech had a *purpose*.

First, he would find the remains of Sam, Granny Nell, and his other siblings, and give them proper rest.

Then, because he was the Wolf, he would hunt.

There would be no peace for Bad Whiskey, and no peace for his wicked men.

One by one, Keech would send them to their doom.

PART 2

THE YOUNG RIDERS

WHISKEY ON THE TRAIL

The crow stood motionless on the lowest branch of the oak. Its wings were folded inward, as birds do when not in flight, but these wings were so abnormally long their tips jutted well below the branch. To Whiskey Nelson, they gave the crow a barbed, carving-knife appearance.

The creature would have been invisible in the night, had Whiskey not held one of the burning torches used on Raines's orphanage. In the firelight, he could see the crow staring at him, its eyes black as gunpowder, peering into his mind.

The *P'mola*, the Reverend Rose called them. A name derived from the Abenaki tribes who had once welcomed him into their villages—till the Reverend's lust for power betrayed their trust. The *P'mola* were his emissaries, the darkest of all creatures. When the Reverend had awakened in the Palace of the Thunders, they were the first things he had created.

You lost the amulet shard, the crow said now. The words were not spoken aloud, but came to Whiskey as a terrible rasp—the *Reverend's* rasp—deep inside his head.

"I'm sorry, boss," Whiskey muttered. He had fallen to his knees to address the crow. "It won't happen again."

No. It will not.

Whiskey had taken his gang southwest down an all-but-forgotten Indian buffalo trail. It would be the quickest route to the village of Whistler, the location of the nearest graveyard, according to information acquired from one of the *P'mola*. The gang had only half a day's ride to reach Whistler, and with any luck, the resting place of the Char Stone.

You let a boy defeat you, the crow said.

"The kid's a green bean," Whiskey said. "He splashes in rivers and plays with sticks."

He was raised by Isaiah Raines, taught the ways of the Enforcer.

"And I took Raines down," Whiskey said, then promptly regretted the boast. To speak to the messenger crow was to speak to the Reverend, and the Reverend cared little for arrogance.

In response, the crow flapped its immense wings. *Careful how you speak to me, Nelson. I could have this* P'mola *tear you limb from limb.*

"The boy's just a pup, boss."

The crow cackled. *You fool. The boy is Blackwood's son.*

The voice in Whiskey's head was terrible, but hearing that old name—*Blackwood*—was somehow worse. His entire body went rigid at the sound of it. "That's impossible!" he croaked.

When Raines fled with the Char Stone, he must have taken the boy as well.

Whiskey fell silent. His good eye dropped to the dead leaves swirling between his boots. He could hardly believe it. The foolish pup with the claw hammer was the son of Screamin' Bill Blackwood.

The crow shifted slowly upon the oak branch. After a moment, the Reverend's terrible voice raked across Whiskey's mind again.

You failed me.

"No, boss, I'm close!"

The crow screeched. *You have dined on my vitality for too long, Nelson.*

"I just need to raise more thralls!"

I gave you the Prime. I taught you the Black Verse. And you failed me.

"We'll have the Stone by next nightfall, boss!"

The Prime is mine for the giving. You are no longer worthy.

Whiskey felt the stone of his heart skip two beats. "Boss, no! Don't take it!"

The *P'mola* screeched again, an agonizing noise that speared Whiskey's brain. This time a cold, watery sensation trickled through his veins, filling his body with hollows. Memories from his childhood flickered, and then snuffed out, lost forever. He wobbled upon his knees, struggling not to pitch over.

He knew what had just happened. The Reverend had begun to drain the invisible essence that kept him whole, the force known only as the Prime, the darkest of all the chaos magics.

Terrified, Whiskey remembered the happiest song from his youth, the song his father had taught him when he was a young boatsman on the Mississippi. He clung to the memory as if it were gold treasure:

> *How happy the soldier who lives on his pay,*
> *And spends half a crown on six pence a day;*

He fears neither justices, warrants nor bums,
But pays all his debts with a roll of the drums . . .

The song began to slip. He tucked it down, his only posses-
sion, his only connection to the old life.

The Reverend Rose could enter a man's head, round up his
thoughts, and burn his sweetest memories to ash. The Reverend
Rose could tread on a man's soul and cut it to ribbons with the
rowels of his spurs.

But Whiskey could not let the Reverend have everything.

"Don't drain me, boss!" he pleaded. "I'm sorry! I'll make it
right!"

The crow cawed, then took flight, rising high above the oak
tree, high above the Missouri forest, and vanished into the wild
darkness.

Whiskey climbed back to his feet. He took a tall breath to
calm his mind.

"Master?"

Whiskey spun, his hand dropping instinctively to his Dragoon.
The speaker was Dixon, one of the first thralls he'd ever raised.
The other thralls lurked behind him.

"I thought I told you all to stay on the trail."

"Yessir, it's just that—" The thrall grimaced in the torchlight,
as though scared to continue. "Them dead'uns we rounded up are
startin' to stiff up. Your stallion and the packhorses don't like it
none. Want us to go ahead and bury 'em?"

Whiskey said nothing at first. The Prime was seeping from
his bones, but the power to raise was still inside, pulsing just

under his flesh. The Reverend Rose had left him just enough to get the job done.

"Bury 'em," Whiskey said. "Be sure to leave no sign."

Dixon lowered his head, obedient. "And Raines? Want us to bury him, too?"

"No, leave him," Whiskey said. "I'll see to him later."

"Yes, Master."

The thralls began to ramble back through the woods.

"One more thing," Whiskey called.

"Master?"

Whiskey raised his voice. "You all failed me. You let the pup escape and lost the shard."

"Not me, Master!" Dixon whimpered. "It was the others! I wanted to find 'im!" The other thralls shuffled back, hoping to avoid Whiskey's wrath.

"I've told you worms the amulet cannot come together. Thanks to yer blunderin', Raines's shard is still in the wild. An example must be made."

Without raising a finger, Whiskey pulled at the invisible ropes around Dixon's mind. The thrall gave a choking sound. He raised his hands to pry at his throat, but Whiskey forced the arms back down to his sides. There was no other struggle. Dixon dropped to his knees.

"I give, an' I take away," Whiskey growled.

The thrall crumpled to the ground, and was still. Bad Whiskey looked at the other thralls and sneered, "Go."

The thralls hurried away.

CHAPTER 10

AMBUSH AT COPPERHEAD ROCK

Pa *Abner stands before Keech and Sam in the deep forest, two miles north of Low Hill, the quiet place he brings them to train. He holds an object up to the faint sunlight, a freshly sharpened iron tomahawk, the same one that had grazed Sam's cheek in the fighting circle one season before. The sun flashes on the blade like a silver wound cut into the air.*

"Ready yourselves, boys," Pa says firmly. "Prepare your minds."

"Yessir," Keech and Sam respond in unison.

"Keech, mind your feet," Pa warns. "I won't tell you again."

"Sorry, Pa," Keech says, and checks his stance. Over the sounds of distant loons and Missouri warblers, he can hear the apprehension in his own voice, a small pang of worry that hasn't gone away since Pa began their weapons training. He has done well in their lessons on land and water navigation, and the teachings on tool and weapon building, but he has never accepted the warrior's way, has never fully embraced the side that makes you fearless in combat. Sam is the confident one, more willing to

accept the pain of a battle. Keech knows he still has so much to learn, even from his brother.

"Study the blade; visualize the swing," Pa tells them, then takes a menacing step forward.

Keech and Sam draw deep breaths, again in unison. They hold no weapons of their own. The only protection they're allowed in the fighting circle is that of mental preparation.

"We don't leave this ground till you've seized the weapon," Pa says.

Off to the west, a whip-poor-will calls out a lonely ballad.

Pa grips the iron tomahawk, and speaks the phrase that opens the game.

"Now, my young warriors, let's begin."

~

A cold dampness caressed Keech's cheek, pulling him out of the ghostly memory from three summers ago. He opened his eyes to find himself staring at one of the runt shoats from the pigpen. The shoat grunted and nudged Keech with his snout, probably hoping for a bucket of slop.

Keech pushed the curious shoat away and sat up. The charred skeleton of the farmhouse, billowing heaps of buckled timber, lay before him. He had apparently collapsed again in the front yard, either from exhaustion or from the shock of seeing his family, his home, destroyed. The heat from Whiskey's fire had dried his clothes and coat. To the east, a cautious light spread across the sky. Clouds covered the void, but they couldn't hold back the approaching morning.

He stood and rubbed his eyes.

He knew what this morning would bring. Might as well get it done.

Keech went to the woodshed, retrieved one of Pa's shovels, and set about combing through the rubble of the Home for his family's remains. In the nearby coop, Pa's blue hens fussed at the empty dirt. Somewhere north, a friendless bird cackled.

Minutes after he began, the billowing smoke and lingering heat from the buried cinders forced him away. There was no way he would be able to dig through the Home for their remains. He would have to wait for the wreckage to stop smoking and cool down, and by that time Bad Whiskey Nelson would be long gone. Keech spat in frustration, and hunkered down on his haunches to think.

The wind shifted and pushed the black smoke south, and in that moment Keech's eye caught something small and thin poking out of the Home's ashes. He walked over carefully and used Pa's shovel to reach over the cinders and lift out the object.

It was Patrick's stick-and-ball, the toy that Robby had whittled for him. It was still intact, barely even grazed by the fire.

Keech clutched the toy with both hands and decided this should be the moment to say something and then shed his tears.

But Keech could find no words, no tears. The sign that hung over the shakepole fence was still there—PROTECT US, ST. JUDE, FROM HARM—and he remembered all the times he and Sam had slapped that sign for good luck—but everything had changed. All he felt now was a confusing sort of rage.

After a long silence, the words came. But they weren't for Sam or Granny Nell or the others. Not yet. He addressed Pa Abner.

"You kept too many secrets, Pa. Now Sam and the family are

gone. You must have had your reasons, but now it's too late to save anyone."

Keech's hands began to quiver around Patrick's toy.

"I have to go hunting now. You put this on my shoulders. I have to finish it."

He looked at the mountain of black timber where his family lay buried under cinder.

"Vengeance will come," he said to them. "I swear it on my life."

Buttoning his coat, Keech crossed the property and headed for Big Timber Road to retrieve poor Felix and Minerva. With everything that had taken place, he had almost forgotten they were still tied to the pignut hickory behind Copperhead Rock.

As he hiked up the road, he slipped his hand into his coat pocket and Pa's silver pendant grazed his fingers. He'd forgotten all about it. He pulled it out and gave it a look. Bad Whiskey had wanted this something fierce. When Keech had escaped with it, Whiskey had yelled at his thralls, *Get the shard, you fools! The Reverend'll have our heads!*

Maybe he shouldn't be touching it. Maybe Pa Abner should have gotten rid of the thing a long time ago. A good luck charm didn't bring misery and destruction.

A curious shiver ran through Keech, as if he were being watched. The shadows were long inside the elms, and he didn't like the way the trees moaned and snarled when the wind kicked up. Clutching the pendant, he walked faster.

Behind Copperhead Rock, Keech felt relieved to see the ponies standing exactly where he and Sam had left them. They had tangled their ropes around the hickory, and Minerva had suffered a small gash above her left hock; otherwise, the ponies were in passable shape.

Stowing Pa's charm inside Felix's saddlebag, he set about untangling their ropes. Midway up the tree bark, the sight of his own carving—the head and face of the Wolf—gave him a lonely feeling. He had never thought of himself as the Wolf without Sam as the Rabbit. They had always been inseparable, ever since Sam had been dropped off at the Home as a toddler.

From deep in the woods Keech heard a blunt crack. Felix and Minerva blustered.

"Easy now," Keech said. He stood still, ears cocked toward the sound.

Nothing.

As soon as he turned back to the ponies, the forest exploded behind him. Limbs cracked and leaves shattered. Keech spun around to see three figures leap out from behind Copperhead Rock.

The trio hollered and yelped, and Keech's only thought was that Bad Whiskey and his thralls had returned to finish their treacherous work. His eye caught a gleam of sharp metal—a giant, nasty blade in one of the figures' hands.

Keech scrambled backward, midway to turning about and forming the proper fight stance, but his heel snagged Minerva's rope and he tumbled. His bowler hat flew off his head and landed in a blanket of leaves. As soon as he was on his back, the trio descended upon him. The one with the knife sprang like a bobcat.

The figure straddled his stomach and pressed the razor-sharp blade against the side of his neck. Keech tried to lift his body, but the goon bounced a little, using his weight to drive the wind out of Keech's gut.

"Move a muscle and you're dead," the attacker snarled.

The other two figures gathered around their partner. Recovering a quick breath, Keech took a closer look at them. He blinked in surprise when he realized he wasn't staring at Whiskey's gang of thralls.

He was staring at three boys.

One of Pa's first rules of fighting sounded in his head: *If possible, reduce the danger.*

Keech unclenched his fists.

"Hey there, fellas," he said. The attacker's bulk on top of him pinched his words. "If you aim to rob me, I'm only holding a few pennies."

The trio glanced at one another, then rumbled with laughter. The boy with the giant knife leaned downward, pushing breath that smelled like salted beef up Keech's nostrils. "We ain't after your pennies," he said, his voice revealing a light, nimble accent. The blade in his hand had to be a full thirteen inches long.

"You think we're pickpockets?" said the largest of the boys. This one stood six feet tall in his muddy boots, and his stomach was as round as an oak barrel. Keech put this boy at fifteen, despite his size—too young for a beard but old enough for puppy fuzz.

The third boy—the mousiest of the trio—looked no older than ten. "Even if we were thieves," the kid said, "we wouldn't want a bunch of no-account pennies."

The boy with the knife said to his large trailmate, "What should we do with him, John Wesley? Feed him to the wild boars?"

"Dangit, you ain't supposed to use names! He might be one of them killers!"

"Yeah, no names, *Cutter*," mocked the youngest.

The boy who apparently went by John Wesley tossed a hand in the direction of the Home. "Was that blaze down yonder your handiwork?" he asked Keech.

"Hang on a dang second—you think I'm responsible for *that*?" Anger knotted Keech's stomach. He struggled against the boy with the knife. "You'll want to get off me now," he said.

"Oh yeah? What happens if I don't?"

"I'll make you eat that knife is what."

Cutter chortled. "I'd like to see you try, *chavo*."

Without taking his eyes off the boy's face, Keech used both hands to grab the blade-wielder's right wrist and forearm. He shoved the arm and wrist violently upward, twisting the business side of the blade away from his neck. Then he kicked up his left leg and hip to toss the kid off his stomach.

The boy yelped in pain and went tumbling. Before he could reposition himself, Keech pivoted perfectly, landed on top of him, and pinned the hand still clumsily holding the knife to the ground. One final turn of the wrist, and Keech wrenched the blade out of the hand. He tossed it safely to the side.

Nearby, the mousy boy released a surprised gasp.

"My knife!" the boy beneath him shouted. He lifted his other arm to strike, but Keech moved quickly, securing the boy's fist with his free hand.

"Knock it off, all of you," another voice called out from behind Copperhead Rock.

Keech glanced back. A fourth boy appeared around the boulder, a long muzzle-loading rifle propped in the crook of one arm.

"Kid, we don't mean you no trouble. Now kindly release my friend, and we'll leave you in peace."

This new boy was even taller than John Wesley, but a good deal slimmer. The weapon on his arm was a long-barrel musket, a Hawken rifle with a polished wood stock. Keech recognized the rifle because stories had it that Daniel Boone and Davy Crockett both had carried one.

"You have my word no harm will come to you," the tall boy said to Keech. "Please. Let him stand."

Positioning one knee on the attacker's chest, Keech shoved himself up. His rising motion drove a loud wheeze out of Cutter's throat. Keech backed away, and held up his hands in a gesture of appeasement.

Cursing under his breath and shaking his hurt wrist, Cutter got to his feet. He gave Keech a furious look, then went to retrieve his giant knife. He slid the blade over the arm of his coat to clean the dirt off and returned it to a long leather scabbard upon his hip. Keech noticed that the knife's handle was a twisted brown-and-white grip of solid bone. There were hints of an old design, some kind of engraving, at the base.

"Much obliged," the rifleman said to Keech. "Sorry for the tempers. My trailmates get jumpy when they run across a stranger." He offered a large hand for Keech to shake.

"No harm, I reckon." Though deep down, Keech wanted to give a bona fide lickin' to the boy with the knife for pinning him down.

Letting the rifleman stand with his hand in the air, he took a moment to collect his bowler hat and brush the dirt off his rump. He had no wish to trust any of these scamps, but there was something about the tall boy—a solid confidence—that reminded him of Pa Abner. Warily, he offered his own hand for proper shaking.

"Name's Keech Blackwood."

"Keech, glad to know you. My name's Nathaniel, but everybody calls me Nat."

As they shook hands, Keech took a second to size up Nat. The boy looked sixteen, perhaps older, with dark mahogany hair that fell the length of his neck. His rawhide clothes were shabby and faded by the sun—a rancher's garb, full of dust and hard work—and the brim of his gray hat cast a wide shade over a pair of fierce blue eyes, so deep and severe they were almost unsettling.

Keech noticed a peculiar marking on Nat's coat. A small egg-shaped patch, brown on the top, yellow on the bottom, sewn tightly onto the coat's breast pocket. Inside the oval was a symbol:

Keech had never seen it before. He figured it for a rancher's mark.

A loud bluster from the ponies drew his attention away from the patch. He gestured at the animals, still tied to the pignut hickory. "That's my horse Felix. And that's Minerva. Her owner was Sam, but he—" He paused to swallow a lump. "He died down yonder."

Nat frowned. "So that was *your* house."

From their vantage point, Keech couldn't see any traces of the Home itself, only the rising black smoke through the white elm trees. But the outline of the orphanage was strong in his mind, standing tall and happy and defiant in the clearing below the peak.

"It wasn't just a house," he said. "It was an orphanage. We called it the Home for Lost Causes."

"'Lost Causes,'" the smallest boy mused. His voice had not yet dropped. "Named after Saint Jude?"

Keech smiled, impressed by the kid's knowledge. "That's right."

The mousy boy returned the smile, then cast his eyes to the ground. Like Nat's, his eyes were a fierce blue, honed to sharpness by hard days. "We lost our families, too. They all got killed."

"Sorry to hear it," Keech said.

The boy shrugged. "No more time for sorry," he said. "There's only time for vengeance."

Keech took a few moments to finish untangling his ponies. As he worked, the mousy boy walked over and pulled a small leather pouch out of his black woolen coat. He opened up the pouch, revealing a thick, greasy medicine inside.

"I bought some salve back in Saline County. My horse cut his muzzle on a jack pine branch." He gestured to the gash above Minerva's hock.

"Much obliged," Keech said.

The small boy applied some of the cream to Minerva's wound. When he was done, he wiped his fingers on his trousers. He noticed Keech's carving of the Wolf head on the pignut hickory.

"What's that?"

"Nothing," Keech replied.

Nat summoned everyone back together. "I think it's high time we have proper introductions," he said to Keech. "The small one there"—he pointed to the mousy boy—"that there is Duck."

Keech nodded to Duck, who smiled bashfully and doffed his blue hat, a head covering so large it concealed nearly every strand of the boy's short brown hair. Around his neck the scrawny lad wore a knotted green scarf, cinched up tighter than a croc's mouth. His trousers were mud-blotted, and both of his boots were cracked along the toes, soon to be in shambles. Keech immediately pegged Duck as Nat's brother, on account of the eyes and hair color. "You two siblings?" he asked.

Nat flashed a small grin. "How could you tell?"

"There's a family look about you."

Nat turned and gestured behind him. "The big one yonder, that's John Wesley." The heavy boy dropped his eyes to his boots at being called out by name. He wore a yellow straw hat pulled low over a pair of bushy eyebrows, and the hair beneath the hat was a curly reddish blond, full of knots and tangles. He looked just as disheveled and trail-muddy as Duck. "He's hunting the outlaw who killed his ma."

Keech offered John Wesley a small nod. "I'm sorry to hear it. Who's the one responsible?"

An aggrieved look crossed John Wesley's face. "I don't speak his name."

"Ain't nobody's business anyway," Cutter said, and patted John Wesley on the back. He then added, "Ain't you gonna introduce *me*, Nat?"

Nat sighed, not so much an exasperated sound, but a light

mocking one. "That there is Cutter," he said. "He thinks his knife is magic, but he's an ace with it."

"It is magic!"

Nat ignored him. "Cutter's only his nickname, though. He's too stubborn to tell us what his real name is."

"You cowhands know it's bad luck to ask for a fella's full name. You have to earn that," the boy said, and chortled. Cutter's boots, coat, and hat were a dusty tan, and a bright blue bandana hung around his neck. In place of a belt, he wore a dull red sash made of woven silk, tied in a half-bow knot on his left hip.

"Cutter's chasing the man who killed his friend," Nat continued. "He and John Wesley was on the trail together before they met me and Duck. They're thick as thieves, those two."

Cutter was still rubbing his offended wrist. "Don't you even *think* about trying that move again," he growled at Keech, "or I'll have my compadre pull your arms off." He gestured to John Wesley, who offered Keech his meanest scowl.

Not the friendliest pair, Keech thought. Still, there was something about them, the whole pack. They seemed strong together, united. Maybe they could help in some way.

"So what do you call your outfit?" Keech asked Nat.

"We ain't settled on a proper name. We never expected to be on the trail for so many weeks."

Keech nodded.

Nat sent John Wesley off to fetch the gang's horses, concealed up Big Timber Road behind a thicket. While he was gone, Keech and the others assembled around Copperhead Rock. Nat explained that their group had been traveling on a northwest track, avoiding main roads and large towns. A few miles south of Big Timber they had spotted columns of dark smoke rising from a nearby valley. When they stashed their mounts and moved closer, they had found Keech and his ponies near the big rock.

"What happened down there, anyway?" Nat asked. He stooped to one knee and leaned on his Hawken rifle like a staff.

Keech hated to speak about his family's murderer. But if he wanted their help, they would have to hear as much as he could tell.

"A fella named Bad Whiskey Nelson is what happened. My pa said he rides with a cruel pack who call themselves the *Gita-Skog*. It's some kind of wicked militia, though Pa never told me where they come from or how many make up the outfit."

"I've heard the name," Nat said, glancing at his brother. "Their deeds are known farther down the state."

Keech pondered the comment. "The sheriff of Big Timber did say a terrible band of murderers had been sweeping the Territories. Just yesterday there was an incident over in Big Timber. A strange man shot up the telegraph and threatened the clerk."

"Same kind of thing happened down in Arkansas," Cutter said.

Nat grunted. "No coincidence, I reckon. Keep going, Keech."

"Whiskey rides a chestnut broomtail, but the horse looks sick, like it hasn't been fed for months. And there's a brand on its forehead."

"On the *forehead*?" Duck gasped. "That's awful!"

"It looks something like this—" Keech stooped and drew the brand in the dirt.

The group studied the marking.

"A spiral?" said Cutter.

"More like a rose," Keech said. "I just can't draw for spit. Whatever it is, I've never seen a brand like it in these parts."

Nat gave the symbol Keech had drawn a long look. "A rose," he muttered, as if a dark thought had crossed his mind. "Describe this Bad Whiskey. What's he look like?"

"He's no handsome man, that's for sure. He dresses in black and wears a pointy goatee. Carries a Dragoon, and smells like a ripe sty." Keech turned to Duck. "Was this the same man who killed your family?"

Duck opened his mouth to answer, but Nat put a hand on his shoulder, stopping him.

"The one who killed our folks goes by the name of Big Ben," Nat said. "A grizzly of a man who wears a tan riding coat and a long red beard, parted halfways in the middle like a lizard's forked tongue."

Keech thought back to the night before. No man among Whiskey's number had worn a parted red beard. And the largest goon in Whiskey's horde had been the thrall with the gold nose ring, the one Keech had thought of as Bull.

"All I know is, when the law finds Bad Whiskey, I want to lead him to the gallows myself," Keech said. "I want to look in his one good eye so he knows it was me who laid him low."

A visible shock registered on Cutter's face. "What do you mean, 'one good eye'?"

"Bad Whiskey is blind in one eye. He's got a filthy yellow glaze over the left one, like somebody took a rotted egg and smeared it over his eyeball."

Cutter dropped his head. "*El Ojo*," he murmured. His hand lowered to the bone grip of his giant knife, as though by habit.

"El what?" Keech looked at Nat and Duck, but the brothers said nothing.

Cutter gazed across the forest. "Maybe someday I'll tell you a story," he said to Keech. "A story about a boy named Bishop, my *amigo*, my one true friend—till he was put down by a cruel, murdering *bandido*. The one who killed him, I call him *El Ojo*. The Eye."

Cutter spoke the rest through a vicious scowl.

"The man in black you describe—I believe your Bad Whiskey is *El Ojo*. And he ain't yours for the taking, Blackwood. He's mine."

CHAPTER 11

I AM THE WOLF

Keech stepped closer to Cutter. "Not a chance," he said. "Hunting this man is all I have left."

Cutter's lips drew upward. "This ain't no debate, Lost Cause. I've been planning revenge on *El Ojo* for months. No way some orphan's gonna steal it."

Hearing Cutter use the name of the Home in a disparaging way sparked a brand-new flame of anger. "Don't you call me 'Lost Cause' again," Keech said.

"Or what, *Lost Cause*?"

The flame sizzled to a brush fire. Keech broadened his stance to scuffle again, but Nat stepped between them. "Settle down, both of you. Fighting won't bring anyone back. It certainly won't get you closer to your one-eyed outlaw."

A high whistle sounded nearby. Everyone looked around.

John Wesley came galloping up Big Timber Road, mounted on a fat calico gelding. Beside him trotted three other horses—a slender palomino mare, and a fine-looking pair of buckskin Fox Trotters.

As he rode up, John Wesley gestured over his shoulder. "Horses!" he shouted. "Approaching from the east!"

Keech scrambled up Copperhead Rock to get a glimpse. Though he couldn't see proper details yet, the sound of clopping hooves and clattering spurs galloped on the wind. Riders were indeed approaching, and traveling fast.

Nat whistled a shrill melody. In response, Cutter and Duck mounted their horses, preparing to light out.

When the first of the travelers galloped into Keech's view, he grinned. "It's the sheriff!" He climbed down Copperhead Rock. "Bose Turner is a good man. You can trust him."

Cutter snorted. "Ain't no such thing as a trusty lawdog."

Mounting his horse, Nat pointed toward Pa Abner's property. "We'll ride down to your land and water our mules. You talk to your sheriff, Keech. Explain who we are, what we're after. Maybe he'll help us track the outlaws. But if he tries to slow us, we'll scatter."

Keech found the plan agreeable. As the four young riders headed over White Elm Peak and down to the Home, he guided Felix and Minerva to the middle of Big Timber Road and stood facing east.

Give me strength, Sam, he thought, as four men led by Sheriff Turner galloped toward him, stirring dust clouds in their wake. When the sheriff saw him, he gave a sharp whistle and the company came to a stop in the road.

Keech doffed his hat. "Sheriff." His eyes prickled with relief at the sight of the big man.

"Mr. Blackwood."

Keech took a moment to peruse the troop. On Turner's left sat Deputy Goodlet, a pudgy, mean-faced lawman who'd never spoken a kind word to Keech or Pa Abner in his life. On the sheriff's right sat Deputy Ballard, the skinny man who had assisted Turner on Main Street.

Keech had assumed the other two men in the company would be lawmen as well. He was pleasantly surprised to see the third man was the white-haired clerk, Frosty Potter.

When Keech saw the fourth man, his stomach lurched with surprise and disgust.

The fourth rider was none other than Tommy Claymore, the peg-leg bandit.

The creature was hunched atop a speckled mustang, iron shackles binding his wrists to the pommel of his saddle. Keech couldn't believe how different he looked compared to the day before on Main Street. His pale face had turned the color of stale prunes, and his eyes had become two murky hollows, full of gloom and resentment. At first it appeared his mouth had fallen right off his face, but the lips were indeed there, just curled beneath his filthy beard, like a dried-up cicada shell.

Revulsion burned away any relief Keech had felt. "Sheriff, it sure is good to see you and your men," he said. "But why is *he* with you?"

Tommy Claymore cackled at the question. "'Cause judgment has come, you foolish tyke."

Frosty Potter leaned from his saddle and swatted the fiend's head. "That'll be enough out of you," the clerk said.

Claymore chuckled again and then quieted down.

Turner said, "This rascal is the reason we rode out. Last night he started babbling in his jail cell about some kind of attack. At first we thought he was trying to get a rise out of us, but when he mentioned a 'massacre,' I started asking questions."

Deputy Ballard said, "He offered enough details to make us think we oughta ride out and look."

Not wanting to be left out, Deputy Goodlet continued, "We had to bring him along 'cause he wouldn't tell us where the killin' happened."

"No sooner did we light out than Claymore mentioned the orphanage," Turner said. "I prayed he was lying, but not long after, we spotted smoke. Tell us everything, son. Spare no details."

Behind the sheriff, Claymore snickered.

Keech tried to ignore the brute. "All right, Sheriff. But please, keep his trap shut."

All strength left his body as he began the story. The fresh memories wrenched out the hot tears that hadn't wanted to fall before, forcing Keech at times to pause the tale, wipe his face with his coat sleeve, and collect his breath.

Turner listened without interrupting. When Keech got to the part about the Char Stone, the sheriff lifted his hand to stop him.

"Why would Whiskey want a blasted rock?" he asked.

Keech considered telling Turner what Pa had said in the study, that the Char Stone was a cursed thing. But he needed these men so that they could form a posse and ride down Whiskey.

For now he simply replied, "It's some kind of treasure."

"Must be worth a lot of *dinero*," Deputy Goodlet said. "Hey, Bose, maybe we'll get ourselves a finder's fee."

"Hush, Goodlet," Turner said.

After Keech had finished, Turner led the troop down to the Home. The air was a burden of churning smoke. The men gazed in disbelief at the mangled black heap that had once been the farmhouse.

"When I lay hands on this Whiskey Nelson, he'll regret the day he was born," Turner said.

Leading Minerva by her rope, Keech trotted Felix to the shake-pole fence, then stopped at the gate to let the lawmen proceed. He grimaced when Claymore passed, beaming his coyote grin.

"Lookit my master's fine work!" Claymore cheered. He rattled his shackles at the rubble, then leaned over his saddle to get closer to Keech. "You," the bandit whispered. "You have somethin' he wants."

Deputy Ballard took hold of Claymore's chains. "Quiet, you dog," he spat, and pulled on the shackles. "Apologies, Mr. Blackwood. I'll take this slug away and give you some peace."

"Much obliged, Deputy."

Ballard spurred his horse and led the peg-leg bandit out of sight.

Frosty halted beside Keech at the gate as Turner and Goodlet crossed the yard and disappeared around the smoking mountain of rubble. The clerk peered southward, where Ballard had taken Claymore, and said, "Mr. Blackwood, don't let that rattlesnake get under your skin. He ain't worth a lick."

"I sure am trying, Mr. Potter."

"Men who make wicked deeds in life are hollow on the inside."

Keech shuddered at Frosty's words. He remembered Sam's discussion back in Big Timber. *I can't shake a terrible feeling*, his brother had said. *Like that fella didn't have a soul.*

"I think this man is hollow in more ways than one," Keech said.

"Men like Claymore—" Frosty went on, but suddenly an angry shout rose from the backyard, where Bose Turner and Deputy Goodlet had disappeared. The white-haired man looked up. "What in blazes?"

The shout hadn't come from one of the men. The voice had belonged to a boy.

"Nat's gang!" Keech yelled. Claymore had caused such a distraction, he'd forgotten the plan to inform Turner about Nat and the others.

Leaving Minerva at the fence, he sped Felix around the rubble. Frosty followed on his roan. In the backyard they found Turner facing the open barn and leveling his Colt revolver at Nat, who had dropped to one knee and was holding his Hawken rifle to his side. Deputy Goodlet had pulled his own weapon on Cutter, who stood beside Nat, poised to chuck his massive knife. Duck and John Wesley stood behind Nat and Cutter in the barn, frozen in their tracks. Blue hens clucked around their boots, combing the dust for feed, oblivious to the conflict around them.

"Lay down your rifle!" Turner boomed.

"Mister, it ain't even pointed," said Nat.

"You have till the count of three!"

Keech rode up beside Turner. "Sheriff, I know these boys! They came down to water their horses."

In the barn's doorway, Cutter said, "Give the word, Nat. I'll practice my aim."

"Sheriff, these boys ain't your enemies," Keech said. "They're hunting the gang that killed their families."

Turner's steady gaze passed over each of them. "Is that true? You kids are tracking criminals?"

Slowly, Nat lowered his Hawken to the dirt. He gestured for Cutter to sheathe his knife. "Yessir, since early September," he said, rising.

Keech's thumping heart relaxed as Turner and Goodlet holstered their sidearms. Cutter was the only one left clutching his weapon. Nat turned back to him. "Dangit, Cut, put the knife away."

"Or what?"

"Or I'll do it for you."

Muttering, Cutter slid the long blade back into its sheath. One of Granny Nell's pigs came waddling up, fussing at the blue hens around Cutter's feet. Annoyed, he shooed the critters off with the side of his boot.

Keech and Frosty dismounted as Turner and Nat's gang walked carefully toward one another in the yard. Nat introduced his group, then stretched out his hand. Turner sized Nat up with great interest before shaking.

"That symbol," the sheriff said, pointing at the brown-and-yellow patch on Nat's coat. "I recognize it."

Nat glanced down at the patch with a small frown.

Turner opened his mouth to speak again, but a bluster of

horses from the south interrupted. It was Deputy Ballard, returning with Claymore. He was holding the bandit's chain in one hand and what appeared to be a scrap of black cloth in the other.

"Hey, Bose, I found this cloth back yonder," Ballard said.

"Where?" Turner asked.

"Over to the south. On a buckthorn bush."

"Maybe a strip of Whiskey's overcoat," Keech mused.

"I think I've located the gang's tracks, too. No thanks to this varmint." Ballard jostled Claymore's chain.

Turner eyeballed the patch on Nat's coat one last time before moving his gaze to the black scrap in Ballard's hand. "So what do you think?"

Ballard pointed back to the property's southern edge. "There's a path at the wood line. The weeds are pushed back there, and a few of those buckthorns have been trampled. Looks like Whiskey and his crew are headed straight for Farnham."

Beside the deputy, Tommy Claymore chuckled.

Duck clutched his coat at the sight of Claymore, looking quite uncomfortable just being near the scoundrel. "What is wrong with that fella?"

A voice of warning sounded in Keech's head. He had already tried, the morning before, to send Bad Whiskey down to Farnham on a wild-goose chase. But the man had seen through that deception. He wouldn't pursue that direction again, especially if he was acting on Pa's clues about this Char Stone and seeking the nearest graveyards. *A sullied place. A place of death*, Pa had told him. *I can feel its wickedness pulling at me from the west.* Farnham was a long ride, and the country along the way was empty of graveyards.

If Keech had to guess, the gang would be riding for Whistler, a peaceful village deep in the western forest. Many of its settlers were German immigrants. Keech had been there once, on a business trip with Pa to trade furniture for rice and salt pork.

"What now, Sheriff?" Frosty asked.

"I reckon it's time to find some good men, form a posse, and hunt these killers down."

The sheriff's words baffled Keech. Did Turner intend to ride all the way back to Big Timber simply to round up townsfolk? Such a thing would take hours, maybe a full day.

"Sheriff, we can't afford to lose time," Keech said. "Bad Whiskey is half a day's ride away. My hunch is he's ridden west to Whistler. If we don't ride now, he could destroy the place. Those people are defenseless."

Turner wrinkled his brow. "I know of Whistler. But Jake's found the trail south."

"It's a false one," Keech said. "The black cloth, the trampled weeds—it's all intended to throw us off. Whistler is where he's headed, I know it."

Deputy Goodlet snorted. "Ain't nothin' at Whistler but a bunch of plowchasers."

But Keech would not be bullied. "Sheriff, Whistler is in trouble. And after Whiskey's done there, he'll disappear."

"Keech, by your own words, there are half a dozen men in the outfit," Turner said. "We'd be outgunned."

"I have my Hawken," said Nat.

Turner wagged his head. "Absolutely not. I will not bring along a gaggle of hasty kids to track and arrest murderers. We're just not outfitted. We could be on the trail for days. I'm sorry, boys, but we do this by the book. We seek proper volunteers. We need full-grown *men*, and we need them well-armed."

Cutter pulled his giant knife again. "What do you call this, lawdog—a maple leaf?"

Deputy Goodlet grunted. "Put that knife away, green pea. You're gonna hurt yourself."

In a flash the blade appeared in Cutter's opposite hand. "Call me that again, you bog-trotter."

"Enough," Nat said, then turned back to the sheriff. "No disrespect, sir, but I have to side with Keech. The time to ride is now or never. My gang may be young, but we've been on the trail of these men for weeks. We've been studying their movements, the way they work. They travel in small packs, they strike quick, and they vanish into thin air once they're done."

"I understand the need for haste," Turner said. "But that don't change the fact that we need a posse of men, not boys."

Keech looked Turner straight in the eye. "Sheriff, I may be a greenhorn in your eyes, but I'm far from a child. Pa Abner prepared me well for this day. Please don't attempt to stop me."

"Nobody thinks you're a greenhorn, son," Frosty Potter said. "In fact, you saved every one of our hinds back in Big Timber. We can see the purpose in your eyes, and I am certain you're up to the task. But you can't go chasing after men willing to murder children unless you're equipped proper. They'd tear you apart."

Keech thought about the silver pendant in Felix's saddlebag, the way Pa had used the piece to destroy Whiskey's leprous thralls.

Because the sheriff's revolver might be worthless against the gang, it dawned on him he might be the best-armed person in the hunt.

"Mr. Potter, you're a wise man," he said. "There is no doubt, Bad Whiskey *could* tear us apart. He's a cold-blooded snake, and he's got the taste for blood. But that's exactly why Whiskey will not get the upper hand."

The clerk looked confused. "I don't follow."

"To catch a deadly snake, you need something worse. You need a predator, unafraid of the poison." Keech looked at Sheriff Turner to speak the rest.

"Well, Sheriff, I am the Wolf. And with or without you, I'm gonna find this murderer, and lead him straight to the end of a rope."

CHAPTER 12

A REVELATION AT SWIFT HOLLOW

According to Sheriff Turner's pocket watch, it was just after two o'clock when their posse set out for the village of Whistler. Keech had at last made the sheriff understand that the signs pointed to Whistler's demise. The town needed help, and they needed it quickly. Besides, the grateful folk of Whistler might help them form a proper posse. In the end, Turner made the call to ride west.

The group struck out at the westernmost edge of Pa Abner's property, taking the long path the old settlers had nicknamed Swift Hollow, for its curiously dark and winding terrain.

Eight souls made up the posse: Nat and his gang, Turner and his deputies, and Keech, who found himself riding next to Duck on the trail. The only man absent from the posse was Frosty. He had volunteered to stay behind and look after Pa's livestock. Keech had been so set on chasing Whiskey that he had mounted Felix and forgotten all about the other animals, including poor Minerva. He was happy they would be getting proper care.

The posse rode in silence—except for Duck. He never stopped speaking, but Keech didn't mind. The kid talked about everything—from building rabbit houses to making chokecherry stew.

"You sure do know a lot," Keech told the boy.

Duck smiled proudly. "Everything I know, I learned from my pa."

"Mine too. He had answers for every question."

"'Ask, and it shall be given to you,' my pa used to say. 'Seek, and ye shall find. Knock, and it shall be opened unto you.'"

"The Bible?" Keech said.

Duck nodded. "My pa used to say it all the time, during our lessons. He was the smartest man on Earth."

Keech thought Pa Abner was the smartest, but he knew better than to argue about the dead.

Behind them, Tommy Claymore rode between the deputies. Keech hadn't wanted the foul creature to come along, till he realized Claymore might be able to spill on Bad Whiskey's plans. The mongrel would never betray his master outright, but if someone pressed him for answers, he might just give something valuable.

Duck must have read the revulsion on his face, for he spurred his pony closer and said, "You never told us what's wrong with him. The fella in the chains."

Keech grimaced. "He's a walking dead man, is what's wrong."

Duck looked startled. "Sheriff's gonna lead him to the gallows, you mean?"

"No. I mean the man is *dead*. As in two-bullets-in-the-heart dead."

A few feet away, Cutter called out, "Who's dead?"

"Never mind," Keech returned.

Visibly shaken by Keech's words, Duck gazed off into the woods. After a time he said, "We didn't tell you about the night our folks died."

"Big Ben," Keech said, remembering his conversation with Nat. "Red beard parted like a forked tongue, right?"

"That's the one. Well, the night Big Ben attacked our ranch, he brought *something* with him. Some kind of monster."

"A thrall?"

Duck shrugged. "We never saw it, but Big Ben kept shouting at the woods like he was, I dunno, scolding it. When Nat and I was escaping, we heard it tear down one of our barns. The thing tore it down like the barn was paper."

"There's a mighty big thrall working for Whiskey," Keech said. "I call him Bull. Maybe he was the one responsible."

"Maybe so," Duck said. He pulled up the folds of his thick black coat, then shook his head a bit, as if readjusting his thoughts. Finally, the boy said, "I know you've been through a lot, Keech. We'll find the men who did this to your family. I swear it on my pa's name. We'll find Bad Whiskey."

"'Seek, and ye shall find,'" Keech said, and Duck smiled.

⌒

The first hour drifted by without occurrence—till Sheriff Turner called the posse to a sudden halt. A treacherous gully blocked the group's path, a chasm so deep and wide the trees on each side of the trail had tumbled right in. Tangles of limbs and roots stretched up from the massive void, rendering any sort of travel impossible.

Nat scrutinized the ugly ravine with a blank expression. "What happened here?" he asked. "Earthquake?"

"A great flood," Turner said. "It happened long ago, but the land never recovered. There are sinkholes all over this basin."

The group took a moment to rest the ponies and study the forest for an alternate path. Cutter reached back into his saddlebag and pulled out a wad of beef pemmican wrapped in gray cloth. He tore off small strips of the dried meat and offered some to each member of the outfit.

"Whistler is just beyond this stretch," Keech said. "We need to find a way through."

"We could dip into the woods here," said Turner, chewing a sliver of pemmican and pointing to where the gully stretched to the base of a tall, dismal-looking hill. "I'd rather not risk a deadfall, but the trail's too washed out to continue. Also, rain's approaching."

Dark thunderclouds had indeed amassed overhead. Sparks of lightning surged within them. Keech noticed something else. A trio of black dots were circling inside the clouds.

Crows.

Turner noticed Keech's gaze. He studied the black specks and puckered his long brow. "You're nervous about those birds. Why?"

Keech remembered Pa's warning again: *This world has many crows, and those crows can see far, and take what they see to dangerous places.*

He was about to explain what he knew, but Nat spoke first. "Those things are bad news."

"Your gang has seen the crows?" Keech asked.

Nat nodded gloomily. "First time was in Boone County, then farther north in Caldwell. They never flew down close, but they tracked every move we made, so we decided to ride in the forest, to hide from them."

"What fool talk is this?" Turner said.

Keech recalled how the crow had perched on Bad Whiskey's shoulder and murmured in the outlaw's ear. "They're not birds," he said to Turner. "I don't know what they are, but they're something else." He considered divulging the other peculiar things to the whole group—Pa's deadly silver pendant, the Char Stone that Bad Whiskey desired so badly—but Cutter and John Wesley were shifty sorts, prone to anger. Nat and Duck seemed trustworthy, but the other two boys might try to take the charm.

"The Devil's at work in Missouri," Cutter said. He had finished his ribbon of meat and was now twirling his long blade fretfully between his fingers. "I'd wager those birds even have the Devil's mark. We're in the last days, *hombres*."

"Bunch of baloney," Deputy Goodlet mumbled, rather uncertainly.

Keech paid no mind to the deputy. "What's he talking about, Devil's mark?"

"Did you ever study the Middle Ages?" Duck asked.

"I've read a story or two."

"Well, during the Inquisition, the preachers and holy folk believed the Devil put his mark on his witches to make them impervious to pain."

"That's a load of horse apples," said Nat.

"No, it's true!" said Duck. "Anything evil has to have a mark."

Keech remembered the sinister brand—the mark of the rose—under the forelock of Bad Whiskey's stallion. Goose bumps skittered over his arms. "Last night, I saw one of the crows," he said. "I don't recollect any particular mark, but I do know it was the ugliest bird I ever saw. Bigger than a burlap sack, and its beak was longer than a farmer's scythe."

Sheriff Turner said nothing, only stared at the savage gully in the Swift Hollow trail.

"I don't know if the Devil's in Missouri or not," Nat said to Cutter, "but whatever those critters are, they're here for a reason."

"They came with Bad Whiskey," Keech said. "They're connected to him." *And to a man named Rose*, he considered adding.

Tommy Claymore began to chortle. When Keech looked, the bandit wiggled two bony fingers at him, a malevolent wave. Deputy Ballard yanked the prisoner's chain to quiet him.

Nat turned their attention back to the gully. "So where do we go now?"

"We could send a scout over the hill," Turner said. "See if the woods are passable."

John Wesley had been sipping water from his canteen. At the mention of a scouting mission, he sat up straight and raised his hand. "I'll volunteer, Sheriff!"

"No, I'll go," said Deputy Ballard. "I'll drag Claymore along. If the mangy mutt sinks in a bog, we'll know it ain't safe."

Turner nodded. Ballard grabbed the prisoner's chain, spurred his pony with a loud "Giyyap!" and pulled the mumbling thrall and his mustang up the hill.

Turner pointed at his other deputy. "Goodlet, you follow."

The heavy lawman snorted displeasure. He peered over his shoulder at John Wesley. "That one craves adventure. Let him go."

"Don't make me say it again," Turner said.

Clucking at his horse, Goodlet rambled into the woods to join Ballard. Soon the two deputies and their prisoner disappeared over the hill and into the shivering gloom of the forest.

Once the men were gone, the sheriff turned back to the young riders. "This gives us time to speak private."

Keech and Nat exchanged a curious look.

Turner slid off his mount and smoothed a wrinkle from his riding coat. On Nat's orders, all the boys followed suit and stood by their ponies.

"Sheriff, if this is about us riding in the posse—" Keech began.

"No, it's not about that," Turner interrupted. "It's about something Claymore said, back at the jail. And about something I've seen."

"We're all ears, lawdog," said Cutter.

Turner lifted his hat and patted sweat off his brow. "Claymore didn't speak just about the attack on the orphanage. He mentioned another raid. Something he couldn't have possibly known, because he couldn't have been there. Last night he mentioned the storming of a ranch that took place in *September*. Talked as if he'd been there himself. But I shot and killed Tommy Claymore four months back in Gentry County."

"What do you mean, you killed him?" asked Nat.

"You weren't just putting on about him being dead?" Duck asked Keech.

"I tell you, it's the end of days!" said Cutter. He looked at his closest trailmate, but John Wesley kept silent.

"Never mind all that," continued Turner. "This ranch attack of which Claymore spoke. It happened all the way down the state. In Sainte Genevieve."

Keech felt his heart take a giant leap. Sainte Genevieve was the place where Pa's letter was to be telegrammed.

"Which brings me to the second matter," Turner said. "When I first met you boys, I noticed a symbol on your breast pocket, Nat." He pointed to the brown-and-yellow patch on Nat's coat.

"I bought this old thing in a store for a penny," Nat said. "Don't know why it's a bother."

"I sure was surprised to see it," said Turner. "'Cause I have seen that symbol before. Ten years ago, when a stranger came calling on Big Timber."

"Ten years ago?" Keech said. "That would've been the year Pa took me in."

Turner nodded. "In fact, this stranger was seeking Abner. Said his name was *Noah Embry*, though I recognized the face from a government poster, and the name on the poster was *Bennett Coal*, who was wanted for murder across three territories."

As Turner spoke, Nat's and Duck's faces turned the same pale color. Keech noticed Nat's hands had tucked into fists, and Duck's eyes looked on the verge of tears.

Turner continued. "Strange thing is, that fella who claimed to be Noah Embry wore a brown-and-yellow patch on his pocket. One that looked just like *that*." And again he pointed to the colorful emblem.

"What you're wearing, son, is the badge of the Cattleman's League of Sainte Genevieve. The badge a man wears when he builds a ranch in Sainte Genevieve County, pays his fees, and joins the League."

Nat hitched a breath. "Now wait a second, Sheriff."

"Which tells me," said Turner, allowing no interruption, "you have a connection to that old murderer, Bennett Coal. And I've got a feeling I know what that connection is."

The sheriff said nothing more. But there was no need. The answer struck Keech at once.

"You!" he exclaimed to Nat and Duck. "You're Noah Embry's kids!"

CHAPTER 13

THE ESCAPE

More answers tumbled into place in Keech's mind. Ten years ago, 1845, Noah Embry—whose real name was Bennett Coal, just like Pa's real name was Isaiah Raines—had come to north-west Missouri to find Pa. Both men had already said good-bye to their old lives, and had taken on new names, new identities. Noah Embry had tracked Pa back to Big Timber, because they'd stolen something from the Reverend Rose and had to conceal it.

They had to bury the Char Stone.

Now, Bad Whiskey's boss was back. *Your standing here tells me the Reverend's woken in the Palace*, Pa Abner had said to the man. Wherever this "Palace" was, Rose was now awake there and sending his militia across the country to hunt his property. The *Gita-Skog* had killed Embry before Pa could send the warning telegram.

Keech could tell Nat and Duck were feeling a perplexing sort of rage—the same rage he too had felt after Pa's secrets had been laid bare. But how much did the boys know? How much had their father, Noah Embry, told them about his old life as an Enforcer for Reverend Rose?

Duck responded to this unspoken question by jabbing a finger at Bose Turner.

"Pa was no murderer! He died a hero!"

Turner gave the boy a firm but sympathetic look. "Your father was a wanted man, Duck."

Nat growled at Keech, "And just what do *you* know about our pa, Blackwood?"

"Nothing that can help."

"You're a fighting liar."

"Now, boys, let's be civil," said Turner.

"Nat, believe it or not," Keech said, "our fathers knew each other."

Nat appeared to reach deep back into his memories. "Pa never mentioned yours at all," he said. "Not a word."

"I believe they rode together, a long time ago. They worked for a man named Rose."

Nat suddenly frowned. "*Rose*," he murmured, the same way he had spoken the word back at Copperhead Rock. "This name I do know. I've heard it in whispers." He looked to Duck, but the small boy only shook his head. "Pa had bad dreams. He talked in his sleep. He used to mutter things about a 'Rose' and a place called 'the Palace.'"

"My pa mentioned that place, too," Keech said.

"You best tell us everything you know," Nat demanded.

Turner said, "Yes, Mr. Blackwood, no more secrets."

The only peaceful solution at this point was to reveal the

telegram. Pa had been very specific about keeping the letter secret, and Keech didn't know whom to trust yet, but there was nothing for it. If he didn't talk, there would be trouble.

Before he could begin, a loud squeal tore across Swift Hollow.

"Help!" a voice caterwauled.

The posse spun around to see Deputy Goodlet, running on foot down the big hill. His pony was nowhere in sight.

Turner sprinted toward the deputy. Keech dashed after him, the four young riders close on his heels.

"What's happened?" Turner hollered.

"Murder!" Goodlet screamed. At the bottom of the hill the heavyset deputy tripped on a root and skidded in the dirt in front of Turner. A miserable grunt spilled out of the man.

"For God's sake, Goodlet, find your wits," Turner said.

The deputy rolled onto his back and pointed up the hill. "He—he killed Jake!"

Turner pulled his handgun. He ordered the posse back onto their horses. Everyone complied except Goodlet, who refused to budge from the ground. Turner scowled at him.

"Don't just sit in the dirt, deputy."

"But I ain't got my horse!"

"Mount up with me, then. Till we find your mule, leastways."

The deputy shook his jowls. "I ain't goin', Bose! That foul prisoner ain't natural!"

"If you don't mount up, you'll go straight back to Big Timber, where you'll be known as a coward."

"Dandy!" the deputy bawled. "Just don't make me enner them woods again."

Turner waved at the posse to gather behind him. "I have no time for yellow-bellies," he declared, and led the young riders off the trail and toward the hill.

Keech glanced back at Goodlet—but the man was now racing up the Swift Hollow road, the very way they'd come.

Hordes of trees cluttered the hillside, but Turner was quick to find the surest path. Once they made the top, Keech spotted Goodlet's horse, standing lost and bewildered, at the bottom of the other side. Ballard's pony and Claymore's mustang stood a few yards away. The bandit was nowhere in sight.

When the group reached the horses, Turner noticed something in a thornbush ahead of them and dismounted. He walked a few feet—then halted in his tracks.

"Keep away, boys!" he gasped, staring down into the brush.

They didn't have to move closer to see the pair of slender brown boots sticking out of the undergrowth. The toes of the boots pointed straight up to the heavens, frozen, lifeless. Though Keech couldn't see the man, he knew the body was Deputy Ballard.

"Deputy!" cried Duck.

The young riders hopped off their horses. Upon seeing the motionless feet in the brush, John Wesley turned a ghastly shade of white.

Turner knelt beside his fallen deputy, slipped off his hat, and took a moment to collect his emotions. "So sorry, old friend," he said to the man in the brush, then rolled Ballard onto his side. The sheriff looked up, surprised, and said, "He's lying on a full holster. Claymore rushed off so quick he forgot to steal Jake's revolver." He reached beneath the body and tugged. The handgun snagged inside the holster, but after a strain it came free.

Something on the ground caught Keech's eye—a curious hunk of meat lying near his boot in the dead grass.

"Um, Sheriff?" He pointed to the white lump. "What is this?"

Turner walked over and dropped to his haunches. His face scrunched.

"That, Mr. Blackwood, is a *thumb*."

Turner picked up the severed digit and held it up to the hazy sunlight. It looked like a fat, white slug in the sheriff's glove. A glimpse of the gruesome discovery made John Wesley heave.

Turner inspected the grimy digit. He peered back up the wooded hill.

"What do you think happened?" Nat asked.

Turner tossed the horrid thing back into the grass and wiped his glove on his trousers. "It appears our prisoner bit off his own thumb."

The young riders groaned.

"Why would he do such a foul thing?" Cutter asked.

"So he could slip a hand out of his shackles," Turner replied. "I'm guessing the moment Jake turned his back, that rascal whipped him in the head with the fetter. Looks like he then used the chain to strangle him."

Duck pointed to a row of trampled weeds nearby. "There! He left a trail! A powerful obvious one, too."

Keech grew excited when he saw Claymore's path. Two winters ago, Pa Abner had taken him and Sam on a hunting expedition through Swift Hollow, so this whole swath of land was familiar. These particular slopes formed a rough circle, a loop of forest so thick the hills themselves offered little for good hunting. It was only when Pa had led them into the midst of the circle, a glade full of poppies and wild onions, that they had found the small game they wanted.

Based on the track left behind by his peg leg, Tommy Claymore was taking the easiest path available to him. Most likely without knowing, he was headed straight for the glade.

Turner gripped a revolver in each hand. "Listen up," he said. "The slopes will wear the horses down, so we'll leave them here. We'll keep together and watch each other's backs." He then leveled a concerned gaze at Nat's Hawken. "Don't bother with that rifle if you see Claymore. If my Colt couldn't kill him months back, cracking off a musket shot certainly won't either. We'll act together, tackle him down as a team."

Nat nodded.

The posse started through the forest, up the next hill. Nat, Duck, and John Wesley moved close behind Turner, but Keech held back, letting them move ahead. There was a cutoff to the glade. He could stop Claymore in his tracks. No one else would have to get hurt.

Cutter was the last in line to follow the others. He saw Keech lingering, and jogged back. "What are you up to, Lost Cause?"

"You go on. I'll catch up."

Cutter gave him a suspicious look. "You aim to track this *demonio* yourself!"

"I know these woods like the back of my hand," Keech replied. "Now go. I'll cut him off at the next hill and push him back to you fellas."

Cutter lingered a moment longer, frowning, then hurried away to rejoin the others.

The moment the posse disappeared, Keech ran back to Felix and grabbed the silver pendant from his saddlebag. He slung its cord around his neck and stowed the charm inside his coat. Then he bolted toward the cutoff around the hill. He knew Turner would scold him for going off on his own, but if it meant capturing Claymore, Keech would take his chances.

It was time to get information.

Thick branches crossed overhead, blocking out the gray sky. To the untrained eye, there was no obvious path here—it was really nothing more than a jackrabbit run—but Keech's eye had been trained to read the trail toward the clearing. He sprinted over the land, putting Turner and the troop a good distance away.

All the red poppies that had once peppered the glade were dead, but the wild onions were still in bloom, giving the dell a rowdy fragrance. Surrounding the area was a thick ring of tall redbuds. The cool glow of the late afternoon sunlight fumed through the branches, filling the space with dusky hues.

Keech paused beside one of the redbuds to catch his breath. Claymore had to be close.

Unnatural cold suddenly burned his chest. Gasping for breath, Keech ripped at the front of his coat. His first thought was that he'd been shot through the heart. But then he realized it was the silver charm stinging him. He snatched the pendant out of his shirt. Though the light was dim in the glade, the shard yielded a bright yellow and gold in his hand, even as it sent icy pulses over his flesh.

He stuffed it back down into his shirt, grimacing, the cold on his skin sharper than ever.

"Howdy, boy," came a voice from behind him.

The speaker had taken him by surprise, but Keech's mind and body flashed back to his training. Pa Abner swinging the tomahawk.

Keech ducked.

No sooner did he move than a whooshing sound droned over his head, followed by a loud *clunk*. The black iron of a shackle cuff had bitten deep into the bark of the redbud he'd been standing beside.

Keech wheeled around to see Tommy Claymore before him, grinning. The thrall had just swung his shackle like a spiked metal ball. The iron was stuck, buried in the wood.

"I've been waitin' for ya," the bandit said. "I felt ya comin'." He tugged at the iron, but the cuff held firm in the trunk. "You've somethin' the Master wants."

"Claymore," Keech hissed. "You'll pay for killing Deputy Ballard."

"You foolish waif. Hand over the shard." He yanked at the iron again. The cuff tore loose, showering splinters across the ground. He swung the shackle back and forth, a deadly pendulum.

Keech looked left and right. Redbud trees and thick underbrush were blocking the clear paths on each side.

The bandit loomed closer. The shackle whooshed back, building cruel momentum.

Pa's voice sounded in Keech's mind: *Watch the eyes, the shoulders. Keep your feet steady.* Mindful of his stance, he concentrated on the sway of the iron. No different from the training woods beyond Low Hill. He lifted one arm to shield his head, knowing the iron would demolish every bone in his wrist and forearm, but hopefully it would be enough to protect his skull if the shackle struck.

Claymore's iron came whistling down, a near invisible arc. Visualizing Pa's tomahawk, Keech sidestepped to the left, keeping his breath composed. The cuff mauled the ground beside his boot. The bandit pulled back, yanking fresh earth with the metal, and began swinging the chain all over again.

"Stand still!" Claymore growled. The claw dropped again, this time clipping the redbud so hard a limb sheared away.

Keech heard a vicious yell and saw a figure leap out of the redbud thicket. The figure slammed into Claymore's side. The thrall and the assailant tumbled to the ground.

In the blur, Keech spotted a red sash and a blue bandana.

"Cutter!" he yelled. The boy had emerged from the same path Keech had used to get ahead of Claymore. He must have backtracked and followed.

After hog-rolling the bandit onto his back, Cutter planted a fist between the thrall's eyes. Claymore squawked and flailed his arms, trying to squirm free.

"Back in Big Timber I beaned this monster with a shovel," Keech said. "You have to hit him hard enough to really clean his plow."

Cutter dropped his fist a second time, then a third. At last Claymore stopped thrashing and he fell back, dazed and muttering, into the wild onions. Chest heaving, Cutter stood. He brushed dirt off his coat, then smirked at Keech.

"Thanks for the tip, Lost Cause."

Keech would have been cross at the nickname were he not so relieved. "Much obliged for the help."

"Nothing to it," Cutter replied. "Now, let's get some answers before Mr. Lawdog finds out we slipped away."

CHAPTER 14

THE INTERROGATION

The stench wafting off the bandit made Keech's eyes water. He wrinkled his nose.

"Ugh, what a stink," Cutter said, lifting his bandana over his mouth.

"It's worse today. It's like he's falling apart."

Cutter noticed the holes in Claymore's chest. "Blackwood, he's been shot! How can a man still breathe with holes in his heart?"

"Because this is no man."

"What is he, then?"

Back at the Home, Bad Whiskey had used a name that sounded like *See-New*, but Keech only knew them as one thing. "He's a thrall."

"What's that?"

"An abomination. A dead man Bad Whiskey raised from the grave, and commands. And unless we stop him, Whiskey will use more like him to kill every last person in his path."

Cutter crossed himself.

"Let's get this over with," Keech said, and kicked the dazed bandit's wooden stub. The creature's eyelids fluttered. He lifted his hand as if to block the sunlight, saw he was missing his digit, and gave a confused bluster.

"Where in tarnation's my thumb?"

"You bit it off," Keech said.

"I don't recollect doin' that."

Keech dared one step closer. Again, he became aware of the pulsating chill inside his shirt.

The thrall's dark eyes started wide as Keech moved in. Claymore scurried backward on his rump, his flimsy arms flailing. "Don't come any closer!" he screeched. He scooted till his back ran against a redbud. Having nowhere else to go, he thrashed his head and kicked his left leg.

"I'm not going anywhere. You're gonna tell me about Bad Whiskey."

Claymore paused his flailing to give Keech a curious look. "The Master?"

"Yes, your rotten master. What's he planning?"

Claymore looked off into the woods.

"Speak, Claymore. I'm warning you."

"Warn all ya want! I shall not bend. The Master won't allow it."

Keech wondered if the creature had any measure of his own free will. During the raid on the Home, Whiskey's demons had appeared to be acting of their own accord, without the outlaw having to compel them.

If thralls could indeed make their own choices, perhaps friendly reason could work.

"Bad Whiskey left you back in Big Timber to rot in jail," Keech said. "All he wants is to command you, turn you about like a branded steer. He couldn't care less if we killed you for good and left your body for the buzzards. Defy him, Claymore. Tell me what he's planning. If you do that, maybe Sheriff Turner can even take you back to Gentry County, where you can start a new life, find some purpose."

Claymore lowered his filthy brow, as if considering the offer. But just as quickly, the frown turned to a hateful smile.

"Foolish boy. The Master *is* my purpose."

Keech reckoned thralls made their decisions only to serve the one who had called them forth. He would have to try a different tactic. "You're falling apart, Claymore. Your master must not be feeding you any more life. How do you feel about that?"

"The Master raised me from the pit. He won't let me rot and die."

Cutter's hand dropped on Keech's shoulder. "My turn," he said, and drew his long blade. A devilish grin flashed behind his bandana. It took no imagination to know exactly what Cutter wanted to do.

The bandit hawked a ball of black spit between Cutter's boots. "You won't bend me neither, kid! Yer all gurgle and no guts!"

"Let's find out," Cutter said.

But as he moved in, Keech held up his arm. "No. Put the knife away."

"Step aside, Lost Cause. I can get us every answer we need."

"Poking him with that blade will do no good. A thump on his head can clean his plow, I reckon, but back at the Home I wounded two of these monsters and they just kept coming. They don't care much about pain."

"He'll feel this, all right. My blade is special. It'll make this snake talk."

Keech considered his next action carefully. There was something in Cutter's eyes, a kind of fretting darkness that looked ravenous for blood. And if what he'd said about his friend Bishop was true, that Bad Whiskey had murdered him in cold blood, Cutter had as much right to seek revenge as the next person. *My amigo, my one true friend*, Cutter had said. If Keech appreciated one thing, it was the power of brotherhood and friendship. He would not leave Cutter in the dark for the sake of lone retribution.

"There's another reason we don't need the knife," Keech said.

Cutter smirked. "What's that?"

Keech rummaged down the neck of his coat and fished out Pa's pendant. The freezing silver captured the wan sunlight and glowed a fiery golden-orange.

"If anything can get him to talk, this will."

A peculiar look crossed Cutter's face. The hand holding the knife dropped to his side.

He's seen this before, Keech thought, but before he could ask about his expression, Tommy Claymore jumped to his one good foot, shoved Keech off balance, and hobbled off through the forest.

The boys didn't have to run far. They pushed the thrall back on his rump, against another redbud. For the moment, Keech forgot all about the look on Cutter's face when he saw Pa's charm.

"It's time you talk, you filth." He nodded at Cutter. "Grab him."

Cutter seized the bandit's arms.

Keech leaned in close, resisting the impulse to turn away from the smell. "You should have minded," he told the thrall, and dangled Pa's pendant in front of Claymore's face.

Numbing cold traveled up the cord and infiltrated Keech's palm. Claymore let loose the most despicable scream Keech had ever heard, a cry that would surely bring Turner running. Though it could have been a trick of the light through the branches, Keech thought he could see spiderwebs of broken black veins appear along Claymore's face and neck.

"Get it away!" the thrall shrieked.

"Give me answers, I remove the charm."

"If I talk, the Master will know!"

Cutter made a huffing sound. "Your master ain't here."

The black veins along the thrall's face and neck were now pulsing, as though on the verge of bursting. "The Master knows all!"

Keech drew back the charm. He needed the thrall to give answers, not spit curses and warnings. The black veins stopped pulsing and Claymore slumped, exhausted.

"Has Bad Whiskey found the Char Stone, Claymore?"

In the distance there came a loud call, booming across the forest. Sheriff Turner was shouting Keech's name.

Cutter gave him a confused look. "What's a Char Stone?"

Keech ignored the boy's question. "Has he gone to Whistler? Has he found the Stone there?"

"I shan't speak another word," Claymore said.

Keech shoved the pendant forward again, to where the silver almost touched the bandit's cheek. The creature screeched in pain.

"Talk," Keech growled.

"The Master is done at Whistler!" Claymore hollered.

Keech's heart gave a stutter. The posse was too late. Bad Whiskey had already found Whistler, and had finished his work there.

"He's movin' on to the Sullied Place!" the bandit sputtered. "Where all men wither!"

Keech knew what Claymore was suggesting, and his blood ran cold at the thought of it. But there was one last question to ask.

"The Char Stone, Claymore. What is it? Is it a weapon of some sort?"

There was a silence. Then the thrall answered, "Life. The Stone is *life*."

Life? Perhaps the Stone was some kind of healing charm?

Keech opened his mouth to pose his next question, but then something strange fell over the thrall's expression. A delighted sort of smile, as if he was seeing someone he hadn't seen in a long time. He twisted his face toward the sky and beamed. His eyes rolled like marbles in their sockets. The pendant began to pulse again, pushing cold deeper into Keech's hand.

Cutter took a step back. "We should get out of here."

Claymore arched his back and wailed.

The pendant was so cold it was now burning Keech's flesh.

"Let's go," Cutter said.

Claymore spoke then—but with a meaner, lower voice. When Keech heard it, he stiffened down to his boots. For the voice was all too familiar.

"Hello, pilgrim."

Tommy Claymore leaned back against the tree. The bandit's

wrinkled mouth stretched into a vicious grin. Keech was horrified to see the left eye on the creature had glazed over a dull yellow.

"Bad Whiskey?" said Keech.

"You've been talkin' to my thrall," the bandit said, in Bad Whiskey's voice.

"What do you mean 'Bad Whiskey'?" Cutter hissed. "Are you telling me this is *El Ojo*?"

Bad Whiskey turned Claymore's right eye toward Cutter. "*Herrera!* Good to see ya again! How's life as a free man?"

Cutter's mouth dropped into a bewildered O. He raised his knife, but for once he looked confused regarding what to do with it.

"You should be more careful about yer trailmates," Bad Whiskey said to Keech. "Herrera will sink that knife in yer back soon as spit in yer face."

Keech was still so bewildered that Bad Whiskey was using the bandit's body to see and talk that few of the outlaw's words even registered. But fury soon overpowered his shock and confusion. "*This* is how your thrall knew about my family's murder!"

Bad Whiskey grinned. "We share a bond, my thralls and me. They slaughter the pig, I cook the bacon. This one here has proved useful, so ever' now and then, I sneak a few peeks to see what he knows. Except he's been tellin' you pilgrims too much. Ol' Tommy's use, I'm afraid, has run out."

Keech felt his face turn flame red. "It's a fine trick, Bad Whiskey. But I heard what my pa said. You have no power of your own. You borrowed power from the Reverend Rose."

Bad Whiskey shook Claymore's head. "Arrogant boy. I was like you once. An orphan. Cast off, sunk in the mud. Believin' I knew it all. Then the world showed me true wisdom. Showed me the magics that hide in the dark, the hollow places where men refuse to go, but where the best treasures lay hid, waitin' for the right hand to seize 'em."

Keech bared his teeth. "I'm gonna find you, Bad. I swear upon my family's honor I'll make you pay."

Whiskey offered another black grin. "Fool toddler, I'll have the Stone in hand before yer posse can find the first horse track."

Keech recoiled at the monster's words. "You know about the posse?"

"Like I told Raines, little pilgrim, I got me a thousand eyes."

Through the forest canopy Keech spotted at least four of the dreadful crows under the dark thundercloud, circling, watching. *They take what they see to dangerous places*, he thought.

Cutter's tongue at last thawed. "You killed my friend Bishop!"

Bad Whiskey paused to think. "Don't recollect the name. Then again, I kill lots of folks."

"You'll recollect it when I find you," Cutter said. "I know where you're headed next."

Bad Whiskey chortled. "You don't know nothin'." The thrall rose to his lone foot, his wooden leg stabbing the earth. Both boys took a fighting stance, but the outlaw didn't attack. Instead he crooned, "You boys think this world is good. You think folks are worth protectin'. But even the good turn bad in the end."

"What are you talking about?" Keech asked.

"Had me a little peek through Tommy's eye, and I saw who yer ridin' with. The children of a backstabbin' double-crosser."

Keech guessed he was talking about Nat and Duck. But what did he mean by double-crosser? "You don't make any sense," Keech said.

"Oh? Ever wonder how I found yer Home for Lost Causes?"

Keech narrowed his eyes.

Bad Whiskey sneered. "Bennett Coal gave up your so-called pa, pilgrim. Poor Raines put his trust in the wrong Enforcer."

Keech was dumbstruck. "You're lying!"

"When the *Gita-Skog* came callin', Bennett Coal—or Noah Embry, or whatever name he was usin'—told us right where to look."

Keech staggered back at Whiskey's words. To think the very man Pa Abner had tried to warn had betrayed his location to the *Gita-Skog*.

He turned to Cutter. "Is that true? Did Nat and Duck's father squeal on my pa?"

"No clue, Blackwood."

Keech seized the boy's coat by one sleeve. "Tell me!"

Cutter struggled in his grip. "I don't know! Even if he did, I'm sure *they* don't know. Now turn me loose!"

Keech released Cutter's coat and spun back to the outlaw. "I don't believe a word you're saying."

Bad Whiskey chuckled again. "You may think me a rattle-snake, little pilgrim, but I don't spit corral dust."

Shaking with uncontainable anger, Keech leaned in closer. He wanted so badly for the creature before him to be Bad Whiskey, but the one-eyed outlaw was across the countryside, stealing closer toward the Char Stone.

"You'll regret the day you met me, Whiskey Nelson. I swear you will."

"Strong lip for a pup! I am the *Gita-Skog*, boy, the Big Snake that consumes all. I regret nothin'."

"You're not the *Gita-Skog*. You're nothing but a low worm."

The outlaw considered the insult, then gazed deep into Keech's eyes. He muttered five final words: "Yer all going to die."

There was a brief silence, then Claymore's left eye returned, only to roll back again to its cloudy white, along with his right one. Death spilled into his gaze, and the creature toppled to the ground in a heap. Two small tendrils of dark smoke rolled out of the thrall's nostrils, reminding Keech of the black dust that had billowed from Cooper's mouth after Pa vanquished him on the Home's porch.

The boys waited, eyes focused on the lifeless form. But the creature lay still.

"What happened?" Cutter said.

"I think Bad Whiskey killed Claymore. For good."

Somewhere to the north, the whimper of a loon filled the deep ravines and bottoms of Swift Hollow.

Then a deep commanding voice invaded the glade.

"Keech Blackwood!"

The boys spun to see Sheriff Turner, marching toward them through the clearing. His revolver was drawn but not aimed, and Deputy Ballard's gun jutted from his belt. Nat and Duck and John Wesley stood in the distance, watching at the forest's edge.

As Turner crossed the clearing, Keech whispered urgently to Cutter. "If he blames us for killing Claymore, no need for both of us to go to jail. I'll take responsibility."

"I don't like you, Lost Cause," Cutter said. "But I don't reckon it'd be right to let you take a fall."

The sheriff approached with a jangle of spurs. Keech braced himself for judgment, but none came. Instead the man put away his revolver and set a hand on Keech's shoulder. "Thank goodness you kids are all right," he said. His face was gray, his gun hand slightly trembling. "We heard the commotion across the hills and started running. We got here just in time to see what happened to this wretch." He stretched one tall leg over, nudged the corpse's wooden peg with a boot. "Looks to be all the way dead now."

"Sheriff, I'll explain everything soon," Keech said. "But first you have to listen. I know where Bad Whiskey's headed. Before he died, Claymore mentioned a 'sullied place' where Whiskey's riding, a place where 'all men wither.'"

Even as he spoke the words, the old childhood rhyme fluttered into Keech's mind:

Should you be there in deepest night ... in moon as dim as candlelight ...

"Sullied place?" Turner said.

"We have to ride on west," Keech said. "And we have to ride fast. Bad Whiskey is headed for the Withers graveyard, Sheriff. He's headed for Bone Ridge."

CHAPTER 15

WHAT HAPPENED AT WHISTLER

The day was slipping to a cold, early darkness. Rounding the deep gully on the trail had stolen some time, but the posse galloped through the forest to make it up. Keech noticed a strange warmth, a heat that was far from comforting. It was the heat of cinder and flame, drifting like a dragon's gasp over the land. He knew the feel of fire in the air too well.

The group soon emerged onto a flat valley, separated by a narrow river. Alongside its bank stretched a wide gravel road, choked on each side by runs of high thistle. Turner gazed up and down the road. "This path looks familiar, but it's been a long time since I've been in these parts."

"This road is called the Old Meriwether," Keech explained. "Up ahead is the Whistler cutoff. We'll have to cross the river, but the waters should be low enough."

The sheriff steered the posse up the Old Meriwether till the forest dipped to the river. The broad trench created by the dip churned with muddy water. This was the opening to the river that would lead them to Whistler.

"Everyone hang on," Turner said.

The posse drove their horses into the river. John Wesley sucked in a loud breath as icy water filled his boots. "I don't like water none," he said, but continued on. One by one they trudged across the channel, the horses whickering at the harsh bath.

"The settlers here nicknamed this river the 'Little Wild Boy,'" Keech said, as the group navigated the channel. "It loops around the countryside and feeds into the Platte River."

"That's dandy," said John Wesley. "But the Little Wild Boy's freezing my gizzard."

Moments later the horses made the opposite bank. As they slogged up the shore, Keech saw the first signs of billowing smoke, just over the western tree line.

"We're too late," he said.

Crackling thunder spoke of rain as they galloped into the settlement. Though their quarry was nowhere in sight, Sheriff Turner pulled his revolver and held it close to his side. "Stay alert," he told the group. He tossed a pressing glance at Nat. "You're the only one who can offer backup if I get into a gunfight. How fast are you at the reload?" He pointed to the Hawken in Nat's hand.

"Fast enough," Nat said.

Buildings blazed on each side of Whistler's main thoroughfare, and behind the buildings, rows of beleaguered cabins and tents smoldered and sputtered. Only a couple of structures remained untouched: a decrepit tack-and-saddle shop and a leaning white gazebo standing in the middle of Main Street.

Beneath the gazebo, a dozen of the residents huddled together under blankets, watching the fires incinerate their village. It was a desolate sight. One of the settlers noticed the posse and cried out in terror. He exclaimed something in another language—German, Keech reckoned—and the townsfolk uttered a collective shriek. They bolted out of the gazebo and scattered to the hills.

Cutter's eyes widened. "Why are they running?"

"They think we're part of Whiskey's gang," Nat said.

Duck gazed at the village in disbelief. Reflection from the fires turned his small face into a wavering mask of sorrow. "Poor folks never knew what hit them."

"What was Whiskey even doing here?" John Wesley asked.

Keech knew it was now time to divulge the rest of Pa Abner's information. If he kept the rest of what he knew silent, it could end up getting someone hurt. Or worse.

"He's hunting an object called the Char Stone," he told them. "He wants it more than anything."

John Wesley frowned. "What in heck's a Char Stone?"

Cutter wiped grime off his face with the back of his hand. "That dead man with the wood leg spoke of it. Back in the clearing. He called it 'life.'"

"You've heard your pa speak from dreams about Rose," Keech told Nat. "Did you ever hear him mention the Char Stone?"

Nat and Duck exchanged a quick look, then Nat said, "Our pa never spoke about his past. He didn't speak much at all."

Never spoke much except to betray Pa Abner, Keech thought

sullenly. Instead he said, "Whatever it is, my pa believed it to be cursed, a thing that shouldn't be touched by man. Whiskey came here to sack graves for it. There was nothing to find, so he's headed to the next graveyard up the trail."

"Bone Ridge," Turner said.

Keech nodded, but a skeptical look had returned to the lawman's face. "This is all real, Sheriff," Keech added. "My pa died protecting this thing's location."

"Magic stones and dead outlaws walking about." Turner shook his head. "Let's just look for wounded, shall we? There could be someone in need."

Down the far end of Main Street stood a small white church, a building Keech had seen before, back when he and Pa had paid their visit. Heavy smoke billowed from the church's busted-out windows.

"The church," Keech said. "There's a graveyard behind it. I'd wager Bad Whiskey aimed his search there for the Char Stone."

"All right, let's check it out," Turner said.

The fire in the church had strengthened by the time they arrived. Keech skirted the property on the blaze's windward side, watching for signs of a shift in the wind. Behind the church stood a crumbling fieldstone wall, no higher than a man's thigh. The Whistler cemetery lay on the other side. Several yards beyond the cemetery snaked the Little Wild Boy, meandering off through the valley.

The posse dismounted. Leaving their horses untethered at the wall, they moved quietly into the graveyard. At least two dozen graves had been disturbed. Tall mounds of earth stood beside each hole, resembling tiny mountains all along the pitted ground. Stepping to a grave, Keech looked down. At the bottom of the hole rested a wooden casket, smashed open. The rotten corpse inside had been turned over, almost crushed to pieces. Horrific proof that Bad Whiskey knew no bounds of decency.

Standing over another pit, Duck shouted, "Nobody's in this one!"

"Same goes here," Cutter called, peering into a third grave.

Waiting at the boneyard's entrance, John Wesley asked, "Why would some of the bodies be missing?"

Keech understood right away. Bad Whiskey had lost half his gang when Pa Abner faced them. Not only had he come to search for the Stone, he'd come to replenish his army.

"He turned them into thralls, like Claymore," he said.

"Swell," John Wesley mumbled.

Nat pointed to a stand of oak trees beyond the graveyard. "Look!"

An old man with a mess of shaggy white hair had emerged from behind the brush. He took slow, deliberate steps toward them, favoring his right foot from a slight limp. He wore a pair of ragged bib overalls, the kind with the apron sewn to his trouser waist. The right side of his head trickled blood.

"Hello, the graveyard!" the stranger called.

Turner raised his Colt. "That's far enough, mister."

The stranger held up his hands but didn't stop walking. "Don't shoot! I don't mean no harm!"

"What were you doing out there in the trees?" Turner asked.

"Ran for cover when them others started shooting up the

town," the old man said. He stumbled over a small root. "I confess to having little pluck. I ain't no gunfighter."

"Your name?"

The stranger shuffled to the cemetery wall. Now that he was close, Keech could see the blood was running from a terrible gash across his hairline.

"Melvin Twiggs. I'm the mayor here. I gather y'all ain't with that one-eyed feller?"

Turner lowered his revolver. "No, sir. My name's Bose Turner, sheriff over to Big Timber. These are my"—he glanced around at the boys—"deputies. We're here to bring the men responsible for this to justice."

Mayor Twiggs shook his wounded head. "You're a bit tardy, I'm afeared. Them long riders done already come and gone."

"How long ago?" Nat asked.

The old man considered. "No more'n a half hour, I'd say."

"We're close!" Duck said.

"Did you see which way they rode?" Keech asked.

Mayor Twiggs pointed across the river, to a deep, ominous-looking wilderness. Thunderclouds filled the dusky sky and cast dark shadows over the valley. The idea of riding into that horrid thicket under rain and lightning made Keech's skin crawl.

The old man pulled a yellow kerchief out of his overalls. As if he had just realized he was cut, he began to wipe the blood off his brow. "You can't mean to pursue 'em," he said.

Turner nodded. "We do."

"But your posse's just kids and such!"

"We're no more kids than you're a mayor," Cutter grumbled. He glanced back at John Wesley and chortled.

Turner glared at the boy. "Be cordial. He's been hurt."

Mayor Twiggs shrugged at Cutter. "Whatever ya say, kid. There's a problem, anyhow. That forest where the gang rode . . ." An uncomfortable pause hung on the next word, as the old man drew a fear-soaked breath. "It's known as Floodwood." He sighed bitterly, as if the name explained everything.

"So?" Turner said.

"Ain't you heard?" The old man flashed a single brown tooth. "Floodwood is *cursed*."

The company swapped a mixture of concerned and confused looks. Cutter wagged his head. "Nuh-uh, no way I'm riding into a cursed forest. Bad enough I gotta follow walking, talking dead men." He spun on his heel and stomped back to his horse.

"That's the biggest load of codswallop I ever heard," Turner said to the old man.

"No, sir, it's true!" said Mayor Twiggs. Heaving with the effort, he lifted one leg and struggled over the fieldstone wall. Keech put a hand out to help him over. After gaining his breath, the old man continued. "Past ten years, nobody who's rid into Floodwood has ever come back to Whistler."

"What makes it so dangerous?" John Wesley asked.

"Yer guess is as good as mine," Mayor Twiggs replied. "I've never stepped a toe in there. But some folk claim they've heard a monster's roar come from the heart of that forest."

A fat drop of rain plopped on Keech's cheek. He looked up at the dark clouds. The rains would douse the remaining fires in

Whistler, but the damage had been done. The village was now just a memory, a ghost story to be shared around a campfire.

"We should ride while we still have some light left," Keech said.

"But we have to help the survivors!" Duck scolded. "Their lives are ruined because your pa told Whiskey to head west."

Boiling anger suddenly flooded every vein. Before he could stop himself, Keech bounded two steps closer and shoved the kid.

Duck lost his balance, tripped backward, and landed in the mud beside a gravestone. His clumsy blue hat rolled off his head, exposing the brown fuzz of his hair. "Why'd you go and do that?"

"Don't you blame my pa for this," Keech said. "If anyone's to blame, it's *your* yellow-belly father."

A large fist came flying at his face and struck Keech square on the cheek. He tumbled to the ground on his rump. A loud ringing, like Granny's supper bell, fluttered through his ears.

Nat loomed over him. "Don't you talk about our pa like that," he snarled. "And never lay a hand on Duck again."

Keech blinked up, dazed. "You hit me."

Duck jumped back to his feet and grabbed his hat, ready to rejoin the battle. "Our pa was no yellow-belly! If you say it again you'll get another fist!" He stuffed his hat back on.

"But I'm telling the truth."

Nat raised his fist again, then hesitated. "What are you talking about?"

"Your father ratted on my pa, is what." Keech rubbed his throbbing cheek. "He told the *Gita-Skog* where to find my home."

"Liar!" Duck screeched.

"It's no lie. Your father betrayed my whole family."

Nat reared back to let knuckles fly again. But this time Turner stepped between them. "Stop this now! There'll be no more dissension in my outfit."

"But Sheriff—" Nat began.

"Back away," Turner said. "Right now."

The rancher raised his hands and complied. "You don't understand, Sheriff. I just didn't like Keech shoving my sister."

The past two days had been plenty confusing, but Keech couldn't, for the life of him, figure out why Nat had called Duck his *sister*. But then he considered Duck's heavy hat, the short haircut, the green scarf knotted up to the chin, and sudden awareness dawned.

"Wait a danged second! You're a *girl*!" Keech sputtered.

"I know," said Duck.

"But you're dressed like a boy!"

"I reckon that's the point," said Duck.

A tickled laugh filled the air. Keech turned to see John Wesley bent over, shaking. "I saw Duck was a girl the second I met her," he cackled.

"Truth be told," said the old man, Mayor Twiggs, "I thought she was a boy, too."

Nat put a hand on Duck's shoulder. "It's hard enough riding with a kid," he explained. "But at least no one thinks twice about a boy. I keep her dressed like that, and her hair short, to keep her safe."

Duck shoved her brother's hand away. "I keep my own self this way, thank you," she said tartly. "And I can handle whatever you can, *Nathaniel*."

Nat frowned at her, then turned to Keech. "You can go hang, Blackwood. We did just fine before you came along."

"You were the ones who tackled me!" said Keech. "I never asked for you to show up!"

"For Pete's sake, get your heads on straight," Turner said. "You're all acting like a bunch of toddlers. Remember who the real enemy is."

Another drop of rain plunked on Keech's nose. The grumble of distant thunder ripped across the valley.

"Rain's coming," Turner said. "You boys calm?"

Nat shrugged. "I reckon."

Keech wanted to shout at the whole gang to jump in a lake. He had suffered too much misery to be chided like a naughty kid. Of course, throwing tantrums would only prove he was a child. And when he thought about it, these kids were suffering their own fears and losses, so everything they were feeling was just as defensible as Keech's anger.

"I'll be okay," he said.

Then a heavy crack broke the evening air.

Keech thought a lightning bolt had struck nearby. But then a circle of dark red blossomed on Sheriff Turner's left shoulder.

"Keech?" Turner said, and slumped to his knees.

The sheriff had been shot.

"Get down!" Nat hollered, as a second gunshot boomed over the valley. A lead ball crashed into the graveyard wall, sending chips of gray stone flying.

Keech dropped to his stomach. John Wesley froze, unsure what to do. Another shot fractured the sky. Mayor Twiggs, already in the act of pitching forward in the mud, avoided the lead ball just in time.

The young riders broke for cover. Nat and Duck dived behind the yard wall and John Wesley joined Keech on his belly. Back by the horses, Cutter drew his knife. He looked curiously calm and dangerous, even though he held the wrong weapon for such a long-distance attack. "Come out and fight!" he snarled at their unseen attackers.

The sheriff's face was already turning pale. Laboriously, he lifted his revolver, took aim in the direction of the barrage, and pulled the trigger. The gun didn't fire. Gritting his teeth, Turner slapped the side of the Colt against his thigh, re-aimed, and squeezed off again. This time the gun bellowed, lobbing a wild bullet across the valley.

Keech shuffled to Turner on hands and knees. He grabbed the arm not wounded and hauled the big man to his feet. They reached the graveyard wall in a matter of seconds and ducked behind the fieldstone. "Rifles, long range," Keech huffed, then peeked over the barrier.

Fifty yards to the west, on the other side of the river, stood a wall of black locust trees—the entrance to Floodwood. The forest was menacing and bleak, and somewhere in that cluster of dark wood lurked the gunmen. Judging by the gunfire roaring from different angles, there were at least two men out there.

Another volley erupted from the trees. Slugs pinged into the stone wall.

"It's a bushwhack!" Mayor Twiggs yelled from the mud.

Hunched next to Duck, Nat said, "Looks like our outlaw's come to us."

"Your Hawken's with the horses," Duck told her brother. "We need to get to it."

Turner pressed a hand against his wounded shoulder. "We have to ride for better cover!" he called out.

All at once, the attack ceased. A peculiar silence hung in the air. The assailants were most likely reloading. Which meant the posse had little time to escape the graveyard. The longer they tarried by the wall, the more likely they were to get trapped.

"Sheriff's right. We have to ride," Keech said.

Nat looked at Duck. "Ready to skedaddle?"

The girl nodded. Mayor Twiggs hopped to his feet, panting heavily, but he looked ready.

"What do I do?" cried John Wesley, still flattened on his belly. "I'm the biggest target!"

John Wesley was right—they would aim right for him—but there was no time to debate. "I'll stay and help the sheriff," Keech told the boy. "Get to the horses. Take Mr. Twiggs."

Nat waved at John Wesley and the flustered Mayor Twiggs to head back toward the burning church. Once John Wesley was back on his feet, the group began to zigzag through gravestones to reach the exit. Keech dared another glance over the wall at the Floodwood tree line, then turned back to watch the others flee.

Cutter was sprinting back toward the village, chasing their horses. The animals had panicked at the gunfire and were racing back to the east.

"Our ponies!" cried Duck as she ran.

"Don't stop! Keep going!" Keech yelled.

"What's wrong?" asked Sheriff Turner, drooping against the wall.

"The horses. They spooked."

Keech winced in panic when Mayor Twiggs stumbled to one knee on the road beside the church. John Wesley scooped low and hauled the man back up to his feet.

Once he saw that the gang had reached a safe distance, Keech looked out again across the river. Standing in the open were two of Bad Whiskey's thralls. One wore a long frock coat, the other had what appeared to be a golden ring glinting from his nose.

The gunmen were none other than Scurvy and Bull.

The brewing thunderstorm at last ruptured. Sheets of hard, steady rain poured from the sky, turning Whistler's graveyard to instant slop.

"*Blackwood!*" Scurvy bellowed. "*We've come to claim ya!*"

Though the thralls were quite a distance off, Keech could still see they were holding long Harper's Ferry muskets. The dead men had to be decent marksmen to hit Turner.

Propped against the wall, Turner said, "I'm sorry, son, but I'm afraid they've taken me out of the hunt." He touched Keech's arm apologetically.

Keech swallowed back a lump. "It's all right, Sheriff." He peeked over the wall. The thralls were lurching steadily toward the graveyard. Soon they would enter the shallow river and then trudge up the bank. Once they reached the wall, the desperadoes would kill Turner where he sat. Then they would finish the young riders and all the other survivors at Whistler.

The solution to their situation was now obvious. Keech saw no other choice.

"I have to draw them away."

"You'll do no such thing!" Turner shouted, then coughed.

"Those monsters are here for me. I reckon once they kill me, they might leave the rest of you alone."

"Stop talking like that."

"I'm not gonna get everyone killed today."

Turner shook his head. "There's a better way. If you could get past them, you could hide in the forest. They'll double back and give chase. That'll give us time to collect ourselves and prepare an ambush while you're hiding."

Keech knew it was a better plan than simply walking out to meet his death. He didn't figure the odds were good for skirting the thralls, but he could try. He readied himself to stand and run.

"Wait. Take this." Turner held out his revolver.

Keech pushed the gun aside. "No, Sheriff, you're wounded. You'll need it. Besides, I have this." He tapped the side of his head. "It's all I need."

Again he prepared to stand, but Turner seized his wrist. "Mr. Blackwood," he said, drawing Keech closer. "Keep fighting. Be strong. Don't give up."

Keech folded a hand over Turner's glove. The knuckles were crimson with the sheriff's blood. "I'll see you soon."

Saying no more, he stripped off his bowler hat and stood.

Across the river Scurvy and Bull quickened their pace, raising their muskets the moment they spotted him.

Be with me, Sam. Show me the way of the Rabbit.

Gripping his hat tight, Keech ran. He vaulted over the graveyard wall and sprinted toward the river. To anyone looking, it may have appeared he was running straight for them, but the map in his mind was certain: One more moment and he would run a diagonal line for the northern curve of the river. On their side, Scurvy and Bull were almost to the bank. By the time the thralls made the water, Keech would take the river's curve and the thralls would lose sight of him.

A hornet sounded near his left ear. Another rifle shot, but no lead touched him. He twisted north along the bank and toward the river's curve. The thralls cursed when they realized his course. They wheeled back around.

Keech was fully exposed now. Glancing over his shoulder, he saw that Scurvy and Bull had taken the bait. They had dropped their muskets and were now shuffling with revolvers held out.

Rainwater soaked his body as he ran. He slid down a short slope and lost the thralls from his view. Floodwood forest was just across the river.

He dived into the freezing water and began to swim, praying with every stroke that the others were taking advantage of his distraction. All around there were treacherous sounds: the slosh of the river, the grumble of thunder, the bellow of gunfire. The thralls were approaching the shoreline, the place he would end up once he reached the bank. Keech paddled harder. Another slug whizzed by overhead.

His boots raked gravel bottom. He dug into the murk and propelled himself out of the river.

Scurvy and Bull were now so close he could see their horrible decay, much worse today than their pale ghost faces back at the Home.

Keech dashed across the field. A lead ball nibbled his coat sleeve. He pushed his legs harder. *Dodge, weave, run*, Pa used to say. *Movement spoils even the best aim.*

The dark line of black locust trees loomed ahead.

Floodwood is cursed, Mayor Twiggs had warned.

Cursed or no, Keech had to get to cover. He sprinted for the gloomy tree line.

CHAPTER 16
FLOODWOOD

The moment he entered the woods, Keech knew the forest felt wrong. A terrible pressure filled his head, as if someone had crammed his ears with sawdust, and a dull, relentless murmur tainted the air, too low to be a whistle, but too high to be thunder. It reminded Keech of a bumblebee stuck on a windowpane.

He stopped to clear his head and catch his bearings. But then Whiskey's thralls appeared less than ten yards away, muttering to each other at the wood's edge. The blustery sky silhouetted their ragged clothes and raised revolvers. Keech dived behind a tree. He waited, motionless, and realized he was no longer holding his hat. He looked around frantically and spotted it lying in the wet leaves a couple of yards away, in plain sight.

The dead men shambled closer, inspecting the wooded border, kicking around the riverbank grass. So far they made no attempt to cross Floodwood's threshold.

"He's close," murmured Scurvy, his frock coat rippling in the hard wind. "I can feel the amulet shard. Strange, though. My skin feels pulled in two directions."

Inside Keech's shirt, the silver began to seep its uncanny chill.

"I feel it, too," said Bull, his voice dark, cavernous.

Scurvy sniffed at the rain and cocked his speckled white head. "What's this?" He pointed to a dollop of dark red liquid on a grass blade.

Keech hadn't noticed a moment ago, but now he realized his right arm was stinging just above the elbow. He touched the injured spot and winced. Wet crimson returned on his fingertip.

The lead ball at the river had not merely nicked his coat.

He had been shot.

Scurvy dabbed at the blood drop. "I knew I hit 'im!" he crowed. "He's powerful close." The thrall started toward the tree line, but his partner hesitated, as if scared to enter Floodwood.

"Master said to stay outta the woods till we kilt the Black-wood boy."

"How we gonna kill 'im if we don't go in?" Scurvy said. He stretched a rotting black finger to Bull's face, snatched the gold nose ring, and yanked the thrall forward. Bull yelped in surprise, but followed Scurvy across the boundary.

Pa Abner had once said fear was the most binding of all emotions. Keech appreciated those words all too well now. He tried to remember Pa's training, the lesson of the rattlesnake in his bed—*Stay in the moment, accept the danger, doubt sparks panic, panic sparks death*—but a blinding fear padlocked every muscle in his body.

There was nowhere to run.

He took a deep breath. To stay in the moment you had to take in your surroundings, find anything useful for survival. A piece of black locust bark lay between his boots. It wouldn't serve as a weapon, but the bark was tough and heavy, perhaps a fine distraction.

He stooped and grabbed the bark. Angling the chunk to fly south, Keech flicked his wrist. The pain from the gunshot wound was sharp, but he managed not to make a noise. The bark snickered through the woods. Over the pounding rain, the sound of the bark splashing in a puddle was enough to grab the monsters' attention.

"Over yonder!" Scurvy yelped. The creatures lumbered south.

Keech ran as hard as he could. He counted every yard he traveled—a habit taken from Pa Abner's lessons. Soon he lost sight of the thralls.

Before long, Keech's eyes began to fall upon perplexing land markers in the forest, and he found himself too distracted to remember his yards. The first curious thing he saw was a twisted willow tree, standing out nearly sideways on a steep hill. The drooping leaves of the willow were a strange color, neither green nor brown, but a dull gray, like a wilted dandelion. Keech stopped to investigate. He went to pull one of the leaves toward his eyes but stopped, and yanked his hand back.

The leaves were covered in silvery prickles. Tiny spikes that seemed to be alive, moving as if blown by a wind that did not disturb the leaves themselves.

Keech backed away. He had never seen a tree like this before. It was like the willow belonged to another world.

He pressed on. Farther north, he stumbled through a patch of black locust trees and up to a small clearing. He pushed back a few branches and found himself at a muddy gray beach. A tiny pond lay a few feet away, its water so black it could have been wagon grease. He stepped across the beach to the water's edge. The pool was still; no bubbling foam at the edges, no ripples or waves, not even a splashing fish. A terrible odor wafted off the water, a smell like burned gunpowder. He suspected it was nothing but poison, and that if he walked into it he would not come out the other side alive.

Keech's boots shifted in the mud. He realized he'd sunk all the way to his ankles. The beach was dragging him toward the smelly water. He struggled backward, almost losing his balance. He tugged his feet up enough to spin around and took three lumbering steps over the beach. He lunged back for the wood line.

Poison ponds and tainted willows? Floodwood truly was cursed.

He had to push on, especially if he hoped to find a safe shelter before the evening's last light snuffed out.

He continued north till his trek brought him to another peculiar landmark, this time a steep embankment where a tall stone outcropping stood at the top, a red mountain of rock that climbed as high as Floodwood's trees.

Keech stopped and stared at the mountain. Something seemed familiar about it. He couldn't put his finger on what, but the red stones, the embankment, the outcropping gave him a dark, lonely feeling.

He groaned at the thought of climbing that long slope. But a high vantage point would offer a good lookout. The rock afforded a meager overhang, as well, so he could rest up there and tend his wound.

His arm cradled, he started up the embankment. The climb was perilous, a slope of loose mud that offered few footholds, just the occasional tree whose roots threatened to trip him and send him tumbling back down. By the time he reached the stone outcropping, he was smeared in muck and his arm felt like it was covered in biting ants.

Huddling under the rock wall's overhang, he pulled off his coat and examined the wound. The lead ball had sheared away a good amount of hide, drawing enough blood to soak his elbow, but thankfully the ball hadn't touched muscle or bone. Tearing a piece of cloth from his shirttail, Keech wrapped the wound and tied off the bandage with a reef knot. Then he tugged his coat back on, rested against the rock, and closed his eyes.

Floodwood's eerie droning engulfed his tired ears and mind. He shrugged it off as best he could, and suddenly wished for Little Eugena's bugle. Just one more time. Keech was sorry he had ever found it terrible. He would have given anything to hear its delightful noise again.

He was asleep in less than a minute.

When he awoke, the woods had slipped toward dusk. The rain was still pouring and ropes of lightning charged across the sky.

He sat upright and silently cursed. He hadn't meant to fall

asleep at a vulnerable location. He had been foolish and lowered his guard.

Time to move.

Stepping out from the rock, Keech looked for signs of the dead men. When he turned his gaze to the outcropping, he noticed something. A dark smudge on the stone just above where he'd been resting.

Keech leaned in close to the smudge. It was no mere blemish. Scrawled on the stone was a series of numbers. The digits were black as if drawn in charcoal, but when he ran his hand over them, he discovered it was black paint, so old it chipped when touched.

The numbers read:

40 7:7

Astonishment raced over Keech's mind. These numbers had been drawn by Pa Abner's hand! But that wasn't the only revelation. He now understood why the red outcropping had been so familiar.

It was the mountain from Pa's portrait. The one in the study, painted over the old page of the *Daily Missouri Republican*.

Keech looked at the numbers on the rock again and realized he was seeing another Bible verse, just like the ones in Pa's telegram.

The number 40 was Matthew. Pa's letter to Noah Embry had included Matthew 24:42, the secret warning that Bad Whiskey was on the prowl.

But what did 7:7 say?

Cold shimmered upon his chest. Keech was so focused on the numbers, he barely noticed.

Behind him, a slimy voice crooned, "Look, it's our chickabiddy!"

Keech wheeled around. As he did, a flash of lightning lit up the entire woodland. Scurvy and Bull stood ten feet away. Bull was wearing Keech's bowler hat, and both of them were aiming their revolvers at him.

Keech didn't let himself think—he acted.

Using one leg to launch himself off the rock wall, he sprang straight for the smaller of the creatures. He crashed into Scurvy's midsection and they went tumbling down the embankment. Flimsy brush cracked beneath their weight. Keech bowled over a flat stone, the impact driving out his breath. Above them, Bull roared.

For a dead man, Scurvy's grip was astounding. The second Keech had tackled him, Scurvy had thrown his arms around Keech's waist and squeezed. As they plummeted together down the slope, Keech thought he would split open under the strength of those skeletal arms.

"Yer mine," Scurvy hissed.

"I don't think so," Keech said. To force the thrall to release him, he did the only thing he knew to do: he head-butted the creature. A white-hot spike of pain shot through his forehead and he heard a crack. The thrall's arms loosened.

They stopped rolling at the foot of the embankment and Keech shoved himself away.

"You cracked my noggin!" Scurvy yelled, throwing a hand over a jagged dent in his skull.

Keech tackled him again, this time throwing fists. The skinny thrall screamed as Keech's coat parted and Pa's pendant spilled out of his shirt. It dangled by its cord, brightly shimmering. Without fully meaning to, Keech dipped his body and dropped the silver so it rested against Scurvy's cheek.

The squeal that poured from the fiend was too much to bear, but Keech didn't have to endure it for long. As the pendant radiated its violent cold, black veins pulsed and bubbled along Scurvy's flesh. He shuddered, flopped once like a fish, then went limp. The charm had returned him back to the dead.

"That's for Sheriff Turner!" Keech shouted.

But it wasn't time yet to celebrate. Bull was on his way. The brute was stampeding down the slope with breakneck momentum. "Yer mine, runt!"

Midway down the hill, Bull squeezed the trigger of his revolver, but the gun clicked empty. The thrall bellowed in fury and tossed away the gun.

There would be no wrestling or punching this opponent. There would be no holding him down and touching him with the pendant. Bull was too powerful.

Keech had to run. Only this time, he wouldn't be running to escape. The time for fleeing like a rabbit was over. Pa Abner had taught him a hundred ways to overcome an enemy. It was time to put those lessons to work.

It was time to be the Wolf.

CHAPTER 17
A BREAD-CRUMB TRAIL

Instinct told Keech backtracking wouldn't be the best plan. Bull had already covered the ground to the south, and might have grown familiar with shortcuts, so he decided to hold to his northern course. *The expanse of a forest is your friend*, Pa Abner used to tell him and Sam, when teaching them ways to engage enemies in a woodland. *Win yourself distance, win time to think.* He needed to keep moving at all costs.

The problem was, Keech began to suspect that Pa's pendant, his only weapon, was acting as a beacon, guiding the thrall to him.

Eventually Keech came to a sharp rise and noticed a frosted willow tree tilting sideways toward the ground. He stopped in his tracks, the rain battering his uncovered head.

"What in blazes?" he muttered.

He approached the willow cautiously. The tree was identical to the one he'd come across before. The dull-gray leaves, the silvery prickles that moved as if alive—all the same.

He was standing at the very same tree.

Keech rubbed his eyes in disbelief. "That's impossible."

A coincidence, was all it was. Floodwood probably grew a thousand willow trees just like it. Or perhaps the nagging pressure in the forest air was making his thoughts go all skew-whiff.

Slathering his face with cold rainwater, he started back on his northern trek. He just had to keep traveling, gain enough distance to get the drop on his quarry.

Bull's furious voice echoed in the distance, "Gonna find ya, runt!"

Keech stepped up his pace.

Ten minutes later that peculiar pressure bore down upon his brain again as he approached a steep, familiar-looking rise. Once again he came to a halt on his path.

He was staring at the silver willow tree, leaning out from its hill.

"No! That can't be."

Keech advanced toward the willow, as if walking up to his own gallows. He gave the tree a long study, then slumped where he stood.

There was no doubt in his mind now. Somehow, his path through Floodwood had bent him back to where he had started.

One Sunday morning before their day's training—a freezing Christmas Eve—Pa Abner had sat Keech and Sam down at the place they were camping, and had gone over all the elemental rules they had covered since the first day of their forest lessons as children. *When survival's at stake, the mind can deceive*, Pa had told them. *Accept what is real. Recognize the lies. Cast them aside, boys. Never let them in.*

Keech struggled to devise a way to cast the deceptions of Floodwood aside. The logical answer was that he'd backtracked by accident. His tumble down the embankment with Scurvy had scrambled his sense of direction.

But that wasn't possible. The rock formation with "40 7:7" painted on the wall had been angled *north*—the direction he'd chosen to run. After leaving the willow the second time, he had continued that northern track, not veering in the slightest.

Keech plopped to the ground in exhaustion and heard a jangle inside his inner coat pocket. In the distance, Bull bellowed a litany of curses. Keech wouldn't be able to linger, but he was so lost he could no longer recognize north from south.

Recognize the lies. Cast them aside.

Keech peeked into his coat pocket to see what had jangled.

Inside was the leather purse holding thirty-one pennies—the last thing Pa Abner had ever given him. Thirty-one pennies to send the telegram and buy licorice wheels for the orphans. He couldn't believe he'd forgotten about them.

Keech stood and brushed wet leaves off his rump. He had a plan.

He could use the pennies. He could place a penny every hundred yards, like a trail of bread crumbs. They'd be tricky to spot in the dark, but if his path led him back again to where he started, at least he would be sure of his location.

Keech dropped the first piece of copper at the knotted base of the troublesome willow. He started moving again.

Lightning cascaded across the sky, lighting up the woods and revealing scores of twisted black roots and gnarled boughs.

Somewhere behind him, Keech heard Bull howl, "You got nowhere to hide!"

Sprinting over the rutted earth, Keech dropped another penny at the foot of a tall, V-shaped mulberry tree. He stopped to examine the black berries on the tree, but found them wriggling with tiny yellow worms.

He scattered three more pennies over the next three hundred yards, and then one more at the base of a tall white mushroom—a poisonous monstrosity Pa Abner used to call a Destroying Angel. According to Pa, many a frontiersman had perished because they'd mistaken the Destroying Angel for a tasty morsel.

Perhaps that was the curse infecting Floodwood. Everything was poison. You ran in circles till north became south, then at the end of your tether, the woods killed you with its venom. The trees, the roots, the mushrooms—

"And the water," Keech muttered, as he walked into a grimy thicket.

Nearby, the sound of shattering tree limbs told him Bull was looming closer.

Keech was forming a new plan, a way to stop the massive thrall once and for all, when he passed through a narrow opening in the undergrowth. He walked another few steps, feeling that strange unnerving pressure in his head again, and realized he had just moved through a dense line of black locust trees, not a thicket at all. Before him now lay the muddy quicksand beach of the black pond.

The very place he had wanted to find.

He stopped at the beach's rim and examined his surroundings.

His plan would require close contact, and just the right amount of force. The black locust trees were in good position for his plan. The tree canopies were thick on all sides, so if Bull happened to glance over from the trail he'd been following, he would only see limbs and branches. He wouldn't see the pond till he was right upon it.

Now for the lure.

Keech set a penny on the forest floor, at the spot where the ground turned to quagmire. Then he climbed up a nearby tree and perched on a thick limb. A bright memory came of Patrick, scuttling up the stairway balusters of the Home for Lost Causes and balancing on the handrail. *I'm a monkey!*

Keech smiled, feeling curiously buoyant. *I hope you can see me now, flapjack*, he thought.

Moments later the thrall approached the clearing. Keech could hear branches scratch across the fabric of Bull's coat. The creature stopped to listen. Every sound seemed to freeze in Floodwood, save the unremitting buzz in Keech's ears.

"I know yer close, runt. I can feel ya."

A branch cracked as Bull lurched another step. His gold nose ring sparkled in the storm's lightning, and Keech felt outrage when he saw that the monster was still wearing his bowler hat.

"You think I won't find ya. But I will," Bull murmured, rummaging through the brush.

Keech's penny shimmered at the edge of the sand. Surely the thrall would notice.

"You must be important, runt. The Master wants you somethin' fierce. Show yerself an' I'll take ya to him alive. No need to die just yet."

A blinding shaft of lightning crashed into a tree not ten feet from Keech's perch. Branches shattered and wood exploded across the grove. The flash momentarily blinded him. Shadows swarmed his vision and he swiped at his eyes. When he looked in the direction where Bull had been standing, he saw the dead man's silhouette at the mouth of the clearing. The large thrall shambled toward the quicksand, rubbing madly at his own eyes.

Keech prayed he would spot the penny.

The thrall stopped just shy of the sand. He was directly under Keech's limb, so close Keech could smell rotting flesh. Pa Abner's pendant burned cold upon his chest.

The creature removed his hands from his eyes. "The shard betrays ya, runt. It *calls* to me."

Keech held his breath. One more step.

"What's this?" Bull lumbered forward and bent down to inspect the penny.

Grasping the branch with both hands, Keech dropped, swung down in a wide arc, and slammed his feet full force into Bull's backside. The impact felt like driving into a stone wall, but his momentum was enough. The thrall careened face-first into the quicksand. Keech landed safely on the ground at the sand's edge.

The beach wasted no time in engulfing the heavy thrall. There was a snarl as the quicksand swallowed the creature whole, gulping down his stomach, then his legs; and now a Bull-sized lump of muddy sand slipped off toward the black pond. The gray beach sucked its prey deep into the poison water. The black liquid churned and gurgled.

One last great bubble rose from the center of the pond and belched a disgusting spray of black liquid. Keech leaped backward. As he did, his heel kicked his hat. It had fallen off Bull's head. He snatched it up and brushed dirt off the brim.

"*Granny* gave me this hat," he grumbled at the pond, and crammed it back on his head.

CHAPTER 18

THE RED MOUNTAIN

Keech tried to mark how many hours had passed as he stumbled through an unrelenting labyrinth of trees, hills, and gulches, but the task was impossible. At least the rain clouds had parted, revealing a deep purple sky full of silver stars to help guide his way. Exhaustion weighed upon his body. He needed to hole up in a safe camp and sleep a few more hours till daylight. A campfire would be ideal, but any flame or column of smoke could expose him. Somewhere in Floodwood, Bad Whiskey Nelson was stalking about. He could almost feel the outlaw's prowling eye, searching for him.

Keech stopped walking and assessed his location. He now found himself in the center of a ring of evergreens, trees that put off a sulfur-like smell and bent inward, as if bowing to one another.

This place would have to do.

Working as fast as his wounded arm would allow, Keech tore down three armloads of thick evergreen branches. He sat for a spell and interwove their twigs into a crude blanket. The needles were scratchy against his hands and cheeks, but for the most part the boughs made a passable cover. He put his back against one of the tree trunks, gauged his line of sight from each direction, and then drew the stinky evergreen covering up to his neck. If Bad Whiskey or his thralls happened to walk near, they should only see a haphazard pile of branches, smothered in darkness. The outlaw's monsters would sense the pendant, of course, but then again Keech would feel the shard's coldness, so he should have time to react.

He rested in the still of the night and tried to ignore the sulfury stench and his own discomfort. In time he lifted his eyes to the night sky. He gazed up in wonder as Floodwood's heavenly bodies appeared to drift at once backward and forward, creating both a turmoil and a beauty in the cursed firmament. A forlorn wind circled through the evergreen canopy above him, sounding like whispers full of meaningless words. *Zhahhhh*, the wind spoke, a peaceful serenade. Before long, the tree whispers began to shape themselves in his ears, become something Keech had heard during lessons in Pa's study.

Zha Sape, the wind said.

No longer meaningless, but a language, beloved to him. The Osage tongue.

A tha no ko. Listen. *Shto be*. See.

Listen and see, the tree whispers told him.

Keech raised one finger and pretended to touch the moving stars. Perhaps it was there, among those brilliant lights, that the souls of fallen braves encountered their next home, the hunting land where they found their spirits reunited with the lost warriors of old. The idea reminded Keech of his brothers. Tears formed in his eyes—and through that fog of tears he thought he saw the Floodwood stars begin to form images. Turning, rolling, murmuring constellations that seemed to be enacting some kind of grand story.

Shto be, the wind murmured. *See*.

Keech sat upright, mesmerized, and wiped his eyes. The silver images in the sky were still there, still moving. Dancing, almost.

"What in blazes?"

In the stars he thought he saw his own Pa Abner, lifting what appeared to be a bear cub from the dark of a lonely den. Other sparkling characters gathered around Pa, and they whispered to the tiny cub. Before Keech's eyes, the cub began to grow. It became the shape of a giant bear, a monstrous form, something that should not be.

Keech blinked over and over, thinking, *None of this is real. I'm asleep and Floodwood is giving me strange dreams*. But all he could see was the starry image of Pa Abner and his companions, whispering to the stolen cub, creating the great bear.

Wasape, the group whispered.

He squeezed his eyes shut, hoping the peculiar images would disappear. And when he opened them again, there was only Floodwood forest and he was still beneath his evergreen blanket. Clouds had once again folded over the purple sky, dropping a curtain over the night's impossible tale. Nothing stirred in the heavens but the gloomy haze. And the wind no longer murmured to him.

Keech tried to go back to sleep, if he had ever slept at all, and realized he was no longer sleepy. He decided to move again. He shoved the makeshift covering off his body and stood, noticing as he did a muted predawn glow behind the clouds. As the light deepened, a gray drizzle began to fall. Sighing in misery, Keech inspected the bandage around his arm. The cloth was already in tatters, so he ripped another strip from his shirt and secured a fresh dressing.

He began to travel. The morning's light turned the clouded sky a slate color, pledging more misery for the new day. Pushing dull fatigue out of his bones, Keech waded through a narrow thicket of sumac. As he emerged from the brush, he felt Floodwood's throbbing heaviness surge in his head and saw in the distance, for the second time since entering the wood, the red mountain where Pa had painted his clue.

Motion at the top of the embankment made him drop to one knee in the brush. Three dark figures shambled around the rock. It was hard to see details, but Keech thought he recognized the leather coat one of them wore.

Keeping to the shadows, he moved closer.

The figure in leather was Rance, the thrall who had helped Bull shoot up the Home's front door. He was investigating the place where Keech had tackled Scurvy. So far the thralls seemed oblivious to the painted numbers above their heads.

"A body!"

The voice took Keech by surprise. It had come from the base of the hill.

John Wesley.

"One of the dead outlaws," someone else said. This time it was Duck.

"Something caved his head in," came another voice. Cutter's.

The young riders were near, and had found Scurvy's corpse.

Keech wanted to shout with relief. But Rance and his companions were glancing down the embankment. They must have heard the young riders' voices, too. Breaking from the trees, Keech sprinted toward the gang.

Throwing a glance up the hill, he saw the dead men draw their revolvers. The trio started down the slope. The fresh mud hindered their progress, but the rotting outlaws moved with purpose.

"Run!" Keech shouted to the kids. "They're coming!" He gritted his teeth and picked up his speed.

Midway down the embankment, Rance bellowed, "Lay 'em low, boys!" The hill erupted with gunfire.

Surprised by the ambush, the young riders dived for cover. A lead ball whizzed over John Wesley's head and knocked his straw hat off. He squealed, grabbed the hat, and scrambled on his hands and knees in search of concealment.

From his cover behind a low rock, Nat drew a Colt revolver from a holster buckled to his hip. He aimed the revolver at a fat tree standing askew on the embankment. He fired twice at one of the tree's thorny limbs. The rotten wood splintered and crashed down on top of the two creatures accompanying Rance. They tumbled to the ground.

Rance yelped a curse and sidestepped the fallen limb. His revolver thundered. When it clicked empty, he slid to a stop and began reloading.

Keech at last reached the young riders. "Come with me!" If he could make them follow, Floodwood's twisted pathways might hide them. He cut a western path away from the embankment, waving them frantically along as he went.

The young riders chased after him, and soon Nat caught up. "Where are we going?"

"No time to explain!"

Hot lead rumbled around them.

The young riders rushed into a dark thicket. With each step the pressure in Keech's ears intensified again. Colorful dots sparkled his vision, and the murmuring of the forest air grew louder.

"I think he's catching up!" Duck cried.

"Trust me," Keech called back. "Keep moving."

They stomped through a stand of high brush. On the other side, Keech found himself looking at a silver willow tree standing sideways on a hill. He slid to a stop. The others gathered around him, panting.

John Wesley hunched over and dry heaved. "I think I'm gonna die," he wheezed.

"Where's the thrall?" Nat asked, glancing back the way they'd come. Rance's gunfire had fallen silent.

Keech smiled. Yet again, Floodwood had worked its dark magic, this time leading him back to the willow. But this time the curse had saved them. Rance had been sent down another path.

Under the willow's drooping shade, the group escaped the drizzle and rested as Keech explained what had happened.

"The old man at Whistler was right. Floodwood's got a curse on it. No matter where you want to go, you can never escape. You find yourself doubling back over your own rotten trail a dozen times."

The young riders contemplated Keech's words.

"No wonder I've felt so turned around," Duck said, scratching her cheek.

"So what about the thrall who was barkin' iron?" asked John Wesley.

"My guess is, Floodwood led him to a different marker," Keech replied.

Nat frowned. "Marker?"

Keech gestured to the willow tree, careful not to touch any of its wriggling silver leaves. "I've been running from thralls for hours, and several times now I've come across this same confounded willow. But not every time. Twice I stumbled on a quicksand beach with a black pond. That's where I stopped the big thrall. And just before I saw you, Floodwood carried me back to that red mountain. It's like the curse only takes you to certain land markers."

"This is *loco*," Cutter said.

"No doubt about it."

"You mean the forest sent the dead fella shooting at us down another trail," said Duck.

Keech shrugged. "I took a chance it would work."

"A chance? You said 'trust me.' We thought you had a plan!" John Wesley said. There was a pea-sized hole in the high center of his straw hat, the place where a lead ball had struck it. The boy was lucky to be alive.

Nat changed the subject by pointing to Keech's penny at the base of the willow. "We saw your pennies. Started following them last night, a couple hours after we entered the woods to find you. Downright smart to leave a trail."

"I hoped you would find them," Keech said, scooping up his penny and dropping it into his coat pocket.

Nat took his hat off, mopped a bead of sweat off his brow. "Duck spotted the first one under a big white mushroom. We figured it belonged to you. At first we wanted to bring it, but Duck said we oughta leave it, in case you needed to find your way. We traveled what we thought was north, but we got lost as a bunch of geese. We found three more before we came to the red mountain and saw the dead outlaw."

Keech turned to Duck. "I've been using them to keep the markers sorted in my head." Humiliation for attacking the girl at Whistler stole into his gut. "I'm sorry for the way I acted. I didn't mean to say those things about your pa."

"It was sure mean," Duck said, but she patted Keech's arm. When he winced at the touch, her eyes widened. "Are you hurt?"

The arm of Keech's coat had turned scarlet. "I got nicked back at the river."

Duck reached into her coat pocket and pulled out her pouch of horse salve, the medicine she'd put on Minerva's hock wound. She motioned for Keech to peel off the coat.

"I'm no horse!" Keech protested.

"You sure smell like one," Cutter said, and chuckled.

"Just take off the dang coat," Duck said.

Keech did as he was told. Pulling down his crude bandage, he let Duck apply a generous portion of the salve. The medicine stung like a yellow jacket, but after a moment it cooled. He tugged his bandage back over the wound, then dragged his coat back on.

"Much obliged," he said, then pointed at the revolver on Nat's hip. "That's Turner's gun. What happened to him after I ran?"

"We left him in town with a nice family," Nat said. "They promised to tend his wound and fetch our horses. Sheriff handed me this and told us to find you."

John Wesley had peeled off his hat to examine the ragged hole in the crown. After putting it back on, he scrunched his face as if deep in thought. "So how'd you do it?" he asked Keech.

"How'd I do what?"

"How did you stop the thrall we found? I thought they was unstoppable and all."

Hearing his question, Keech knew he had to make a choice. He'd been unwilling to trust Nat's gang or divulge anything Pa had wanted kept secret, but they had taken fire for him, had plunged into a cursed forest just to rescue him. So from here on out there would be no more secrets.

"We have more weapons than a six-shooter and Cutter's blade. I have this," Keech said. He pulled Pa's pendant out of his shirt. The tarnished silver was dull under the gray sky. "*This* is the reason Bad Whiskey is chasing me. He took it from Pa when he stormed the orphanage. I stole it back."

Nat, Duck, and John Wesley stared in wonderment at the shard. Cutter was the only one who didn't appear surprised, since he had seen the pendant back at Swift Hollow.

"Nat, he's got an amulet piece!" Duck said.

Keech blinked in surprise. "What did you say?"

Nat turned to his sister. "Go ahead. Show him, Duck."

Duck pulled a long, thick strand of twine out of her black coat. She showed Keech the object at the end of the twine.

A silver crescent moon. The ornament was almost the twin of Pa Abner's pendant.

"Where did you get that?" Keech asked, stupefied.

"It's a family heirloom," Duck said. "Our pa gave it to us a few days before he died."

"Now it's obvious he meant to keep it away from the *Gita-Skog*," Nat added.

"May I see it?" Keech asked. He held out his hand. The girl gave him the silver and Keech placed the two pieces side by side. The only difference lay in the jagged teeth of the inside edges. The two fragments didn't fit together.

"It looks like with two or three more pieces, we could connect these shards," he said.

"Into a perfect circle," John Wesley added.

"Our pa wore that thing every day of his life," Nat said. "I've always wondered what the lines and weird shapes mean. Some kind of language, I reckon."

"It's no language I ever saw," Cutter said.

Keech handed the shard back to Duck. When the girl slid it

back into her coat, her face scrunched a little. "Now that I think about it, something mighty strange happened to the necklace back at your orphanage, when Tommy Claymore got near."

"Let me guess, you felt it get cold," Keech said.

Duck nodded. "Yeah. On the trail I had to slip it off and tuck it away, it chilled me so bad. It started up again when those thralls attacked on the hill."

"Did it ever get cold before, when your pa kept it?" Keech asked.

Duck shook her head. "Not that I recollect. But Pa always wore it, never let us around it."

A cold wind whispered across Floodwood, bristling the hairs on Keech's arms. He glanced at the cloudy sky. A crow zigzagged overhead, doubling back on its own trail as if it didn't know how to fly straight.

Keech guessed Floodwood's curse was confusing the bird, mixing up its sense of direction the same way it confused human travelers.

He nudged a finger at the sky. "We're being watched."

Nat frowned. "I reckon we need to move."

"But which way?" asked John Wesley.

The gang looked to Keech. After a night of stumbling over his own tracks, there was no easy way to respond.

Then Keech remembered the stone outcropping. The answer to navigating Floodwood lay in Pa's painted cipher—he was sure of it.

"We need to get back to the red mountain."

"But that's where *El Ojo*'s dead men attacked us," said Cutter.

Keech shrugged. "It's a risk, but we'll find the path to Bone Ridge there. When we do, we'll end this once and for all."

The morning had passed to noon before the young riders found their way to the red mountain. Twice the forest had twisted them back to the willow tree, each sodden step accompanied by the terrible pressure in their ears and the maddening swell of the bumblebee noise.

At last they came to the mountain. "About time," Cutter groaned. By the time they made the embankment and reached the outcropping, everyone was covered in grime. From their elevated position, they could see the wild expanse of Floodwood, bathed by the gray light, a sea of black locust wilderness. But not a perpetual sea, as the curse wanted you to believe. Back to the south, Keech could see dark smoke billowing from the tree-lined horizon. The remnants of Whistler.

The young riders gathered around Pa's message on the rock, and Keech explained that the numbers were a code.

"This will show us the way out. I'm sure of it."

Nat peered intently at the digits. "So how does it work?"

"Most codes communicate through a common source," Keech said. "This one uses the Bible. The first number—forty—means the book of Matthew."

"What do those sevens mean?" John Wesley asked.

"Chapter 7, verse 7."

"How do you know the code uses the Bible?" Nat asked.

"This isn't the first time my pa used the Bible to send a message. He also wrote a letter, all in coded numbers. The letter was supposed to be a secret telegram to your pa, Nat. On the way to Mr. Potter's office, my brother Sam and I broke the code. It was a warning, intended to alert your pa that the *Gita-Skog* was on the way."

Nat said nothing, only stared at the numbers on the rock.

"I'm sorry I didn't mention it before," Keech added, expecting Nat to be angry. "But when I saw this message on the rock, I knew I had to tell you."

Nat surprised him by smiling sadly. "I just wish the warning could've made it to us."

"Me too," Keech said.

"*Amigos*, this doesn't solve our problem," Cutter said. "We don't have a Bible. We don't know what the message on the rock means."

"I do," said a small voice.

The boys turned to see Duck, gazing at the numbers on the stone wall.

"And you know it too, Keech. I told it to you back at Swift Hollow. Matthew 7:7. It's the verse Pa made me memorize. 'Ask, and it shall be given to you. Seek, and ye shall find. Knock, and it shall be opened unto you.'"

Nat looked puzzled at his sister's revelation. "I don't understand. Pa never said a word about that verse to me. If it's so important, why wouldn't he involve me?"

"'Cause I got the good memory," Duck said, grinning. "You got the steady hand."

"Fair enough. So, how does this message help us?" asked Nat.

"Maybe it means we should search for a door to knock on," Duck said.

John Wesley tugged at his chin hairs. "We're in the middle of nowheres on top of a rocky hill. Where are we gonna find a door?"

"I reckon that's the first challenge of the clue," Keech answered. "We have to *seek* and see what there is to *find*."

CHAPTER 19

THE CLIMB

The freezing drizzle had stopped by the time the young riders began their search. Cutter stood watch atop the embankment as the rest of them started north, exploring the red wall around the painted code. The stone wall was too solid to offer any kind of door, so they turned toward the west, where a long row of sumac made a natural circle around the outcropping. The sumac bled down to a heavy stand of hawthorn trees that carpeted the hillside all the way down to level ground. At the edge of the tree line the group paused, and Nat looked glumly at the thicket.

"We'd be foolish to push into that," he said. "The forest could scatter us to kingdom come."

"You're right. Let's double back and search the east," Keech said.

The gang started back the way they had come. They found Cutter sitting on his knees at the muddy edge of the embankment, fidgeting with his bone-handled knife. He said nothing as they passed, only shook his head as if he couldn't believe they were on such a harebrained mission.

To the east the gang found a small critter path and followed it up the mountain for several yards, till they came to a tall, jagged slope of wet boulders, a treacherous mound that stretched upward at least two hundred feet or more. From all appearances, the higher point of this entire peak had tumbled loose a long time ago, creating a pelt of precarious rock that sat on the skin of the mountain. Toward the middle of this pile—at least a hundred feet up from the critter path—a colossal boulder jutted severely outward, shiny from the drizzle. It was almost twice the size of Copperhead Rock, and its rounded surface reminded Keech of a hunchback giant. Another hundred feet beyond, a long, thin mantel of stone capped the whole ensemble, as if the hunchback were wearing a brimmed hat made of granite.

"Pa's door could be up there somewhere, beyond that top ledge," Keech said.

Nat gave him a skeptical look. "Those rocks would go catawampus the first step."

"It's not straight up. The climb wouldn't be bad. We have to try."

"Fellas, I can't climb that," John Wesley said. "I'd topple the whole dang thing. Or just tumble down the hill and die. I don't reckon I'd like to do neither."

Nat surveyed the pile again and wagged his head. "John's right. It's a fool's errand."

"Oh, bully on that," said Duck, and sprang past them. Before Nat could stop her, she hopped onto the boulders and started scurrying up the rain-slick mound.

"Duck, stop!" Nat scolded. He reached out to grab her leg, but Duck was already several stones up. Nimble as a cricket, she hurtled up the untidy slope, not once looking down, planting her feet on moss-covered stones that appeared to sit only by threads and blind faith. In this fashion, she covered four wagons' lengths in no time.

"I demand you come down at once!" Nat yelled, as Duck clambered higher.

Duck shouted down, "It ain't so bad as it looks! Mighty slippery, but not too steep. Stop being chickens and come on."

Nat grumbled crossly and started to climb, but the slimy stones were too wobbly. He tried again, but a plate-sized rock tore out of his grip and landed with a crash beside John Wesley. He glanced at Keech with concern. "This was your idea, Blackwood. If something happens to her—"

"I'm almost halfway!" Duck called. To Keech's astonishment, she had already made it to the hunchback, the vast plump stone bulging midway up the pile. "I think I can make the top. Wait there and I'll scout the rest of the mountain."

"No, you will not!" Nat yelled. "I don't want you out of my sight!" He turned to Keech again, his face now a world of worry. "If the forest leads her off somewhere strange, I might not ever find her."

It was a valid fear, but when they looked up again, Keech saw it was too late to remind Duck of the curse. She scrambled over the top ledge, the final hurdle. Bits of granite chunked off the shelf and peppered the slope, but the ledge was firm enough to let Duck gain her feet.

As she stood on the crest, which appeared to be level ground again, she wiped her hands on her trousers and waved her big hat at them. "I'll be back in two shakes!" She turned and ran.

After she had disappeared, Nat stood rigid on the path and stared up at the ledge. He tapped two fingers nervously on the grip of Turner's pistol.

"Don't worry, Nat, she'll be back," John Wesley said.

The rancher shook his head. "You don't understand. She's all I got. If something happened to her, I'd never forgive myself."

A cooing noise, like a mourning dove, echoed in the distance. Keech cocked his head. "Did y'all hear that?"

The sound came again: *coo-COO. coo-COO.*

John Wesley pointed back to the northern side of the mountain. "I'd know that signal anywhere. It's Cutter!"

"We have to go back," Keech said. "He could be in danger."

"Not without Duck," Nat said.

But when the cooing noise came a third time, John Wesley started back down the critter path. Keech followed, then paused when he saw Nat tarry at the mound.

"Go ahead, Blackwood. I ain't leaving Duck."

"John Wesley's right," Keech said. "She'll be okay."

"I ain't leaving her. Go. I'll keep a lookout for the crows."

"All right." Keech hurried after John Wesley.

When the boys reached the embankment, they saw Cutter

stretched out on his stomach and squinting down the long slope. Trouble had surely found them again.

"We got company," Cutter said, his voice muted.

Keech and John Wesley joined him on the ground and peered down the hill.

At the bottom stood a lean figure cloaked in black. A flock of roughly thirty dead men encircled him. The outlaw's dark overcoat rippled in the wind, and he was clutching his Colt Dragoon. A team of five horses, loaded with gear, waited behind the thralls.

Bad Whiskey knelt to inspect the still corpse of his thrall Scurvy.

As soon as Keech had seen Whiskey's dead men, the amulet shard inside his shirt reacted. A pulse of cold went seeping through the cloth and seared upon his chest.

"We can't linger here," he whispered. "Those thralls will feel the charm. They might sense Duck's, too."

"I ain't running," Cutter hissed. "Not when I'm this close to *El Ojo*." Without warning he raised up on both elbows.

John Wesley shoved him back to the ground. "Watch out! He'll gun you down!"

Cutter scowled. "Look at him. He looks sick. My knife can drop him easy."

Even from this distance, Keech could see that Bad Whiskey did look dreadful. His yellowed skin had wrinkled and begun to crack like rotting leather, and his cheeks looked sunken around the bones. Truth told, he looked like one of his own walking corpses.

A bullet spark of memory slammed through Keech's mind.

Something Pa Abner had told the outlaw back at the Home, when they had first confronted each other:

Your standing here tells me the Reverend's woken . . .

Keech's breath hitched in his lungs.

"What's wrong?" asked John Wesley.

Keech finished Pa's words aloud: "'Some devils just don't know when to stay down.'"

The other boys looked bewildered.

Pa Abner had almost revealed the secret in the study. The outlaw looked like a corpse because he was one.

"Bad Whiskey Nelson is not a man," Keech said. "He's a thrall."

Cutter's eyes darkened. "You mean he's already dead?"

No wonder Bad Whiskey had panicked when Pa held the shard near. He was as vulnerable to the charm's power as his rotting goons were.

Cutter scowled with clear disappointment. "No matter. I can end him twice, I reckon."

John Wesley pointed. "Fellas, we're found!"

All three boys flattened on their bellies, but it was too late. Bad Whiskey's horde was staring up the embankment, directly at them.

"Hello, the hill!" the outlaw bellowed. He then hollered a command and the dead army started up the muddy slope. At least a dozen thralls yanked revolvers as they climbed. The ground was loose and rugged, but within minutes they would be close enough to fling lead.

"We have to get out of here!" said John Wesley.

"No, we have to kill them," Cutter said. He stood rebelliously and flicked his knife back and forth.

Bad Whiskey shouted to his goons. "No need to be friendly, boys! Take 'em down!"

A few gunshots crackled up the embankment. The bullets came nowhere close, but Cutter dropped back to his stomach anyway.

"We can't stop them," John Wesley said.

A sour wind swirled up from below, carrying the scent of the dead, while high above, a pair of crows orbited the mountain in chaotic loops.

Keech thought about the stony climb Duck had just accomplished, the thousands of rocks and boulders that speckled the perilous incline.

"There's only one option," he said. "Follow me."

Keech leaped to his feet and took off running.

CHAPTER 20
THE DOORWAY

Nat was already scaling the giant rock pile when Keech came sprinting around the bend.

"I heard the commotion," Nat said, tossing a swift glance down at him. "I have to find Duck." His face burned bright red with concentration, but he had made reasonable progress up the slope.

"Right behind you," Keech said. He vaulted to the pile and began to climb. Cutter and John Wesley came stomping up the footpath a moment later. Both boys froze at the weedy base, as if the sight of Nat ascending the mound had shocked their bones out of movement.

"C'mon, fellas, *pronto*," Keech said.

"You want us to climb *this*?" Cutter asked.

"I done told y'all I can't do that!" John Wesley muttered.

"We climb or die," Keech said. As far as he could see, there was no other way up the side of the mountain.

"We'll likely do both!" Cutter spat.

"Just don't look down. Test each rock before you put your full weight on."

The young riders fell into a silence as their climb began in earnest. Keech focused on the motion of his hands, the shift of his boots, the feel of the damp stones whenever he grabbed for a handhold. He wasn't very high yet, but if one finger slipped or one loose rock fell—if his clumsy body betrayed him in the slightest—he would easily break a leg or even his neck. How Duck had managed to travel so quickly up two hundred feet of slippery, razor-sharp rock was a feat that baffled Keech.

Below him, John Wesley cursed at Cutter, as mossy rocks tore free from Cutter's grasp and tumbled past the larger boy. Keech worried fiercely about John. He was bulky and tiresome, loved to complain, and didn't seem to understand or appreciate his own strength. If anyone got them into trouble, it would be John Wesley.

Keech had climbed nearly to the big rounded boulder—the massive formation he thought of as the hunchback—when he saw a dark stone the size of a ham fly at his face. He recoiled and the rock skimmed his cheek. He tasted chalky dust and sputtered.

"Sorry!" Nat called down. As soon as he said it, the rancher slipped over the bow of the hunchback, which meant he was halfway to the top. Keech felt a flash of envy for the boy's progress. He glanced down momentarily to check on Cutter and John Wesley . . . and saw the thralls.

The quickest of them had reached the mound and were beginning to climb. The rest of Bad Whiskey's army was shuffling up the critter path, accumulating at the foot of the mound, shoving one another, clawing at their turn to ascend.

"John Wesley, heads up!" Keech shouted.

Properly startled, the large boy looked down. Rotting thralls grinned up at him and raised their revolvers. Keech caught a glimpse of leather. It was Rance, leading the pack.

Floodwood once again came alive with gunfire.

"Go faster, Cut!" John Wesley yelled, as ammunition zinged around them. The boy quickened his pace up the rock face. A riotous grunt issued from Cutter's throat as he grabbed for boulders and heaved.

They were sitting ducks on the mound, all of them, a feast of targets. Except for Nat. Since climbing over the hunchback, he was no longer visible. If Keech and the others could only make it to that point, they could gain some momentary cover.

Putrid wind pummeled Keech's face, threatening to rip the hat off his head. He shoved it down tight. He could hear Rance's voice below: "Get 'em, you worms! Don't lose 'em again! All of you, climb!" Grimacing, Keech reached up and touched an inviting stone, only to find that the jagged rock tilted under the lightest touch. He shifted his grip. One wrong move could bring the entire slope down on the heads of Cutter and John Wesley.

Which gave Keech an idea.

A slug whizzed by his ear, so close he felt the wind of it flutter his hat brim. The shot demolished a small stone near his face and he tasted more grit. He heard Pa's faithful voice in his head whisper, *Stay calm*. If he panicked, he would choose the wrong handhold and go slipping off to death.

Nat's voice echoed from above. "I'm at the top!"

Clamping his teeth, Keech at last made the hunchback. It was a tricky endeavor to climb over the big boulder's slippery arch, but he found the holds he needed to lug himself up.

He grabbed a quick breath and rubbed his burning arm. His position didn't allow him to see the other two boys, so he dropped to his stomach and peeked over the drop. His heart thumped when he saw that Bad Whiskey's thralls were slinking closer to John Wesley. One dead man dressed in ragged sheepskin risked drawing his pistol. The mere act of bringing his weapon upward shifted his weight enough that the stone beneath his boot slipped loose. The rock tumble snowballed into a miniature cascade and the thrall was gone in an instant, taking with him another decaying cohort.

"You foolish maggots!"

Bad Whiskey's voice. The one-eyed fiend was now at the mound.

"Mind yer steps!"

A duo of dead men climbed within reach of John Wesley's legs and clawed at the boy's trousers. He screamed and struggled to clutch a piece of shale that crumbled in his grasp. Cutter saw what was happening and stretched down a hand. John Wesley's fingers landed on his wrist and Cutter pulled. The thralls' grip on John Wesley's trousers tore free, and the boy hurried up the next rock.

Keech studied the pile from peak to base. By his estimation, five or six large tumbling stones could cause the whole mound to crumble.

He recalled the nuggets of rock and grit that Duck had shaken loose when climbing over the rocky hat brim. The mantel had been strong enough to support her small frame, and Nat hadn't been heavy enough to collapse the shelf either. But John Wesley was as husky as a horse.

The world below the hunchback was a discord of shouts and curses and thundering revolvers. Soon Keech saw Cutter's head float into view, and he reached down and grabbed the boy's hand. Working together, they boosted him onto the boulder. Needles of broken rock had slashed Cutter's nose, but he grinned anyway, a feral look that both surprised and exhilarated Keech.

"Hey, Lost Cause."

"Hey yourself. I've got a plan. Be ready."

"It better be a dandy."

A second later John Wesley appeared, his face pasty with fear.

"I made it," he moaned.

"We're not out of the woods yet," Keech said. He and Cutter helped John Wesley over the hump, and Keech pointed up to the top of the pile. Nat was nowhere to be seen—no doubt he was searching for his sister.

"I know you're dog-tired, John, but keep climbing," Keech said. "I need you to reach that ledge." He pointed up to the hat brim.

Below, Bad Whiskey called out, "Yer dead meat, little pilgrims!"

John Wesley nodded as if he already understood Keech's plan. He began to scale again, humming a nervous tune as he worked.

A thrall's leathery face appeared like a nightmare over the hunchback. "Found ya!" the dead man muttered. His moldy fingers clawed the stone for purchase.

Before Keech could pull the freezing pendant from his shirt and kill the thing, a dull gleam of steel flashed in Cutter's grip.

Blackened fingers went flying off the thrall's hands, and shock exploded on the dead man's face as he dropped away.

"*Adios*," Cutter said, and sheathed his knife.

More thralls began to scratch at the underside of the hunchback. They would be over the hump in no time. Keech tapped Cutter on the shoulder. "We have to go *now*."

The boys began to climb after John Wesley, who had apparently found one last reserve of energy. He had already made a good distance, and had only a few more feet to go before reaching the top mantel.

"He's gonna do it!" Cutter said.

"Let's just make sure—" Keech began, but a fresh eruption of gunfire clipped the rest of his words. Two dead men had clambered over the hunchback and were firing up at them. Invisible pellets pinged and thudded against the granite.

"Go suck an egg!" shouted a high-pitched voice, and before Keech could register what was happening, a storm of rocks battered the pistols right out of the thralls' hands.

Keech glanced up. Duck was standing on the ledge, side by side with her brother, lobbing stones at Whiskey's goons. Nat was aiming Sheriff Turner's Colt, and fired off two measured rounds. The thralls on the hunchback went tumbling backward off the boulder.

Somewhere below, Bad Whiskey roared in frustration.

"Much obliged!" Keech called to the Embrys.

John Wesley reached the mantel, but when he tried to climb over the lip, his last helping of strength seemed to fail. "I can't make it!" he said, and stretched one hand up to Nat and Duck.

The siblings dropped to their bellies and reached, but the boy was too low even for Nat's long arms.

"We have to help John," Keech said to Cutter.

They climbed as fast as they could. Cutter found a route up the rocks that put him nearly neck and neck with Keech. By the time they reached John Wesley, the stones beneath the boy's feet were clattering, on the verge of tearing out of the mountainside.

Whooshing out a loud breath, John Wesley gripped the edge of the mantel and tried to pull himself up again, but to no avail. The boy was strong, but his own weight worked against him at this angle.

"We're here," Keech told the boy, steadying himself beneath him. "We'll help you up."

"Th-thanks," John Wesley stammered.

The terrible noise of the dead infiltrated the cold air. Keech didn't have to look down to know that Whiskey's thralls were now swarming the hunchback and the final stretch of mound.

Another hail of stones rained on the dead men. Duck and Nat stood on the precipice and launched rocks together, their perfect aim sending more thralls careening down the pile. They would only get back up, of course, but it was a worthy effort to buy John Wesley more time.

Keech stretched up one hand and pushed on John Wesley's left boot to give him a platform. At the same time Cutter fumbled to help him from the other side, scrabbling for a hold on John's right leg.

Steeling himself for one final push, Keech tucked his shoulder under John Wesley's rump. "Hey, watch it!" the boy muttered, but Keech ignored him and shoved.

Just before Keech had spent the end of his strength, John Wesley mercifully lifted. Keech and Cutter shoved him over the edge of the mantel. A terrible noise rumbled above. The hanging shelf wobbled underneath the large boy's weight. Just as Keech had hoped.

"It's coming down on our heads! Move it!" Cutter screamed.

They skittered over the top edge. For one second Keech felt the world go topsy-turvy beneath him, like a tottering tree. He felt the ground slip away and knew that he would tumble along with the heavy stone. He was too slow and would be crushed beneath the slide.

But then John Wesley grabbed his wrist and dragged him over the edge and back to solid ground. Beside him, Nat and Duck were holding on to Cutter.

A devastating crash cracked the air like a thunderbolt.

"Get back," Keech called. "Away from the edge!"

The young riders hurried on hands and knees over tall weeds and burs, away from the precipice. A second later—as a cluster of thralls peeked over the edge—the splitting overhang tilted. The heavy mantel separated from the rest of the mountainside. A look of shock crossed the decayed faces.

The shelf stones barreled down the slope and shoved the hunchback out of its decades-old cavity, loosening the giant boulder like a bad tooth. And when the hunchback began to roll free, the entire mound collapsed. Every remaining thrall careened down the ruined slope inside a tempest of stone and moss and roots and dirt. It may have been his imagination, but Keech thought he heard Bad Whiskey scream as the rubble buried the critter path.

Sweaty and exhausted, the young riders bellowed in victory.

"Leave it to John Wesley to knock down a whole mountain!" Cutter cackled.

Resting on their hands and knees, both Nat and Duck laughed.

"Shut your mouth," John Wesley said. But he was also grinning, and before long he broke into his own fit of laughter.

Lying on his back in the weeds, Keech allowed himself to join in the merriment. But only for a moment. A mile of Floodwood rubble had just entombed a small army of Bad Whiskey's thralls—and most likely Whiskey himself—but their fight was hardly over. And the Reverend's crows were still prowling the cursed clouds.

"We have to keep moving," he said. "The door out of here is close, I know it."

"Can't we rest up a second?" said John Wesley.

This time it was Duck who answered. "Keech is right. There's no time," she said. The girl stood and pointed to a stand of tall brown thistle behind her. A narrow footpath, no wider than a deer trail, led through the weeds and farther up the remaining peak of the mountain, away from the stone mound that had just crumbled.

She smiled. "I think I found our doorway."

Duck led the gang up the path, which was almost invisible under the wall of thistle. The tall weeds had been swept back in several places, a sign that someone might have traveled through here, and not long ago.

The footpath ventured upward, winding in a rough semicircle around the tallest point of the mountain, till it appeared to stop abruptly at another wall, a craggy barrier that blocked their way.

"Okay, so what now?" asked Cutter.

Duck pointed to a fallen oak trunk as wide as a horse leaning against the stone wall. The wood was near black with rot and slick from Floodwood's constant rain.

"That log ain't what it looks like," she said.

Despite the trunk's rotting black bark, the dead oak looked as solid as the stone it leaned against. Duck rapped on the trunk with one knuckle. Keech was surprised to hear a dull echo inside.

"How can a log be a door?" Nat asked.

"Not sure, but I think it's man-made," said Duck.

John Wesley stepped to the massive trunk and knocked on it. There was no mistaking the hollow clunk that resonated back. "Maybe it's just a rotted-out tree."

Keech stepped up and ran a hand along the wet bark. His fingertips dipped into a dark fissure. The indenture was oddly notched, as if it had been cut. As he felt inside the groove, the image of Pa Abner using the silver pendant to open the wooden chest in the study came to mind. He felt a dizzying flood of excitement. He had seen woodwork like this before. Pa Abner frequently used the bark of old trees to finish furniture. This was no rotted log; this was Pa's handiwork. Only the finest woodworker in Missouri could build a door disguised as a fallen oak trunk. Robby would have been proud.

Duck had apparently been thinking similar thoughts. She pointed to the fissure where Keech had slipped his fingers. "A key," she said almost breathlessly. "It's for a key."

Keech pulled the shard from his coat. "You mean this?"

Holding his breath, he thrust the pendant, jagged edge first, into the deep indent. The match was precise. The quarter moon slid into the furrow with no resistance. There was a *click* as the charm found a stopping point. Less than an inch of silver jutted from the cavity, but it was enough to give Keech a handhold.

He gazed proudly at Duck. "You were right!"

"Go ahead," said Nat. "Open 'er up."

Keech twisted the pendant clockwise. There was a clonking noise as a set of wooden cogs turned with a loud grind behind the hollow wood.

"It's working!" Duck said.

When the charm stopped, a deep rattling sound reverberated from the other side of the trunk. Keech felt a second of panic when nothing else happened. But then a large section of the log swung inward, receding into the stone wall behind the trunk. A cloud of gray dust flew all around them. As Keech's vision cleared, he saw a large circle of black.

A long, deep darkness burrowed into the hillside.

"Ain't that swell," said John Wesley. "Our door out of Floodwood is a *cave*."

CHAPTER 21
CUTTER'S DECISION

Keech dared to make the first step into the darkness.

"The floor is solid," he said. "I think it's safe."

As he took another step into the cave, Cutter yanked at his coat sleeve. "Don't go in. It smells like skunk-water in there."

Keech sniffed at the darkness. At first, all he smelled was old cave grime. But then he perceived a scent beneath the grime, an odor that reminded him of Claymore.

Nat appeared beside him in the opening. "There's something dead in there. Some critter, most likely."

"How would it have gotten in?" asked Duck. "The door was shut tight before we got here."

John Wesley backed away. "I got me a bad feeling."

"Ditto," Cutter said.

"We don't have a choice," Keech said. "We have to find a way out of Floodwood, and if the rockslide didn't work, Bad Whiskey will still be on our trail. Whether we like it or not, this cave is our path."

"What if me and John Wesley refuse?" murmured Cutter.

"Why would you refuse?" Keech asked. "You know what'll happen."

Cutter flashed a malicious grin. "That's easy. We kill *El Ojo*."

Keech couldn't take any more of Cutter's pride. "No. We all die. And you'll be the first to go."

Cutter tried to remain stoic, but Keech saw a flash of fear in the boy's eyes.

One by one, the young riders climbed through the hollow trunk. Once they were inside, John Wesley shut the door. The primitive hinges squealed as he did, and there was another turbulent *clack* as the old wood panel lodged back into place.

Whether or not they liked it, they were locked in.

The gang set out into the darkness, prodding at the greasy limestone walls. The cave's mouth opened to a small chamber, no bigger than Pa's barn, but Keech got the feeling eyes could deceive down here. The chamber might be much larger than it looked.

They moved through a darkness blacker than any Keech had ever experienced. The nagging, buzzing heaviness in his head seemed even worse down here, perhaps because the dying light and the enclosed space made him dwell on it all the more.

When their path had completely vanished into the black, Nat called the troop to a halt. "We best make a plan before we go farther," he said, his voice echoing as though he'd spoken into an empty cask.

"This is powerful dangerous," John Wesley said. "We should light torches."

"Where are we gonna find torches?" Duck asked.

"I've got my arm on the right wall," Nat said. "Everyone line up. Put your hand on the shoulder of the person in front of you."

Duck positioned herself behind Nat. Keech found Cutter's back and moved his grip to the boy's shoulder. In turn, John Wesley's heavy mitt landed on Keech's arm.

"Ow! Ease up."

John Wesley's nervous clutch loosened. "Sorry."

"Everyone ready?" Nat asked.

Their boots scuffed across the invisible ground. The path curved and each step felt like a leap of faith. After a few moments of blind shuffling, Keech felt Cutter come to a stop.

"John Wesley's right, this ain't too smart," Cutter said. "We should turn and fight."

"Cut, we've been through this," Nat answered. "They got firepower."

"So what? You got Turner's thumb buster. I got my magic knife."

"That knife ain't no more magic than my little pinky," Duck said. "Besides, weapons are useless against Whiskey's thralls."

"But our amulets aren't," Keech said. He lifted Pa Abner's pendant over his head.

No sooner did he weave the leather cord around his palm than two deafening gunshots rumbled through the cave. The salvo came from everywhere and nowhere. The disturbance jarred the walls, sprinkled dust from the ceiling.

Duck groaned. "How'd they find us?"

"Maybe those blasted crows showed him the way," Cutter said.

"Maybe so. But five of us stomped over that trail and around Pa's door," Keech said. "Whiskey may be blind in one eye, but he's not blind. We should've been more careful about our tracks."

The young riders began to shuffle faster through the cavern. A number of unseen steps led them down a mild slope. When they reached the bottom, the pressure in Keech's ears changed and he sensed they were entering another chamber. A strange chattery noise pervaded the blackness here, like the rustling of a thousand leaves.

Cutter's shoulder dipped, so Keech ducked low. When he swiped through darkness and brushed against the unseen wall, his fingers touched something spongy. He yanked his hand back, only to feel something flutter on the brim of his hat.

"What's that noise?" Cutter asked.

Up ahead, Duck said, "Bats."

John Wesley clutched at Keech's shoulder. "Tell me you're joking. I hate bats!"

"They're all over the walls," Keech said. "Don't make any sudden moves." Gingerly he brushed at the bat fidgeting on his head. There was a tiny protesting screech. Then the critter went flapping away into the darkness.

The chattering never ceased as the troop traversed the invisible chamber. In fact, it grew louder the deeper into the cave they traveled.

Without warning, Cutter stopped again, making Keech bump into him.

"Dangit all, what's wrong now?" he asked.

"I thought I heard something. A growl."

Duck made a gasping noise. "Bats don't growl. Do they?"

"That was my stomach," John Wesley said. "I'm starving."

"How can you think about grub at a time like this?" Cutter asked.

Nat said, "Stay focused."

The gang trudged onward. After a while, Keech stopped trying to make sense of the darkness. The gloom only made him think he was seeing shapes when he knew there was nothing there at all.

The faintest orange glow appeared on his palm.

John Wesley gripped his shoulder. "Keech, your amulet! It's glowing!"

Sure enough, Pa's pendant was pulsing with a strange light, as if it were turning to hot cinder, though the metal felt cold.

The group huddled around his hand. As they watched, the light of the shard grew brighter. Within seconds, it was glowing enough that they could see each other's faces.

"Duck, fetch your charm," Keech said.

There was a shuffling sound as Duck retrieved her pendant. When she laid it across her palm, the same soft orange glow emanated from the shard.

"Why are they glowing like that?" John Wesley asked.

"The pieces react when Bad Whiskey's magic is near," Duck said.

As if to prove her theory, a ragged holler echoed out from the black tunnel: "Keech Blackwood! I know yer near, pilgrim! A pile of rocks can't stop me!"

Over his shoulder, Keech saw traces of a flickering light shimmering in the distance. Whiskey and at least a few of his goons were approaching. They had brought torches to light their way. The glow of the amulets intensified as the torchlight grew brighter.

"We have to go," Nat said.

Keech seized the opportunity to canvass their surroundings. They were shuffling through a long, narrow corridor with a low ceiling. There were no bats here, but the ground sloped up as the corridor progressed, building toward a massive ridge.

Keech noticed something else: the stink of decay was stronger here.

Venomous laughter filled the hollow places. "I'm comin', pilgrim! I can feel ya near! As long as you hold the shard, I'll know where to find ya!" They could hear footsteps, scuffling over limestone.

Nat took his sister's free hand and pulled her along. "Maybe we can find someplace to hide."

Keech and John Wesley moved behind them, but Cutter remained where he stood. "Go ahead and hide. I'm staying," he said.

Nat and Duck spun around. "No, you're not. We go together," Nat replied.

"Just because I ride with you don't mean I take your orders." Cutter pulled his knife. "Don't try to stop me, Embry."

At the sight of the blade, Nat placed his hand on the grip of Turner's revolver. "You want to be careful," he said. "I'm in no mood."

"My brother ain't fooling. I'd listen if I was you," Duck said.

John Wesley tugged on Cutter's coat. "Stop it, Cut. We have to go."

Cutter hawked a ball of spit in the direction of Nat's boot.

"He's a yellow-belly. I came to kill *El Ojo*, not hide in the shadows. We'll take 'im down together, me and you, like we always planned."

John Wesley looked confused about what to do. "We can't just leave them," he told Cutter. "Back at the rocks they didn't leave *us*, did they? We're all a team now."

Cutter scowled. "I do better on my own."

"Cutter, think about what you're doing," Keech pleaded. "You're closed in, no high ground. There'd be no way to escape."

"I don't want to escape," the boy said. "I want *El Ojo* to pay."

"You'll get gunned down if you stay here!" John Wesley said.

"Least I'll die taking a stand. Not running like a coward."

"This isn't running," Keech said. "This is surviving."

"Leave me be, Lost Cause. This is something I gotta do. For my friend Bishop."

Nat took a step closer. "If you're gonna be lunkheaded, at least take a weapon of some use." He offered the sheriff's revolver to Cutter.

The boy looked surprised, but he shook his head. "My knife can take him down."

"Hang your silly knife!" Duck said. "You can't throw a knife at a bullet."

"No, let him have his way." Nat placed the gun back in its holster. "Let's go." Turning back around, he led Duck and a hesitant John Wesley up the corridor.

Keech gave Cutter one last pleading look. "Don't do this."

"I'll be all right, Lost Cause. The very least, I'll slow *El Ojo* down, give y'all a fighting chance to get out of this place and find the Char Stone."

Shaking his head, Keech hurried down the path to join the others. Before rounding the next curve, he ventured a look back. Cutter had spun around to face the other direction. A few yards beyond, chaotic torchlight flickered on the cave walls. Cutter disappeared in the darkness as he hurried toward Bad Whiskey.

CHAPTER 22

WASAPE

As Keech followed the others up the limestone aisle, he listened for gunshots or even screams, but only the sounds of their footsteps touched his ears.

Beside him, John Wesley muttered, "I don't get it. Why can't we hear any fighting?"

Nobody had an answer.

The gang's faces were still lit by the amulet shards, but the light had dimmed somewhat, suggesting they were gaining distance from Whiskey. They continued shuffling along. Soon they emerged into a large, circular room. The stink of death was much heavier in this chamber, and the faintly glowing shards revealed five or six passages that forked away from the room.

"This place is a maze," Nat said.

Keech scrunched his nose. "I think it's something's home."

Swarms of flies buzzed around the room, filling the air with a sickly haze. Beneath the insects, a monstrous carpet of animal bones lay scattered on the floor.

"Just dandy," John Wesley groaned. He raised his boot heel, noticed he was standing on a dingy jawbone, and hopped back with a whimper.

Nat crouched to examine a hefty pair of antlers wedged in the mud. "Mule deer," he said. "Been dead a long time."

"That's what's making that awful smell?" asked John Wesley.

A small scream gave Keech a jolt. "There!" Duck pointed at something across the room.

Slouched against the far wall, still covered in places with flesh, was a human skeleton. Flies surrounded the carcass like a black cloud. The victim's grimy skull gazed across the room. One bony arm reached out beside the body, as though grasping for the darkness.

"Now we know what lives down here," Nat said, grimacing. "A man-eater."

A bundle of cloth lay around the corpse's legs—a pair of deer-skin trouser sleeves and a buffalo-hair breechcloth covered in thick, dried blood. Beside the body lay a slender longbow. Slung over the corpse's shoulder was a quiver made from raccoon pelts. Tucked inside was a single dogwood arrow, its feathers white and brown.

Duck pinched her nose. The light from her shard cast an eerie luster of orange over the skull. "I wonder who it was?" she said, her tone now more curious than frightened.

Keech examined the longbow. He had seen such a weapon many times. He and Pa Abner had constructed one, in fact, on Keech's eleventh birthday.

"He was an Osage warrior."

"How can you tell?" asked John Wesley.

"The bow is made from the wood of a hedge apple tree, and the breechcloth has the Osage design. My hunch is, this fella got lost in Floodwood. He found the cave and got more than he bargained for. But he went down fighting, see?" Keech gestured at the lone arrow inside the quiver. "I'd wager his killer got more than it bargained for, too."

"How'd he get past the door?" Nat wondered.

"Fellas, look!"

Duck pointed to the dead warrior's hand. The bony index finger appeared to be gesturing at the cave wall, directing their attention to a ragged picture painted in dried blood across the mudstone:

When Keech saw it, cold dread rippled down his neck and spine.

"What the heck is it?" asked Duck, squinting at the bloody sketch.

"*Wasape*," Keech said. "The warrior must've died before he could finish the paw." He recalled his vision inside the evergreen ring, the night story etched in the stars.

John Wesley gulped. "What does 'Wasape' mean?"

"Our friend here is telling us what killed him," Keech answered grimly. "A bear."

John Wesley said, in a rushed breath, "Then we have to get out of here. We're standing right in its den!"

"Maybe it's a black bear," Duck said.

"It would have to be a mammoth," Keech said, "to take down a skilled brave with a full quiver."

John Wesley gazed at the network of limestone passages. "One of those tunnels has to lead back to the surface. How else could the bear get outside to hunt?"

"There," Nat said, pointing to the middle passage, an opening shaped like the letter D. "It's the only one that slopes up, not down."

Just then a gigantic roar reverberated through the den. Another shower of pebbles and dust shook from the ceiling.

"Time to go," Keech said, his chest hammering.

The young riders hurried to the D-shaped corridor. Peering inside, Keech saw a natural funnel climbing for several yards. "It's steep, but passable."

Nat nodded. "I'll go first. Duck, you stay behind me."

They started up the passage in single file. After only ten steps, Keech stopped. "Wait." He turned back to the den.

"But that monster could be anywhere," John Wesley murmured. "Just hold up."

Keech sprinted back across the bone-filled room to the fallen Osage warrior. The flies in the den swarmed his face. Swatting them, he crouched to one knee at the skeleton's feet. His amulet piece gleamed hues of yellow and orange.

"I'm sorry about this," he said to the corpse, "but you've got something I might need. If we ever meet on the spirit path, I'll be sure to give you proper thanks." He grabbed the longbow and the quiver and then hightailed it back to the group.

They traveled another hundred yards through the climbing passage and then stepped into another small chamber. The light from both amulets now barely illuminated the area, but Keech could see there was no exit. "Dead end," he groaned.

"Our light's almost gone," Duck said. "We're losing the outlaw."

"That's some luck," John Wesley said. "When we escape, we're blind. When we can see, we're in danger."

"There's no other choice," Nat said. "We have to head back to the den, pick another passage."

John Wesley's eyes widened. "What if the bear shows up?"

Keech raised the dead warrior's longbow. "Then we put the warrior's last arrow to good use."

Reversing direction, they shuffled back through the corridor. After a time, Keech's ears discerned a muffled rumbling, like steady thunder. The hollows of the cave made it impossible to tell the distance to the source, but it sounded close.

"Anyone hear that?" he asked.

"It sounds like a river," said John Wesley.

"I don't recollect passing a river," said Duck.

"Because we didn't," Nat replied. "We made a straight line out of the den and I thought we were taking the same tunnel back. I must be turned around. I reckon we're lost."

"It's the Floodwood curse," Keech said. "We're being led down strange passages."

The gang quickened their pace, careful not to disturb the bats.

Soon the tunnel descended drastically and the rumble of water grew louder.

"I see the next room," Nat said.

Moments later, Keech heaved a sigh of relief when they stepped out of the tunnel and landed on a floor of smooth brown clay. The air smelled fresher here, and the amulet pieces pulsated with stronger light. "Bad Whiskey's getting closer," he said.

"I think we're in a massive chamber. Shine that light around," Nat said.

Duck and Keech held out their charms like lanterns. What stretched before them brought a hitch to Keech's throat. The chamber was bigger than Pa Abner's bean field. Columns of rock jutted from the cavern floor, and thick formations protruded like fangs from the boundless ceiling, which teemed and wriggled with hanging bats. In the distance, a pair of pillars stood side by side, two giant sentinels with fierce limestone faces. Between the pillars, the rumble of water crashed through the room, as loud as a tornado.

"Everyone stay sharp," Nat said.

They walked toward the sound of flowing water.

Water dripped from the jagged ceiling, splashing on thick stone fingers that rose, some as high as a man, from the cave floor. They wove their way through the forest of formations, slipping between the stone teeth, till they came to the giant pillars.

Keech lifted his pendant. The rumbling was a subterranean river, a channel of rapid water that churned in a cradle of black rock.

Stepping carefully toward the water, he stopped where the

muddy floor became wet stone. The shard cast enough light that he could see the water's roiling body, and a few feet ahead, the low facing of rock the river slipped beneath.

"I think this is the Little Wild Boy."

"How could that be?" asked John Wesley.

"The Little Wild Boy runs to the Platte River and cuts a line west through Whistler. I never saw the river again as I was running through Floodwood, which means it must cut underground. And as I recall, the Platte River runs north to south. If we follow the Little Wild Boy, we could find the passage to the Platte."

"And walk right out of here," Nat finished.

"Fellas, take a look!" Duck shouted.

She'd been shining her pendant around the room, casting sheets of light on the walls. There, on the dripping stone of the nearest pillar, was a message painted in black:

43 3:5

They gathered around the pillar, and Keech silently recited the books of the Bible. "It's the book of John."

"Chapter 3, verse 5," Duck added.

Keech nodded. "Do you know it?"

"No, Pa never taught me that one. Nat?"

"Don't look at me," Nat said, shrugging. "I got the steady hand, remember?"

"Surely somebody knows," John Wesley said.

A doleful silence passed.

"So that's it, then?" Duck asked. "We can't solve the clue?"

Keech cursed himself for always being a poor study at Bible

verses. The Scripture had been Sam's joy. It should have been Sam breaking all of Pa's ciphers.

And all at once, the clearest, most delightful answer arrived. Keech looked at the pillar again.

"I know the verse! I know exactly how to get us out of this cave, and out of Floodwood once and for all."

He raised his pendant so he could see Nat's and Duck's faces. The silver's glow was rising in intensity.

"Remember what Sheriff Turner said about Bennett Coal—I mean your pa, Noah—coming to Big Timber ten years back to look for my pa? I think the two men weren't just looking for a way to hide the Char Stone. I think they were setting up these clues along the way to get back to the Stone, if needed. They knew the danger they were facing if one of them was caught, so they scattered the clues between each other."

Duck seemed to know where Keech's next thought was going. "And over the years our fathers were planting the answers to these clues *in our own heads*," she continued, her voice excited. "Each of us got a different piece, a different clue."

Keech grinned at Duck. "Your pa gave you the verse about knocking on the door."

"But what about this message?" Nat asked.

"He gave the clue to my brother Sam. John chapter 3, verse 5. It was one of Sam's favorite Scriptures. 'Except a man be born of water and of the Spirit, he cannot enter into the kingdom of God.' Sam had memorized it because Pa Abner had it underlined in the Bible he gave to him."

John Wesley looked more confused than ever. "But what does it mean?"

"It means"—Keech swallowed hard—"we're supposed to be baptized."

"What?" John Wesley barked.

"Pa Abner is telling us to jump into the Little Wild Boy River."

John Wesley looked green. "You can't expect us to jump in that!"

Nat glanced at the farthest end of the great room, where the whipping water slipped beneath the rock face in a diagonal line. "John's right. That's far too risky. We've got no way of knowing how far we'd have to swim underwater. We could get trapped."

"I didn't sign up to drown in no smelly cave," John Wesley added.

"The river will carry us out," Keech said. "I know it."

Nat stepped over to the bank, dropped to one knee, and sank one arm deep into the sputtering water. "I can't feel the bottom, and the water's cold," he said. "If we didn't get stuck under the rock, we'd freeze to death in minutes."

"This is Pa Abner's plan. I trust him."

"No, Blackwood. I won't let you put my sister in danger on a hunch."

Duck had been listening in silence, her amulet shard held out toward the river. Now she gave her brother an indignant snort. "Stop treating me like a baby. I ain't in no more danger than you. Besides, Keech's hunches have got us through plenty."

"We're not jumping in that river," Nat said, his face stony. "No one's gonna die today on a rickety plan."

"Did somebody say *die*?" a grating voice echoed.

The amulets flared up as bright as lamps. Both Keech and Duck recoiled at the unexpected surge of cold in their hands.

Bad Whiskey and three of his living dead men, including Rance, staggered into the chamber. His henchmen were clutching long torches, and the flames sent shadows dancing about the vast room.

Bad Whiskey looked worse than ever. His black overcoat hung from his wasted body in ribbons, and the hand that gripped his Colt Dragoon was black with decay.

Bad Whiskey saw Keech and sneered. "It's young Jim Bowie!" he said, as if greeting an old friend. "Yer a hard one to catch, boy. Isaiah Raines taught ya good." He pulled his Dragoon and cocked the hammer. "But now I gotcha dead to rights."

Keech's first thought was to protect the shards. There was no point in denying he was holding Pa's charm. Its orange glow was highly visible, but Duck's charm was hidden where she stood behind Keech.

"Put your charm away," Keech whispered. "Don't let him see it!"

Duck quickly stuffed the fragment back into her coat. Keech heard a small whimper escape her throat as the pendant's unnatural cold stung her skin.

The dead men lingered at the chamber's edge. Rugged terrain stood between the thralls and the young riders, providing cover should someone start slinging lead, but with a raging river at their backs, there was nowhere to run.

"Raise yer dirty mitts," Bad Whiskey said. "Nice and high."

Nat pushed Duck behind him. He whispered to Keech and John Wesley, "Find cover."

Before Keech could react, Nat drew Turner's revolver. He pulled the trigger. Keech expected hot bullets to smash through Bad Whiskey and his nameless thralls, but nothing happened. Nat spat a curse and pulled again, but the weapon refused to work. "No, no, no!" he yelled.

Across the chamber the creatures dropped their torches and moved for cover, anticipating Turner's gun ripping holes in them. Bad Whiskey noticed the gun's malfunction and grinned. "It's failed, you fools! His pistol's packin' duds!" He lifted his Dragoon. In response, Rance drew his own Pocket Revolver.

"Everyone, move!" Nat shouted. Keech jumped behind one of the limestone pillars. John Wesley hid behind a wide stone formation.

A hail of gunfire filled the chamber. Gunsmoke billowed through the air, creating a black, dusty fog. Disturbed from their sleep, a thousand bats took flight along the ceiling. A blessing, since their crazed exodus obscured any clear aim. The thralls were hitting nothing but stone.

Keech gripped the Osage warrior's longbow and drew the lone arrow. He would only get one shot, but if he could use the arrow to distract the thralls, perhaps he could rush them with the pendant.

He nocked the arrow.

The gunfire ceased as the thralls stopped to reload. Nat and Duck had joined John Wesley behind his stone formation. Duck was trying to help Nat clear Turner's revolver.

Bad Whiskey's voice echoed through the chamber. "You got no more weapons! Throw out the shard and I'll let ya live!"

Two thralls advanced across the cavern, snatching up their torches as they went. Bad Whiskey stood defiant where he had entered. Next to him, Rance was reloading his revolver.

The creatures would never allow Keech to get close enough to touch them with the charm. They would shoot him to pieces before he could travel half the room. The only thing to do was buy Nat some time to fix Turner's Colt.

Keech stepped out from his cover.

"What're you doing?" Nat hissed.

Keech lifted the bow, drew the string back, and took aim at Bad Whiskey. The outlaw's henchmen stopped, uncertain. Bad Whiskey's good eye fell on Keech's amulet shard, shining like a beacon, and his withering face broke into another sly grin.

Keech said, "It's time to end this, Bad."

"What are ya waitin' for, then? I ain't gettin' any prettier."

Keech took a long breath, exhaled, and with a smooth motion loosed the arrow. It sang across the chamber, whistling between the stone fangs scattered throughout the room.

The arrow sank into Bad Whiskey's heart with a dull thud. The outlaw staggered back and wavered. Keech felt a swell of hope—maybe an arrow to the heart would finish him—but then Whiskey stopped mid-stagger. He grabbed the arrow shaft and tugged the chert-stone tip out of his chest. Chuckling again, he dropped the shaft to the cave floor.

"You took yer shot, pilgrim. Now you all die. Get 'em, boys!"

The thralls lurched forward, sliding past the formations to

where the young riders hid. One ghoulish man tackled John Wesley, who fell hard onto his back. Another bowled into Nat, leaving Duck momentarily exposed, but the strong rancher held his ground.

Across the chamber, Rance cocked his revolver and aimed.

Keech tossed aside the longbow and quiver. He stepped backward to the bank of the underground river.

"Stop!" he yelled.

He dangled the amulet piece over the churning water.

"Tell your scum to back off or I'll drop it!"

Bad Whiskey's good eye squinted. "Yer bluffin'. That shard is yer only defense."

Keech flashed the outlaw his most vicious look. "Try me, Bad. I know the Reverend Rose wants this, like he wants the Char Stone. What happens if you don't deliver?"

After a silence, Bad Whiskey said to his thralls, "Back off, boys," and slipped his Dragoon back into its holster. Rance lowered his own revolver and the two thralls stopped clawing at the boys. John Wesley muttered a frightened curse, but he managed to crawl away.

Bad Whiskey raised his hands. "See, pilgrim? I can be reasoned with. All I want's the shard. What do you want in return?"

Before Keech could consider how to respond, a colossal roar shook the very air of the chamber. Every soul in the great room, including Bad Whiskey and his henchmen, gazed around with trepidation.

"What in blazes?" Whiskey sputtered.

"It's coming!" boomed a nearby voice.

The shout took everyone by surprise. They all turned and saw Cutter race out of the nearest passageway, gripping his knife.

"Cutter!" John Wesley exclaimed.

On Cutter's heels lurched an enormous black shape, roaring at his back and loping on four gigantic legs.

The Wasape.

But this monster was no natural bear. As the Wasape chased Cutter into the chamber, it reared on its hind legs. Upon its paws it stood more than double the height of a Missouri black bear. Its pelt was gray and ragged, its claws as long as daggers, and its eyes burned a diabolical red. All over its misshapen body, skinny brown sticks protruded from its flesh. The Osage warrior's arrows, Keech realized. And suddenly a memory flashed through his mind, a memory of the old Whistler mayor, speaking about the Floodwood curse:

Some folk claim they've heard a monster's roar come from the heart of that forest.

The Wasape, Keech thought, remembering his dream in the evergreen ring. *The Wasape contains the Floodwood curse! That's what Pa was doing in the vision. He and the Osage were putting a blight upon the bear and tying the creature to this area.*

Still in full sprint, Cutter noticed Bad Whiskey, altered his direction, and ran straight for the outlaw. "*El Ojo!*" he shrieked. "You killed my friend!" He raised his long blade.

The Wasape dropped back to all four massive paws and kept after Cutter. The creature's enormous body demolished every stone fang in its path.

Bad Whiskey and Rance leveled revolvers at their attacker. Lead balls tore into the rocks Cutter wove between, but missed the racing boy. A few of the bullets struck the Wasape in its massive shoulders. Furious, the bear roared and chomped after Cutter's heels.

Nat, Duck, and John Wesley took advantage of Cutter's distraction. "To the river!" Nat yelled. The trio moved toward Keech, who stepped away from the water. He didn't know how to help Cutter, but he refused to abandon him again, especially to a cursed bear.

"Cutter!" Keech hollered. "This way!"

A lead slug smashed into a hanging stalactite near Cutter's head, spraying rock shards in a cloud around him. His eyes locked on Keech and suddenly he altered his path again, running toward the other boys and Duck.

A low rumble shook the entire chamber. As the Wasape smashed apart stone pillars, the cave itself began to crumble. A stone the size of a fence post cracked above Keech's head. He leaped sideways. The stone slammed into the floor where he'd been standing.

Keech lifted his amulet shard to see, but a falling chunk of rock struck his hand. The glowing fragment flew out of his grasp. "No!" he yelled. He scrambled for the charm, but already the rubble had buried it and sealed in the light.

The Wasape flailed in fury as the outlaws fired bullets into its hide. With each bat of its mighty arms, pieces of limestone soared. The creature searched the room for the source of the attack and locked in on Bad Whiskey. It loped toward the one-eyed man, growling with rage.

Showing a foolhardy bravery, Rance stepped between the bear

and his master and emptied his revolver into the creature's chest. A single swipe of the Wasape's claws tore the thrall in half.

Bad Whiskey lost his footing and tumbled on his rump. He scampered backward. The Wasape lunged and clamped its jaws around Whiskey's elbow. The outlaw howled.

Keech was combing the ground for his pendant when Cutter reached him.

"Let's go, Keech. We can't linger."

"I lost the charm!" He grabbed rocks and hurled them aside.

"The ceiling's falling."

"We can't leave without the charm!"

Cutter grabbed Keech's wrist. "You didn't want to leave me back in the tunnel," he said. "I'm telling you the same thing you told me. Be smart, *amigo*."

Reluctantly, Keech gave up his search. All five of the young riders assembled at the riverbank, teetering on the edge of the roiling river.

A giant stone formation plunged from the ceiling, crushing the other two ghouls.

The Wasape lunged again. Bad Whiskey barked a curse and scrabbled away. He found the Osage warrior's arrow, grabbed it, and raised it high. The outlaw jabbed the arrow deep into the Wasape's chest. The great bear flung its head back and bellowed.

Keech yelled at Nat, "We have to jump!"

In the dying torchlight, Nat's face looked sick. "If you're wrong, Keech, this river will be our grave."

"If we don't jump, we'll be killed anyway."

"Right," Nat said. He grabbed his sister's hand. "Ready?" he asked Duck, and the girl nodded excitedly. They leaped into the raging river.

Cutter stepped up next and crossed himself. "Now we're jumping in a river," he said, as if trying to make sense of the plan. The boy chuckled and sheathed his knife. "I reckon I've done crazier things. *Adios!*" he shouted, and jumped in.

John Wesley didn't budge. "I can't do it," he cried.

Keech looked at him desperately. "John, this river's our only hope."

"But I ain't sure I can swim!"

Keech felt a sickening panic twist his gut. "Just hold your breath and kick. It's easy."

The Wasape roared behind them as the cavern continued to rain massive chunks of stone. There was no more time for debate. "We'll go together," Keech promised. "I won't let you drown. I swear it."

John shivered. "Okay, let's do this."

Keech grabbed the bottom of John Wesley's coat, clutching the cloth as tightly as he could. John Wesley released a loud cry, then vaulted into the water.

Keech had one last moment to hear Bad Whiskey scream, then he sprang into the river, holding for dear life onto John Wesley. The icy water engulfed him. He began to kick, but the rapids were much too strong for swimming. The river sucked him under. The currents snatched his fingers away from John Wesley's coat. He fumbled for the boy, but there was no use.

Keech tumbled into the unknown.

PART 3

THE SULLIED PLACE

WHISKEY IN THE DARK

The drum is his glory, his joy and delight,
It leads him to pleasure as well as to fight;
No girl, when she hears it, though ever so glum,
But packs up her tatters, and follows the drum.

The song came to Whiskey like a leaf tumbling in the wind. He tried to hold on to it—the song reminded him of warmer days, before the *Gita-Skog*, before the Reverend Rose—but the tune faded.

He knew the song was an old Revolutionary War tune, but Whiskey couldn't remember who had sung it to him. His father? His mother? To be honest, he couldn't remember either of them anymore. Not their faces, their names, not even their voices. His memories were dying.

He opened his eye, saw nothing but darkness, and heard a muffled growl rumble at his feet.

He was lying deep under Floodwood forest. The growling

thing was a bear. The crumbled ceiling had pinned the monster. The bear had swiped off his right arm. Those things were certain.

Whiskey reached out to look through the eyes of a thrall, but no woken vessel remained. The orphan boy—the son of Screamin' Bill—had crushed the last of his *Tsi'noo* under rubble.

However, there was another he could raise. A corpse back in the forest with his stallion and the packhorses. But did he have enough strength? The Prime was near gone. The Reverend had withdrawn so much of the dark energy. Only the smallest spark lingered.

Whiskey coughed up dust and tried to sit, but his body was as weak as a rag doll. He collapsed back to the ground and stared into the darkness.

And he pays all his debts with a roll of his drums . . .

He tried to whistle the song. Nothing came out but a wheeze.

Suddenly, Whiskey realized he couldn't remember his own last name. The darkness of this place was stealing everything from him.

He felt around the stony ground with his left arm. His gloved hand turned up his faithful Dragoon, but nothing else of use.

A tiny fire, no larger than a penny, flickered near his feet.

He was seeing the eye of the great bear, still open. The Wasape, the boy had called it. A glint of light reflected in the bear's eye.

Whiskey looked around for the source of illumination.

Lying in the cave dust was the glowing amulet shard. After all the chasing and battling with Screamin' Bill's orphan, a vital part of Whiskey's mission was lying only a few yards away.

Once he had it, there would be only one last thing to retrieve—the Char Stone, the source of new life. If he found it in time, Whiskey would no longer need the Prime to sustain him. The Stone could put back all that had gone wrong. The Stone could make him a whole man again.

A fluttering noise, the flapping of wings, interrupted his thoughts. The Reverend's dark mouthpiece, one of the emissaries known as the *P'mola*, had found him.

There was a scratching sound at his left ear, followed by a vicious caw. The Reverend's voice bored into the hull of Whiskey's mind.

You've been beaten, Nelson.

Nelson! That was his last name. "No, boss," Whiskey said. "I've got Isaiah's shard! It's here, in the cave!"

You are useless on your own. Ignatio and Big Ben will finish the hunt.

"I won't mess up again! If I just had more time, I could have the Stone by midnight."

After a long, empty silence, the Reverend spoke again.

You have been a loyal hand, Nelson. When the Enforcers betrayed me, you stood beside me. You fought Screamin' Bill, you fought Isaiah, and you died for me. I will give you one more chance. One.

"Yes, boss!"

You have till midnight. Retrieve the Stone.

"I can do it! Please don't let me slip away."

There was another long pause. Then a trickle of power flowed through Whiskey's limbs. The Reverend was feeding him one final taste of the Prime. Enough to raise more men and finish the hunt.

Refreshed, Whiskey stood, stretched his legs, and dusted off his trousers. He searched for the crow but saw nothing but darkness. He knew it was still there, watching. Darkness always felt different when the *P'mola* were about.

"The bear took my arm, boss. I can't swim out by the river's way. Lift the curse or I'll be stuck in Floodwood."

The bear is the Keeper. Finish the bear, and end the magic that binds you here.

Whiskey grinned. Smart of Raines to create such a Curse Keeper. Most men would never be able to defeat it.

He picked up his Dragoon, blew the cave dust off the barrel, and stepped over to the mountain of shadow that was the Wasape. He cocked the gun—but paused. "No," he muttered to the bear. "Not a bullet for you. Prob'ly wouldn't work nohow."

Whiskey stepped to the amulet shard and lifted its cord from the cave dirt. His gloved hand held the fragment away from his body, as a man would hold the tail of a viper.

"This wretched metal works on most magics. Let's see if it does the trick on you, Curse Keeper."

The creature grunted, straining to move, but a stone chunk the size of a thick tree pinned the massive body. Whiskey squatted in front of the creature's head and lowered the shard.

The second the glowing metal touched the monster's snout, the Wasape gave a tremendous roar. It thrashed for a moment as if hoping to flee the inevitable; then it slumped, and moved no more.

Whiskey waited for something—a sound, a feeling, a flash of mystical light—to signal the end of the Floodwood curse, but nothing happened. Nothing visible, leastways. Yet he detected a silence upon the energy imparted here, a stillness under the surface. The obnoxious buzzing that stained the air was gone.

He felt the rustle of wings again as the *P'mola* landed on his shoulder. The creature dug its talons into his flesh.

Go now, the Reverend murmured through the crow. *Retrieve my Stone.*

"Yes, boss."

Midnight, Nelson. Your clock is ticking.

Whiskey found no trouble backtracking through the cave and emerged from the hole he had blasted through Raines's door with his Dragoon. The October sky had darkened. What little sun was left would be setting soon. No time to waste. He had to find the Sullied Place.

His stallion waited for him at the base of the embankment. The other packhorses had fled while he was in the cave. On the ground at the stallion's hooves lay Whiskey's special bundle—the corpse he had hauled from the orphanage.

Whiskey stooped to murmur in the corpse's ear. "I've a special task for ya, old friend."

He then uttered the ancient words from another place, the Black Verse the Reverend Rose had taught him. The drop of Prime stirred in his veins.

A finger slowly curled. Then a hand. Soon there were mutterings. A cough. A blink of an eye.

Isaiah Raines, known by others as Abner Carson, stood. The bullet wounds that had taken his life were still fresh upon his body.

Whiskey said, "Lead me to the Sullied Place, Raines."

The thrall gave Whiskey a curious look, as if it wanted to question the command. But that was impossible. No thrall could oppose its Master.

Like a farmer prodding a stubborn mule, Whiskey nudged the thrall with his mind.

WALK, he commanded.

The dead man grimaced, then shambled forward.

CHAPTER 23
EXĪTE

Keech Blackwood splashed up from the Little Wild Boy River and blinked at the autumn sky. He had lost count of the number of times he'd emerged from a freezing river the last few days. Sputtering, he dug his hands into dark sand at the water's edge. He noticed his hat floating and grabbed it, amazed he hadn't lost it in the river.

Glancing back to the east, Keech spotted their exit and whistled in disbelief. The Little Wild Boy spilled out of a black hole sliced into the foot of the Floodwood mountain, a fissure the shape of an upside-down horseshoe. The back side of the mountain was a jumble of black dirt, half-buried boulders, and gnarled trees—all of which looked on the verge of tumbling into the crazed water.

There was a loud splash nearby as Cutter broke the river's surface and sucked in a giant breath. "What a swim!" he exclaimed, his own hat sagging on his head. "I can't believe we're still kickin'." Shivering, he staggered through the shallow water and stood next to Keech on the bank, his face a mixture of relief and shock. As if by instinct, Cutter's hand dropped to his red sash to make sure his knife was still intact.

Hectic movement near a bend upstream caught Keech's eye. "Oh no," he moaned.

Nat and Duck were working to pull John Wesley out of the river's current. The boy looked unconscious, his arms loose by his sides. Nat stood behind him, arms linked around his chest, heaving the boy onto the bank while Duck cleared the sand of debris.

"John!" Cutter cried. He sprinted up the bank. Keech hurried after him.

Nat and Duck dropped to their knees around the boy. The rancher began to push at the soft base of John Wesley's chest—hard, quick movements. Whenever Nat paused, Duck would bend, pinch John Wesley's nose, and blow into his mouth.

"What in blazes are y'all doing?" Cutter shouted, running up to John Wesley's side. "Leave 'im alone!"

"We're saving him," Duck said. She bent again to John Wesley's mouth and blustered more air down his gullet. "Pa used to say when a fella drowns, you have to push air back into him."

Keech stood at the unconscious boy's feet, gripping his sodden hat. He would never forgive himself if the boy perished.

John Wesley coughed up a lungful of water. His face turned deep purple from the vicious hacking. He muttered two words that sounded like, "*Papa, no,*" but Duck shushed him.

"Easy. Don't talk."

John Wesley struggled to regain his feet, but Cutter pushed

him gently back. "Stop your fussing," he said. "You almost drowned."

John Wesley spluttered, then collapsed on the riverbank.

Keech sat on a fat driftwood log and pried off his boots. As he emptied them of water, Nat, Duck, and Cutter stepped over, trembling in their wet clothes.

Nat joined him on the log. "Your crazy hunch saved our hides back there."

Keech nodded. "We need to find Bone Ridge now. We have to be close."

"We'll find it."

"Thanks for saving John Wesley."

Nat smiled, but it quickly fell to a frown. "He ain't out of the woods yet. We need to dry him up, warm his skin."

"We could build a fire here," Cutter said, gesturing to a flat spot on the bank.

"I don't relish camping where the river spills out," Duck said. "Bad Whiskey could come riding out of that hole any second."

"He won't be coming through there," Cutter said. "Last I saw, he was being torn to bits by the bear."

"Who's to say the bear did him in?"

"If it didn't, the cave-in must have finished him," Cutter said.

But Keech didn't believe for one second that Bad Whiskey was done. That ornery cuss had pulled an arrow out of his own heart.

To make matters worse, Keech had given him a vital tool. The pendant. There had been no choice but to abandon the charm, but if Whiskey had survived, he would have felt the presence of the silver and retrieved it.

Nat must have plucked this thought straight from his mind, for he turned to his sister and asked, "You still have Pa's charm, right?"

Duck lifted the shard out of her shirt. The hand around it was shivering from the cold. "If Whiskey survived, I'll take him down."

"Good." Nat stood and cracked his back. "Let's scout for a safe camp and go to ground for a spell. I don't want to look for Bone Ridge when we still have company." He gestured to the dimming sky north of the Little Wild Boy. Three dark specks floated under the lowest cloud. They were bathed in dying sunlight, and they moved in steady circles, as if sweeping the land for woodland prey.

Keech frowned at the sight of them. "They don't seem confused anymore. Over the forest they were acting all mixed up, like they'd found a bushel of wild berries."

"Come to think of it, I don't hear that awful buzz," said Cutter.

"The weird pressure's gone, too," Duck said, wiggling a finger inside her ear. "Does that mean we're out of the curse?"

"I think we made it out of Floodwood, at least," Keech replied. He slipped his wet boots back on. "Nat's right. We better get a move on."

"Y'all go without me," said a croaky voice.

Everyone wheeled around. John Wesley stood behind them, his legs wobbling.

"John!" Cutter said. "You should be resting."

The boy shambled closer, his big arms clutched around his river-soaked body. He had left his bullet-riddled hat sitting on the ground, and his long curls of strawberry-blond hair clung to his face and neck in wet clumps. "I ain't gonna put no one else in danger. Not anymore. It's best if you go without me."

"Nobody's leaving you behind," Nat said. "We're a team, remember?"

"We ain't no team," John Wesley said. "We're just a rabble of fool orphans. We don't know where we're going, we lost our ponies and our food, and our friend from Big Timber got shot up."

Cutter walked over and stood defiantly before him. "If it weren't for you, I'd still be riding the countryside alone, or dead on the side of some road."

John Wesley dropped his head.

Pa Abner's comforting words came back to Keech as he stood and put a hand on John Wesley's thick shoulder. "Work as two, succeed as one, John."

"Huh?"

"You are Cutter's left hand, and Cutter is your right. Our mission is to stop Bad Whiskey and find the Char Stone. We can't do this without you. *Cutter* can't do this without you. Our posse won't succeed if you stay behind. I honestly believe that."

John Wesley turned his back on the others, as if struggling with a hard thought. A stark silence descended over the group.

Finally, the boy nodded. He turned and pointed at Cutter.

"I'll keep on for you, *amigo*. We made a pact to ride down your desperado, and that's what we're gonna do."

Keech glanced at Cutter, whose calloused lips had cracked into a smile.

"As for the rest, I'll do my best to watch your backs," John Wesley said. "I can't promise I won't mess up, but I'll stand by you as best I can."

Grinning, Keech said, "Then let's get moving and finish this."

The gang made haste up a northern track, taking a fox trail Keech had discovered behind a heavy wall of jimsonweed. Cutter used his knife to chop away the growth as Nat and Duck moved alongside John Wesley, who was slumping on Nat's shoulder and humming a lonely-sounding tune. Keech walked behind Cutter, his eyes locked on the distant crows.

A frigid wind whistled over the trail, shuddering the jimsonweed. Keech raised his coat collar and wished he was riding his horse, Felix. Having his trusty pony would make all this infernal traveling so much easier. It saddened him to think Felix might be forever gone.

A loud curse gave him a jolt. Cutter had paused on the trail and was looking back at him.

"Admit it, Blackwood, you can't see no trail. We're lost." He spat another curse, and continued chopping weeds. "I can find my way through a cave better than you can walk through woods."

"Speaking of the cave, whatever happened to you back there?" Nat asked.

"After you left me in the tunnel, I took off running to face *El*

Ojo. I could see his torchlight getting brighter, but then the light faded and I was standing in darkness as black as tar."

Keech pondered. "The curse must have led you down a different tunnel."

"What'd you do then?" Nat asked.

"I got lost," Cutter said. "I couldn't see my own hands."

"We must've wandered the cave a good hour," Duck said. "You were in the dark the whole time?"

Cutter nodded. "Sometimes I heard noises and tried to track them. I think I even heard y'all at one point."

"You should've called out."

"I did for a spell, but then I heard a rumble. That shut me up."

"The bear?" Duck asked.

"Yep. You know what happened next, I reckon."

Keech had been keeping his eyes focused on the path. He saw something at the edge of the trail and stopped. He stepped closer. A few of the weeds had been bent. "Looks like someone's been ahead of us. We must be on the right trail."

They marched onward. After a sharp turn west, Keech called another halt as the fox trail slipped into a dense thicket. He dropped to one knee, searching for more evidence of passage, but there wasn't even a hint of a broken stalk. Perhaps the secret traveler had realized his mistake with the weeds and squirreled the rest of his movement.

"We have to be careful," Keech told the others. "Watch for an ambush."

Soon the fox trail bent back to the north and the forest opened into a large field, a meadow of tall broomsedge that spread for hundreds of yards. In the distance, the land dropped steeply downhill. Keech studied the sky over the meadow. The crows had disappeared, but he could feel their presence the way a fella could feel a headache behind his eyes.

The gang moved with caution through the meadow. When they came to where the landscape dropped, they stopped and beheld the sight below with astonishment. The valley at the bottom was surrounded on three sides by a steep bluff carved out of grayish white stone, a trinity of high walls that resembled marble or—

"Bone," Keech whispered to himself. "Beware the high ridge made of bone."

The shape of the lowlands had a curved look as if formed by the shoe of God's own horse, a divot stamped into the surrounding woodlands. Nestled inside the valley was a ghost town, a sprawling settlement overtaken by time and decay. The town looked as large as Big Timber, and yet not a single living thing stirred upon its streets.

Duck peeled off her hat. "Ain't that a lonely sight!"

The tall wooden wheel of a gristmill was visible at the ruin's western end, but where the waterwheel would have dipped into a stream, there was nothing but dried-up bedrock, encroached on by desolate forest. All around the town's borders, Keech saw only thick hems of black locust trees, and realized with dismay that the forest engulfed the entire bowl of the valley, obscuring everything else past the settlement.

A gristmill. A waterless brook. He couldn't shake the sudden feeling that he had seen such a village before. But then again, there were many settlements that looked exactly like it: dried up and discarded.

"I wonder what happened down there," Cutter said.

"I reckon the Withers drove them out," Keech said.

"The Withers?"

"As it was told, Bone Ridge was the graveyard where they buried the victims of a wasting disease called the Withers. They say the disease killed so many folks, the graveyard stretches on for miles."

"Sounds like a bunch of nonsense," Cutter said.

Nat turned to Keech. "Daylight's burning. We should move."

By the time they reached the ruins, the sky had faded to a deep purple. Full dark and a hunter's moon would be upon them soon. At the village outskirts, there was no welcoming signboard, but there was a sign at the approach to the settlement's main road, a miserably crooked placard that said POLK STREET.

As the gang shuffled up the old street, they regarded the devastation around them with a hushed reverence. From all appearances, the town had been a respectable outpost in its day, but many of its structures had either burned or collapsed. Weeds clogged the filthy alleyways, and the wooden sidewalks had long ago surrendered to the broomsedge that cluttered the valley floor.

Nat pointed to the town's livery stable, one of the few buildings still intact on Polk Street. "We'll hole up in there," he said. "No one could see a campfire behind the main wall."

A cold feeling of déjà vu swept over Keech when he saw the old stable.

"We could set a watch," John Wesley said, his voice raspy. "I'll sit first."

"You're still blue as a fish," Cutter told the boy. "I'll take first watch."

"A couple hours' rest wouldn't hurt," John Wesley conceded. "And it sure would be nice if we could eat something."

As the gang settled into the stable, Keech searched around the street for some kind of food. He longed for Cutter's pemmican, but the meat had run off with the horses. He settled for a heavy patch of blue chicory, still in its bloom, growing in one of the town's wild alleys. After inspecting the plants and finding them healthy, he brought back a heaping handful. The group nibbled silently on the greens and petals.

"A bunch of weeds ain't really what I had in mind," John Wesley grumbled, but he scarfed down his portion all the same.

After the meal, Keech and Duck struck out across the ruins to gather firewood as Cutter kept watch over Polk Street. Nat stayed back at the livery stable to fashion John Wesley a dry straw bed.

Every stick and branch Keech collected was dark with moisture from the recent rains, but Duck boasted that Nat could get a fire burning even when the wind was high and the day was stormy.

"Maybe we can burn this," she added, kicking at a large brown sign wedged in the mud in the middle of Polk Street.

Keech looked at the sign and felt his mouth go dry. It was the signboard that should have been standing at the town's outskirts, but the valley's high winds must have blown it up Polk Street. The message painted across the cracked wood read:

You Have Ennered
The Villege of SNOW
No Pick Pockets or Horse Thievers!

Keech dropped his firewood. "I've seen that sign before." *In a dream*, he almost added, but the déjà vu was far too strong for him to believe it had merely come from fantasy.

He turned to Duck. "Tell your brother I'll be a little longer coming back. I have something to check out."

Duck scowled. "Keech Blackwood, you're gonna get yourself in trouble."

"I'll be back in a flash."

"Where in tarnation are you headed?"

"West of town, to have a peek at the woods past that old gristmill."

"Don't you dare go in those woods!" Duck warned. "You might get trapped again."

Keech looked up and down the ravaged avenue. "I don't think that's gonna happen. I think Snow is part of a route we're meant to investigate. Call it a hunch."

Keeping to the shadows, Keech moved to the western edge of town, where Snow's lonesome gristmill house stood upon a high foundation of stone.

He approached slowly and touched one of the paddles of the waterwheel. Flashes of Pa Abner's face, younger, struck him as he did.

Keech looked beyond the millhouse and scanned the dense forest of ugly black locust trees that made a veritable wall around the town's boundary. The trees were gnarled and bent, leaning back toward the house and the dried-up stream. Much like the trees on the other side of the Floodwood mountain, he couldn't see ten feet beyond their wrinkled, thorny trunks.

Images of a path behind the mill flashed through his mind, more a feeling than a clear picture.

"West, past the millhouse," Keech murmured aloud. "Has to be."

He descended the dry riverbank, stepped across the barren stream bed, and pushed into the forest. Somewhere in the dark, a slew of wild dogs barked and bayed at the hunter's moon. It was a desolate sound, full of omen, but he kept moving.

Bone Ridge Cemetery was close. Keech could feel a chilling menace creep upon him like the night itself. The feeling grew stronger when the land dipped like a washbowl and pitched him unexpectedly downhill. There was no choice but to pick up speed. Keech raced to the bottom of the short slope, unsure whether to feel panic or exhilaration. He ran through branches and moonlight; he ran through fear and fury. He slowed when he felt his boots scurry over flush earth. He tossed a quick glance behind him, but the old millhouse with its giant wheel was no longer visible.

He expected to see more thick woods ahead of him, an

impossible wall of forest. Instead, the gnarled trees parted slightly to reveal a single, slender footpath.

At the end of the trail stood a black gate, at least fifteen feet high.

Keech's heart pounded as he gazed at the entrance to Bone Ridge, the graveyard Pa Abner had called the Sullied Place.

The gate was made of twisted iron, its intricate bars coiled like strangling vines, converging at the top with dull spearhead points. The gate stood open, but only enough to allow a man to squeeze past, as if the last visitor had slipped out in a hurry and forgotten to seal the way. Beyond the gate, the broomsedge was so tall Keech couldn't make out where the tombstones began.

A thick stone wall surrounded the graveyard, at least ten feet high on each side of the gate. The top of the wall was crumbled in places. Broken fieldstone littered the ground, as if a giant fist had tried to smash the wall in rage. All around the great partition— north, south, east, and west, from all appearances—stood a rugged, gnarled barricade of black locust trees, leaning toward the stone as though ravenous to enter the Bone Ridge yard.

Keech noticed a rusted metal sign hanging crooked from one of the spearheads. The sign simply read:

EXĪTE

The word meant nothing to him, but it still caused a strange, gray feeling to creep over him, like he had seen the word somewhere before.

"It's Latin."

The voice made him jump. Keech spun to face the footpath. Duck stood at the base of the hill. She held a makeshift torch made from an old broom handle.

"Duck! You scared the hair off me."

The girl crossed the footpath. "I had a feeling you were gonna explore. I just couldn't leave you to wander about unprotected."

"It's dangerous out here."

"Exactly. You oughta have your neck wrung for wandering about alone."

Keech smirked. "You sound like my Granny Nell."

"Who?"

"Never mind. Where'd you get that torch?"

"Nat had started a fire. I used some burlap wraps to hold the flame. I told Nat you was still out finding wood. Lucky for you he's distracted by John Wesley or he'd be out here scolding you."

Keech shrugged, then pointed to the rusted sign. "What does that mean?"

Duck shone her torchlight on it. "Back in the Middle Ages, folks who lost family to the Black Death would scrawl that word over the doorways of the dead as a warning." She gave Keech a dismal look. "It means 'Get out.'"

Heavy clouds rolled over the full moon, leaving no illumination at the moment other than Duck's yellow torch flame. Keech examined the sky, but the firelight blinded him. If the crows were flying overhead, they were impossible to see. Frowning, he put a hand on Duck's shoulder.

"This is the place. Bone Ridge. Go round up the others, bring them straight here. If John Wesley's too weak, tell him to stay and rest. Tell them the Char Stone is here."

Duck winced at the mention of the Stone. "I'm scared to find it, Keech. Our fathers went out of their way to hide it, and we're gonna go dig it up? That seems unwise."

Her words sparked a memory of Tommy Claymore, back in the Swift Hollow glade. *The Stone is life*, the thrall had said. If resurrected fiends like Bad Whiskey Nelson were the product of the Char Stone's magic, then there indeed was much to be frightened of. He could hardly imagine what dark purposes the Reverend Rose planned for the Stone.

"Our fathers wanted to protect it," Keech said. "We have to dig it up to keep it out of Bad Whiskey's hands. Besides, the Reverend Rose knows it's here. We can't just leave it. We have no choice. Now go fetch the others."

After she crossed to the base of the hill, Duck paused to look at him. Torchlight shone upon her small face, and Keech caught a glimpse of the real Duck. Not the ten-year-old child Nat wanted to shield, but the fierce, dauntless individual who had been raised by an Enforcer.

Then she headed up the hill and left Keech, once again, alone.

Shuddering, he stood before the tall rusted gate. The clouds parted, liberating the red hues of the hunter's moon. He gazed at the sign in Latin—*Get out*.

Steeling himself, Keech entered Bone Ridge, where the victims of the Withers awaited.

CHAPTER 24

THE REUNION

The sheer size of the old boneyard astounded him. Hundreds of grave markers spread across a vast land of hills and gorges, most of which lay covered in broomsedge. Everywhere Keech looked, his eyes fell upon a gray stone slab, or a wooden tablet, or a cross formed with dry sticks and old twine—markers interrupted only by the occasional statue of a cloaked woman or an angel with stony wings unfurled.

Beware the high ridge made of bone, he thought glumly. *All those who enter turn to stone.*

A smell of ancient rot simmered across the graves, as if the stink of the Withers was too heavy for the wind to sweep off. Perhaps the plague *had* lingered. All over the boneyard, shovels and pickaxes littered the ground, giving Keech the impression that family members and loved ones had fled quickly from the place.

Mindful of his flanks, Keech stepped away from the gate and deep into the chaotic rows of graves. He read the names and dates written across a few of the headstones. The death year was the same for all of them—1832, the year of the outbreak. His stomach churned at the thought of so many people perishing at the same time.

Still reading headstones, Keech stumbled over a patch of weedy, sunken graves. He staggered back when he realized where he was standing. It was terrible luck to walk on someone's resting place.

He held his breath, as the superstition called for, but then he noticed a name on one of the tombstones he had trampled and loosed a gasp. Keech eased closer to inspect the stone and realized his stroke of bad luck couldn't be worse.

The etching on the granite read:

ABRAHAM NELL
Loving Provider
1794–1832

The grave he'd just walked across belonged to Granny Nell's husband.

On top of deeply offending Mr. Abraham, Keech couldn't begin to think about the punishment Granny would have inflicted, had she been alive to find out. There would be dishes to clean, shutters to whitewash, floors to mop. A host of horrible chores for days on end, all for upsetting poor Mr. Abraham's eternal rest.

Then Keech's eyes dropped to the inscription below Mr. Abraham's name and death date—a message engraved downward and sideways to bear the shape of a cross. The tombstone instructed:

> WATCH
> THERE
> FORE
> FOR YE KNOW NOT WHAT HOUR
> YOUR
> LORD
> DOTH
> COME

A tremor of recognition rocked Keech in his boots.

He was looking at Matthew 24:42, the fourth set of numbers in Pa Abner's telegram.

Closing his eyes, Keech let his memory drift back to his first reading of the letter. He visualized the ride with Sam to Big Timber, the conversation at Copperhead Rock. Although he had never been great with memorization—that had been Sam's talent—he found that he was able to recall each letter, each number, the way Pa Abner had written it:

> N E
> 39 3:1.
> 52 5:2.
> 26 7:25.
> 40 24:42.
> A C

He and Sam had figured the code was a warning, a signal to Nat and Duck's father. A warning that never would have reached Noah Embry anyway, considering he'd been killed back in September by Big Ben, another member of the *Gita-Skog*.

But if the code was supposed to be a warning, why engrave the Scripture from Matthew 24:42 on Abraham Nell's tombstone?

"I've missed something," Keech whispered. "Help me find the answer, Pa."

His eyes still closed, he moved his mind back to the hour before the ride to Big Timber, when he and Pa had talked in the study. He saw the silver charm in Pa's hand, the narrow lock on the oak chest. He saw the charm slide into the keyhole, and heard the click of the ancient lock. He saw the letter in Pa's hands, sealed shut with scarlet wax.

Realization struck Keech like a fist to the gut.

The letter was never intended to be a warning. It had been sealed and locked away long before Bad Whiskey had shown up. Years before.

"Which means we never broke the code, not the way it was intended," Keech said, his pulse rushing again.

What was Pa's old proverb? *If you look hard enough, you might find two ways to look at a thing.*

A door opened in Keech's mind and a new answer stepped over the threshold. Perhaps the letter was not a warning, but a set of *coordinates*, a direct path to the Char Stone. Perhaps each of the other Scriptures belonged to engravings on three other graves.

No sooner did the revelation come than a whisper floated to Keech's ears, softer than a touch of silk.

"Hello, son."

Keech spun on one boot heel, his hands clenching into fists. What he saw made him lose his balance. He tumbled backward onto his rump, right on top of Abraham Nell's grave. His palms sank into loose dirt, but he barely noticed.

Pa Abner stood before him, back from the dead.

Keech choked back a cry as the figure lurched forward and the details of his face emerged in the moonlight. Pa Abner looked like a monster, his thick gray beard marbled with dried blood, his eyes clouded white. His face held the same color of death Keech had seen on Bad Whiskey's ghouls back at the Home.

That one-eyed murderer had turned Pa into a thrall.

Pa took another shambling step. His cloudy eyes rolled in their sockets, as if blind. Keech scrambled back till he bumped against Abraham Nell's tombstone. "Don't come any closer!"

The thrall's face took on a pained grimace. "Keech, listen to me." The voice was gravelly, like a man who's hollered himself out. "I don't have much time. Whiskey is near. He thinks he has control of me, but he doesn't. I've learned to block my mind, even in death. But I won't be able to hold out much longer."

His heart was pounding so hard, Keech thought he could feel it through his shirt. He stood. "Pa? Is it really you?"

"Bad Whiskey has the telegram, Keech. If he breaks the cipher, all is lost."

A horrifying notion occurred to Keech. This might be some unspeakable trick. Bad Whiskey had the power to invade his thralls' minds and steer them like dumb horses to his will. If Whiskey was controlling Pa, then the mangy dog could rascal his way into Keech's trust and earn himself a straight shot to the Stone.

Keech needed a surefire test to tell if Whiskey was pulling Pa's strings.

He recalled the glade at Swift Hollow, the way Tommy Claymore had gone blind in one eye when Bad Whiskey stepped into his body, and he realized he knew just the thing.

"If it's really you, Pa, then show me your left eye."

Grimacing, Pa lurched forward, leaning his pale face toward Keech. Both eyes wore the glaze of death, but the left eye could see. Bad Whiskey didn't look to be riding inside Pa's animated body.

Relief flooded over Keech, though he remained cautious. "Pa?"

"Yes, it's me. Now tell me quickly, son, did the others make it out of the fire? Granny Nell? The kids?"

Keech looked down, forlorn. "No one made it out, Pa. Everyone is gone."

The big man gritted his teeth as if in anguish.

Keech said, "Pa, let's escape this. Let's go now, together."

But Pa was already glancing back toward the stone wall. He whispered, "Too late, son. He's here."

The gate of Bone Ridge swung open and in rode Bad Whiskey.

He was missing his right arm, and his left hand gripped a broken broom handle with burlap burning at the top. Keech recognized the torch as the one Duck had been holding when she came to fetch him. Keech's breath stopped when he saw a small body draped over the cantle behind Bad Whiskey.

"Duck!" Keech bellowed.

Bad Whiskey chuckled as he steered his gangly horse into the graveyard. "Relax, pilgrim, she's alive. See?" He bumped Duck with his elbow. A moan escaped the girl's lips and she began to squirm. Keech noticed that her hands and feet had been bound by thick ropes.

Keech hollered, "I'll get you out of this. I'm sorry!"

From the back of the outlaw's saddle, Duck mumbled in a weak voice, "Ain't your fault. I never shoulda got caught."

Keech wondered why Duck hadn't used her silver shard to still the outlaw. He must have bushwhacked her before she could wield it.

Bad Whiskey pushed his steed a few feet closer. Duck cursed him at the back of the saddle, but he paid the girl no attention. A wisp of low wind kicked across the graveyard, making the flame flutter atop the torch.

"Listen up, pilgrim. Yer so-called pa won't show me what I need to know."

Pa Abner stood silent at the foot of Abraham Nell's grave. Pa's face suggested he was concentrating, working hard to keep the wall inside his mind from tumbling.

Keech glared at Bad Whiskey. "I guess my pa is smarter than you, Bad."

"If he's so smart, pilgrim, then why's he a walkin' dead man?"

"He's not the only walking dead man I see."

Bad Whiskey offered a cruel smile. "Scoff all ya want. Yer still gonna tell me how to find the Stone."

Duck shouted, "We'll never help you!"

"You shut yer mouth," Bad Whiskey said, "or I'll shut it for ya."

"You'll pay for it if you try," Duck warned.

Grunting, the outlaw dismounted, a tricky business with only one arm. He plunged the broom handle into the ground. Cinders from the fiery burlap rained on his shabby boots, but he ignored them. As the torchlight burned, he reached into his overcoat and pulled a yellowed piece of paper from his pocket. "Remember this?" he asked. He pondered Pa's telegram with a scowl, then tossed the paper in Keech's direction. It landed near Pa Abner's boot. "Pick it up. Give it to yer pup," he commanded the thrall.

Keech and Pa locked gazes. Then Pa bent, picked up the telegram, and handed it over.

"Break the code," Bad Whiskey ordered. "Now."

"Don't do it!" shouted Duck.

"For the last time, hush yer maw." The outlaw's eye returned to Keech. "Hurry along now. I ain't got all night."

"You're nervous, Bad."

"I said hurry along. I didn't stutter."

"I see fear on your mangy face."

Bad Whiskey's entire body shook. "Yer provokin' me, boy. Break the code or you'll see my *true* face."

Keech crumpled the telegram into a ball and threw it on the ground. "You'll have to kill me."

Bad Whiskey reached for his belt. Again, Keech expected him to pull the Dragoon, but when his hand returned, it held a brown cloth. When he loosed his grip, a leather cord appeared out of the cloth and Pa Abner's silver charm dropped into view. Black veins rippled along Whiskey's neck—a symptom of the amulet shard's magic—but he continued with a grimace.

"I don't have to kill *you*," he said. "I can do the next best thing."

He shoved the pendant toward Pa's face. The magic was prompt. Murky veins bubbled to the surface of Pa's cheeks and neck. Pa recoiled, but Whiskey's hand followed. The smallest touch of the silver and Pa would drop like a stone, forever still.

The sight of his pa quivering before the glowing shard sickened Keech. He couldn't stand to watch another second of the man's whimpering. "Stop!" Keech screamed. "The numbers are verses! From the Bible."

"Verses?" Bad Whiskey squawked.

"The verses are written on tombstones."

"Where?"

"How should I know?"

Whiskey dangled the shard mere inches from Pa's agonized face. "Find 'em."

"That would take days."

Pa lurched back a step. "Don't help him, Keech! I'd rather be dead again!"

Bad Whiskey laughed. "I see Raines found hisself a hidden reserve of courage. So noble! Well, no matter." He tucked away the silver in a coat pocket. Then he pulled his Dragoon and shifted the barrel toward Duck. "Do as I say, pilgrim. Now."

Keech froze. "You won't hurt her." As he spoke, low, hurried movement caught the corner of his vision. His heart leaped and he focused on the outlaw, knowing better than to betray the coming ambush with a flick of his eye.

"Try me—" Bad Whiskey began, but suddenly the iron of a pickax slammed down across his arm. He released a bark of surprise as the Dragoon dropped out of his hand. Nat stepped into the light, holding one of the pickaxes that had been littering the ground.

"Step away from my sister, you filth. We've gotcha surrounded."

Growling at his wounded arm, Bad Whiskey looked north and south. "Sorry, pilgrim. I do not accept yer offer. I know there's only three of ya. You can't stop me."

"You're outnumbered, Bad," Duck said, delighted. "You've got nothing left."

Bad Whiskey squatted to the ground. "Oh, I'm far from finished." The rags of his overcoat ruffled behind him like the wings of a giant bat. "I reckon I got just enough power left to take care of business."

Sneering, the one-eyed thrall whispered something under his breath.

Pa convulsed, bending over and gripping his head, crying in pain. The world was still for a moment, and then Pa Abner charged at Nat.

The rancher tried to swing his pickax in self-defense, but he was too late. Pa Abner barreled into the boy, burying his shoulder into Nat's gut. He lifted him off the ground and carried him back into the night shadows.

"Nat!" Duck screamed.

Keech could see what was happening, but before he could do anything, Bad Whiskey bellowed two words—"*Tsi'noo!* COME!"—and struck the earth with his fist.

A low grumbling filled the air, a muffled wailing that sounded to Keech like hundreds of cicadas trapped and murmuring underground. The earth shuddered under Keech's boots.

"Keech, what's happening?" Duck yelled.

Grinning, Bad Whiskey muttered a string of the darkest, strangest words Keech had ever heard. A chant.

As he spoke it, dozens of graves shattered open. Ancient dirt flew high into the misty air. The ground split beneath Keech and the skeletal arm of Abraham Nell reached from the depths. A rotted hand grabbed Keech's boot and squeezed. Horrified, he kicked the hand away.

"*Tsi'noo*, rise, and git to work!" Bad Whiskey roared.

CHAPTER 25

THE *TSI'NOO*

K eech watched in dazed silence as all across Bone Ridge the victims of the Withers burst from their graves. Their wails and snarls filled the air, a nightmarish symphony. Bad Whiskey had not raised a gang to protect him—he had raised an army.

The creatures rising weren't fresh-bodied thralls like the ones who'd ridden with Bad Whiskey before. These were rotted monstrosities of bone and sinew, held together by the thinnest magic. Some of them wore tattered bonnets, while others shambled in ragged pinafores or torn leather buckskins. The corpse of Abraham Nell hauled itself to the surface, dressed in a threadbare waistcoat.

The rising *Tsi'noo* groaned, surprised by their sudden return to life. Unspeakable faces lifted to the sky and muttered a single word in unison: "Master!"

Keech shivered as Bad Whiskey laughed. The resurrection had drained him. His body appeared to be wasting like a rotted tree succumbing to a hard wind. However, his laughter spoke not of pain and demise, but of victory and pleasure.

Pa Abner staggered back into the circle of torchlight. His face twisted with strain. He lurched toward Keech, opening his mouth to scream, but the sound caught in his throat. The dark power that had brought Pa back to life had corrupted his body, his mind, perhaps his very soul. The spark that had made Abner his father and protector was being snuffed out, replaced by Bad Whiskey's will.

Tears welled up in Keech's eyes. "You're strong, Pa. The strongest man I've ever known. Fight him."

"I can't!" Pa cried, and shook his head. *"Run!"*

Keech heard the sound of thralls scraping their way out of open graves. Abraham Nell staggered in a circle, fussing at the moon. Other thralls crawled toward him, gnashing rotten teeth, crying their damnation.

But Keech could focus only on Pa, who moved with a graceless stagger, his wide eyes hollow and deadly. Keech dug into the dirt and leaped away.

"Come on, you stupid rope!" Duck yelled.

Keech turned and saw the girl struggling against her binds on the back of Bad Whiskey's horse.

The amulet shard. The silver pendant stowed in her coat could send Bad Whiskey back to whatever dark pit he'd risen from.

A stumbling monster with no arms snapped at Keech's neck. Keech knocked the corpse back into another thrall, sending both tumbling into a deep, dark hole. A sharp hissing noise arose behind him. Keech spun to find a creature with its mouth gaped open and black teeth chomping. He twisted away and sprinted toward Duck.

Dozens of rotting thralls approached the bound girl as she struggled. Keech was only a few steps away but didn't know how he could untie her before the horde dug their claws into her.

His dreadful chant complete, Bad Whiskey bounded to his feet. "Where do ya think yer goin'?" he said, stepping into Keech's path.

Screaming in fury, Keech slammed into Whiskey with all his might.

Bad Whiskey grabbed at Keech's coat, but couldn't secure his hold. He crashed to the ground. His hat tumbled away and his mangy head whacked into a wooden grave marker, snapping the plank in half.

Keech stumbled over Whiskey and crossed the final few feet to Duck.

"We gotta help Nat," Duck cried. "He could be dying out there!"

Keech moved to grab the girl around the waist and haul her from the horse, but Duck was already tumbling down. She rolled sideways off the stallion, and landed on her feet in the broomsedge. Her hands still bound, Duck rotated quickly and came face-to-face with an approaching thrall. The creature was small, perhaps a woman once the size of Granny Nell. Duck swerved around the thing's fumbling arms.

Panicked by the commotion, Bad Whiskey's horse bucked. Its hooves struck the short thrall in the head, knocking the skull clean off its shoulders. The stallion rotated its angry hind toward Keech. He flung himself out of the way just as the animal's leg punted the air beside his nose.

"Let's go!" Duck called.

They took off running toward the area where Pa Abner had tackled Nat, dodging and shoving Whiskey's wretched dead along the way. The fresh thralls were weak, ill-formed, their bodies putrid with time, but Whiskey's curse had wrapped them in sinew and meat enough that they continued to creep forward.

Under the red moonlight, Keech scanned the ground for any sign of the rancher. "I don't see Nat."

"Keep looking," Duck panted, holding her tethered hands in front of her.

Somewhere behind them, Bad Whiskey's desperate voice split the night. "Bring 'em to me!"

Keech spotted a tall figure near the stone wall to the south. "I think I see him!" he gasped. "He's alive, by the wall."

A swarm of thralls had clustered at the wall's base and were crowding the rancher, who was throwing wild punches, knocking monsters off their feet. But the numbers were too great. The boy was being overwhelmed.

Duck shouted, "We have to save him!"

Keech threw a glance behind them. At least two dozen thralls were in pursuit.

"The second we can stop, I'll untie you. Then you can fetch your shard," he said—then they both ran into a solid wall. The impact sent them tumbling back with startled grunts.

Keech shook his head, dazed. A second later Keech's vision settled enough for him to see what they had crashed into.

It was no wall.

They had been stopped by Pa Abner.

Shambling creatures crept in on all sides. Duck lay on the ground, moaning. Not fifty yards away, Keech could see the cluster of thralls around Nat closing in. Frightened cries rose into the air as the boy fell beneath a sea of gristle and bone.

A pair of black boots stepped into Keech's view, spurs clattering like nails on glass. Bad Whiskey stood over him, clutching his hat. The remains of his black hair had fallen out of his scalp, leaving him bald. Even his daggerlike goatee was losing strands, exposing a pitted chin beneath.

"Nice effort, Jim Bowie." The outlaw kicked his boot into Keech's gut, driving the breath out of his lungs. "Seize 'im," Bad Whiskey ordered. A pair of large hands grabbed Keech's shoulders and hauled him to his feet. It was Pa Abner.

"Duck!" Keech yelled, but the girl was no longer lying where they had tumbled. Only the ropes that had bound her remained.

Bad Whiskey turned to see what Keech had noticed.

Cutter leaped out from behind a nearby statue of a weeping woman. "Die, *El Ojo!*" he bellowed, and buried his long blade into Bad Whiskey's chest.

Bad Whiskey barely flinched. He looked down at the knife, as though intrigued, and snickered. He shoved the boy backward. Cutter fell onto his backside, disbelief etched across his face. "It should have worked. This blade should have killed you!"

The desperado yanked the knife out of his chest and pointed the blade at Cutter's face. "This ol' thing?" Bad Whiskey turned it over in his hand and examined the intricately carved bone grip. He ran a thumb across the engraving at the base. "Did you think this pigsticker was magic, Herrera?" He laughed.

"I—I don't understand," Cutter cried.

Keech noticed movement near the statue of the woman. Duck was crouching nearby, close enough to end this. "Duck, the charm!" he yelled. He couldn't understand why she hadn't already pulled her shard.

Duck didn't move, and Keech realized that by calling out, he had betrayed her meager hiding spot. A fool's mistake.

Bad Whiskey spotted the girl and jabbed Cutter's knife at her. "You! You have a shard?"

Tucked behind the statue, Duck shook her head. Thralls surrounded her, holding their positions till their master gave his next command.

"Come to me, child," Bad Whiskey ordered.

Duck held her ground, her face desperate for a path.

"Don't make me tell ya again."

"Use the charm!" Keech repeated. "Take him down!"

"Throw it to me! I'll finish him," Cutter called.

"Quiet!" Bad Whiskey kicked at Cutter's chin. The boy's head snapped back and he slumped, dazed. The outlaw's glazed eye darted back to Duck. "A second shard of the amulet?" He raised his eye to the dark sky, where the crows were circling. "Hear that, boss! *A second shard!*" His eye dropped back to Duck. "I knew I felt somethin' strange. Hand it over. My *Tsi'noo* will tear you apart if ya don't."

Around the boneyard, the thralls hissed. The ones surrounding Duck crept closer toward her, awaiting the order to rip and tear.

"I'll never do what you want!" Duck shouted.

Bad Whiskey drew a long breath. "Pity."

"Look out!" Keech hollered, but it was too late. A grinning pair of thralls lunged at Duck. One of them was Granny Nell's dead husband. Before Duck could move, the monsters seized her arms. She screamed and pulled, but she was too small to break free.

Bad Whiskey motioned for the corpses to bring her closer. The thralls yanked her across the yard.

"Give me the shard. Now," he said.

"I don't have it!"

Before Keech could register what she'd said, the thrall on her left side juddered and collapsed. A second later Abraham Nell followed, tumbling back to silent death.

John Wesley stood behind Duck. He held up his right hand. A warm golden light glowed in his palm. He smiled.

"I do."

Keech felt a roar of triumph in his soul as John Wesley stepped forward, the radiant charm tied to his hand by a thin cord. With each step he took, Bad Whiskey retreated, gritting his teeth in rage. The surrounding thralls inched closer, but the large boy wheeled the charm wildly, brandishing its otherworldly light.

"Tell them to back off!" he shouted.

The outlaw flung his arm skyward, more a gesture of panic than surrender. "Stop, you worms, stop!" he squealed to his army. "Come no closer!"

Every thrall in Bone Ridge turned to regard their master.

"Tell them to go back to their holes," John Wesley demanded.

Bad Whiskey hesitated, his good eye sizing up his opponent. Slowly, he dropped his arm. "You ain't gonna kill me. Wanna know why?"

John Wesley wavered, uncertain.

"Let me show ya."

Keech felt his boots leave the earth. The graveyard tilted in his vision; then he found himself flying through the air. Pa had picked him up and heaved him at John Wesley. Keech flailed, hoping somehow to change his course, but Pa's toss had been dead-on. He smashed into the large boy and they toppled to the ground.

Keech struggled to untangle himself, and when he rolled aside, he saw that John Wesley had taken a mean blow to the head and been knocked unconscious. He looked up to see Bad Whiskey bending to retrieve his Dragoon. Stepping almost gingerly toward Duck, the outlaw once again positioned the massive revolver.

"This fight is over," he said.

"Don't you hurt her," came Nat's voice.

A pair of thralls had dragged the rancher, bleeding and bruised, into the torchlight. The battered boy dropped to the ground, his furious eyes locked on Whiskey.

"Don't you hurt my sister."

Duck smiled at her brother. "Don't worry, Nathaniel, I ain't afraid to die."

Bad Whiskey pursed his lips. "You should be, little'un. The other side is pain and torment."

"For the likes of you," Duck spat.

Snickering, Bad Whiskey cocked the Dragoon's hammer. He looked at John Wesley, who was groaning back to a dizzy sort of consciousness. "Toss away the shard, hero. You've got till the count of three."

Even in his daze, John Wesley recognized the danger. He pulled the glowing charm free from his palm, looked at it once, then threw it aside.

"Good boy. Now all of ya, on yer feet. I've decided not to kill ya after all."

From where he lay in the dirt, Keech had a perfect view of the hunter's moon over the surrounding black locust trees. Riding across the moon's face were dozens of crows. The terrible flock cut sharp arcs across the sky, observing the struggle but making no move to intervene.

They hate to be close to the amulets, Keech thought. A thrall could bear the amulets as long as the silver didn't touch flesh, but perhaps the birds were more sensitive. He remembered the monstrous crow that had landed on Bad Whiskey's shoulder at the Home. The way Whiskey had taken five steps back after Pa revealed the shard. Maybe the steps hadn't been for Whiskey. Maybe they had been a precaution for the crow.

A series of screeches fell from their beaks. Something was upsetting them. "The crows seem anxious, Bad," Keech said. "What happens when your clock is up?"

"You should worry about what'll happen when *yers* is up," Bad Whiskey muttered. He peered at the cobalt sky. A hint of fear spread across his face. "To yer feet," he said to Keech, his tone desperate. "Wake Herrera."

The *Tsi'noo* approached, surrounding the young riders. Keech winced at the sight of Pa Abner, his eyes hollow and full of nothingness, standing beside Whiskey.

Kneeling at his side, Keech lightly slapped at Cutter's cheek. The boy's eyes fluttered. He gazed around, confused. "Did we win?"

Keech shook his head.

His hand safely gloved, Bad Whiskey scooped Duck's shard from the dirt and tucked it into a pocket inside his tattered overcoat. "We got some work to do," he said. "Raines, the code."

Pa Abner ambled over, extended his hand, and thrust the crumpled telegram back into Keech's palm. Keech tried to look the thrall in the eye, but Pa refused to gaze back.

"Crack the cipher," Bad Whiskey said. "Time to find my Stone."

"And what happens if we do?" Keech asked.

"Then, little pilgrim, we do us some real magic."

CHAPTER 26

TREASURE HUNT

A freezing wind gusted as the young riders stumbled, defeated and weary, across Bone Ridge's broken hills. Behind them, Bad Whiskey rode his chestnut horse, his left thumb tucked into his gunbelt. In front of the horse walked Pa Abner, holding Duck's broom-handle torch.

The outlaw had commanded the *Tsi'noo* to build their own lights, so now they carried gruesome torches made from stray bones or tombstone planks. The flames burned ghostly red, reminding Keech of the night Granny Nell and his orphan siblings perished.

Since the fourth verse from the telegram had already been discovered on Abraham Nell's marker, Bad Whiskey had forced Nat and Cutter to dig up what remained of the grave. The *Tsi'noo* had thrown the boys two old shovels, and Bad Whiskey had ordered them to jump into the hole. The only thing Nat and Cutter had turned up was the dead man's empty coffin, its heavy lid smashed to splinters by Mr. Abraham himself.

"There's nothing here," Nat growled, his face grimy with dirt.

"The Stone must be in one of the other three graves," Bad Whiskey said. "Let's move west."

The *Tsi'noo* shoved the young riders across the boneyard. The entire gang looked on the verge of collapse. Keech looked at Nat and Duck. The siblings were bruised, skinned up, exhausted, but they nodded at him nonetheless—a signal that they were ready to fight again when the time was right.

A staggering number of tombstones stretched before them, bathed in ruddy moonlight. Many of the graves had opened when Bad Whiskey spoke his chant, but many more remained intact. At the end of every row Whiskey stopped and sent thralls to the graves to inspect the tombstones for writing. Most times the creatures returned, grumbling, "Nothin', Master." One thrall shambled back and described a Scripture verse from Revelation, but Keech only shook his head. They resumed their search.

The longer the hunt dragged on, the more desperate Bad Whiskey seemed. "I'm warnin' ya, pilgrim, don't mess with me. If we don't find the right graves soon, I'm gonna start fillin' some empty holes with yer friends."

"There's too much ground to cover," Keech said. "It'll take the whole night to search every tombstone."

"You ain't got all night," Bad Whiskey said. "You got an hour. The girl will take the north end and Herrera will scout the middle. You, rancher"—he pointed at Nat—"take your hefty friend and search the west. Jim Bowie will stay with me. Now, go fetch my Stone."

The *Tsi'noo* separated the young riders to each corner of the boneyard. Because the landscape was hilly, Keech couldn't make out where the thralls took Cutter and Duck. As he walked off, John Wesley stumbled a few times, still befuddled from the earlier blow to his head. Nat was a short distance off, shuffling through the graves, guarded by five or six thralls. Like the others, he carried a broken shovel. If they discovered one of Pa's verses, their orders were simple: Dig the grave or die.

As they waited, Bad Whiskey snatched the telegram from Keech. He studied the letter again. "Four verses, four graves. But why would Raines mark four?"

"Maybe he broke the Stone into pieces."

Bad Whiskey regarded the silent Pa Abner. "Impossible. The Char Stone contains ancient magic. It ain't some simple object that can be cracked. No, we're missin' a connection."

Bad Whiskey's last word sent a quick idea fluttering through Keech's head.

Connection.

He gazed across the moonlit hills, hoping to see the answer.

A murmur nearby, followed by a shout, broke his concentration. Nat was arguing with one of his thrall guards. Bad Whiskey grinned at the commotion and closed his good eye. His body went rigid, and Keech realized the outlaw was reaching into the thrall's head.

If there was a good time to attack, it would be now. But before Keech could act, Pa Abner's heavy hands gripped his shoulders, holding him in place.

Bad Whiskey opened his eye. "Splitting you boys up worked like a charm. Already the rancher found the Ezekiel verse. And our pal Herrera found Malachi over yonder."

When they reached Nat, Keech saw that he had indeed discovered a wooden grave marker that bore the words of Ezekiel 7:25. Like Abraham Nell's marker, this one too had been fashioned in the shape of a cross:

DESTRUCTION
COMETH
AND THEY SHALL SEEK PEACE
AND
THERE
SHALL
BE
NONE

Nat stood in the hole, throwing out wet dirt with his spade. His feet rested on the base of a split, empty casket.

"Anything?" Bad Whiskey asked.

Nat knelt and rooted around with his hands. He came up empty-handed. "Satisfied?" he hissed at Whiskey. "Your precious Stone ain't here."

Bad Whiskey grumbled and went deathly still. At the same time, Pa Abner rocked back on his boots like he'd been jolted by lightning. Pa's left eye jittered, then calmed, like a spinning marble coming to rest. The outlaw's lips pursed into a quivering line.

Keech realized Whiskey was trying to read Pa's mind, but couldn't. He smiled at the outlaw's frustration.

As soon as Bad Whiskey released his hold on Pa, he slammed

the back of his hand into Keech's face, knocking him sideways. He felt his bottom lip split and tasted blood. Down in the hole Nat cursed, but Whiskey's outburst drowned every word.

"How deep did Raines bury my treasure? Keep diggin'!"

Keech squinted up from the ground, his face stinging. He struggled to his feet and gazed toward the center of the graveyard, at the distant silhouette of a tall angelic statue that stood upon a low hill. The idea he'd gotten a few moments before fluttered back.

Pa Abner's Bible verses were connecting points. But the points were not plainly visible. *Two ways to look at a thing*, he thought. To see the connections, he had to look at Bone Ridge a different way, as if flat on a map. He had to take the bird's-eye view.

Keech now understood. Cutter, Duck, and John Wesley would find nothing. All four of the graves bearing Pa's verses were, in fact, empty. But he said nothing aloud. In fact, he didn't want to blink for fear of betraying one secret thought:

I know the location of the Char Stone.

Bad Whiskey stared at Keech with piercing interest. "You solved it."

"I don't know what you're talking about."

"Speak, or I'll bury the rancher alive."

"Keech, don't give this yellow-belly anything!" Nat shouted.

"Shut up," Bad Whiskey said. With rattlesnake fury, he wrapped his hand around Keech's wounded arm and squeezed the aching flesh. Keech dropped to his knees.

"Where is the Stone hid?"

"I'll never yield!"

"I've got the strength of ten men, boy."

Keech twisted in agony. "And I've got the endurance of twenty."

Cursing, Bad Whiskey released his grip. Keech fell backward, clutching the injured arm. Whiskey glared at the crows in the sky.

"The endurance of twenty men, ya say? Let's put that to the test."

Keech steadied himself for what was to come. Bad Whiskey aimed to torture him. One of Pa Abner's most critical lessons had concerned the presence and reality of physical pain. *When you're faced with suffering of the body,* Pa had said, *place all of your mind in a box, the tiniest box you can imagine, and nail the lid shut. Don't let anything through.*

Keech imagined the box where he would hide.

But then Bad Whiskey turned to Pa Abner and said, "Break yer orphan."

Pa Abner loomed over Keech and began to swing his heavy arms. His fists struck without mercy. Keech backed over rows of graves, his arms raised to shield his face, but Pa was a tornado, relentless and blinding. Somewhere in the background Nat was yelling, and Bad Whiskey was cackling, but all other sounds were secondary to the vicious, inhuman grunts that came from Pa.

"Please, Pa, stop," Keech begged.

But the blows kept coming. Pa's fist slammed into his gut and Keech dropped to his knees. A heavy curtain began to close over his vision, fetching a darkness both gloomy and welcoming.

"Enough, Raines."

Pa Abner stepped away and Bad Whiskey leaned over him, scowling.

"You ready to talk yet, boy?"

"Never. You'll just have to kill me. At least you'll never find the Char Stone."

"Maybe I will kill ya, pilgrim. Then I'll raise ya like I did Raines, search yer mind for the answer. I'd imagine you don't have the guards on yer thoughts like he does."

Bad Whiskey pulled his Dragoon.

In an instant, Keech realized he was defeated. There was no way he could stop Bad from uncovering his solution to the code. The only chance he had of beating the fiend was to keep on living and wait for a better plan to form. He raised his hands. "You win. No point in dying if you can just get the answer anyway."

"Keech, no!" Nat yelled.

Keech spoke through a pained gasp. "Digging the other graves will be useless."

Bad Whiskey sneered expectantly. "*Yes?*"

Holding his aching stomach, Keech began to draw in the dirt.

"*There* is your rotten Char Stone," he said once he was finished. "Hidden at the cross." He pointed to the center of the drawing.

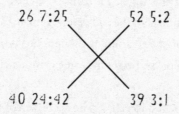

Bad Whiskey started barking orders, instructing the other kids to find and stand at the four graves that were indicated on the telegram code. Then he commanded Pa Abner to drag Keech to the center of the X.

The *Tsi'noo* gathered, carrying torchlights, at the foot of the granite angel Keech had spotted earlier. Overgrown mounds of witchgrass blanketed the ground, obscuring most of the graves.

Keech rubbed his pounding temples. His ribs screamed from Pa's blows.

Holding a fresh bone torch, Bad Whiskey muttered to himself as he stomped around the base of the angel statue. Two thralls approached, leading Duck. Another group escorted Cutter toward the illuminated area. Keech grew worried when he saw no sign of John Wesley—the boy had been badly dazed when they last saw him.

Duck grimaced in concern. "Keech, are you dying?"

Keech slowly stood. He looked to the south. "Not dying. Just awful sore."

"Why'd the thralls bring us here?" Cutter asked.

"Because I want ya together when ya die." Bad Whiskey stepped out from behind the angel. Pa Abner marched dutifully behind him. In one hand Pa held the coded telegram, in the other a pickax. "I reckon the son of Screamin' Bill might be tryin' one last trick," Bad Whiskey said, "so I want me some prisoners to kill if we don't find the Stone."

Confusion rocked Keech. "Who is the 'son of Screamin' Bill'?"

Bad Whiskey spun on his heel and laughed in Keech's face.

"You mean Raines never even told ya the name of your own rotten *padre*? Screamin' Bill Blackwood, terror of the West!"

Cold prickles danced down Keech's spine. Hearing the name of his father for the first time, spoken by a devil, left his mind feeling tangled. He wondered what sort of emotions he ought to have and why he only felt a sort of nauseous panic in his gut.

"I see yer all shook up," Bad Whiskey said. "Raines shoulda told ya, boy. Yer pa was an Enforcer for Rose."

Keech glanced at Pa, wounded that he had never heard the truth. Pa's face remained coldly empty.

Bad Whiskey jerked his head at Pa, who tossed the pickax at Keech's feet. "Well, pilgrim, you can ponder that final betrayal as ya set to work."

"What do you expect me to do?" Keech asked.

Bad Whiskey pointed to the tall angelic statue. "Fetch my Stone."

Keech lifted the pickax with a pained grunt. He shivered when he looked up at the stone figure. The sculpture was one of the most beautiful things he had ever seen, like something he'd dreamed in a perfect sleep. The angel's granite hair flowed down her crumpled robes like frozen water, and she was praying, her hands cupped together in mute supplication. Her wings were folded inward, almost touching at their feathery tips, as if protecting her hands from curious enemies.

While Keech moved around the angel's stone pedestal, studying the granite for strange cracks or openings, a third group of thralls brought Nat over to sit with the captive Duck and Cutter.

"What's happening?" he asked.

"Keech is gonna uncover the Char Stone," Cutter said.

Bad Whiskey stalked behind Keech, his bone torch and foul breath just behind his ear. The outlaw peered at the sky and mumbled a curse. Dozens of crows dissected the clouds, a swarming mass that made the night sky look alive.

"Hurry up. Quit stallin'."

Every inch of the statue appeared to be solid. Keech inspected the pedestal again, but only piles of witchgrass surrounded the slab. "It's not here."

Bad Whiskey dropped his torch and grabbed the pickax from Keech's grasp. "It has to be!" With his one arm he swung the tool at the angel's robes, her wings, the sandaled feet upon the pedestal. Slivers of granite flew. The pickax severed the angel's hands. They landed at the base of the pedestal and shattered below the statue's feet.

Keech glanced down at the broken palms and fingers. Two small squares of blackened cypress peeked up from the ground, barely visible under the witchgrass.

He pushed aside the grass, revealing two identical grave markers. They lay flat against the earth, side by side, and judging by the way the ground had all but swallowed them, their presence was intended to go unnoticed.

Bad Whiskey stopped midswing, his face frantic. "What is it?"

"Two graves," Keech said.

Dropping to his knees, he cleared the loose witchgrass from one of the graves.

The hasty, knife-cut engraving on the cypress marker caused his heart to thump. It read simply:

BILL

My father, Keech thought, feeling those nameless emotions steal over him again.

Still holding the pickax, Bad Whiskey charged over and shoved Keech out of the way. He leaned in and read the name, then staggered back a step, as if the mere sight of it threatened to knock him off his feet. Bad Whiskey bared his black teeth. He pointed to the second wooden marker. "Move the weeds."

Keech swept away the witchgrass. At first he thought the second marker was blank. Then he noticed four letters, carved into the center, obscured by dirt. He rubbed the dirt away with his thumb.

"Erin," he read. He felt he had heard the name before, somehow, somewhere.

"She was yer mother," Bad Whiskey said. He glanced at Pa Abner. "Clever, Raines, to hide the Blackwoods here."

Keech swallowed a heavy lump. This was the place, then. The resting place of the Char Stone. Inside the gravesite of parents he had never known. Erin and Bill. *Screamin' Bill*, Bad Whiskey had called him. *Terror of the West*.

Pa Abner had claimed that his parents had died a decade ago in a gunfight with Bad Whiskey. Why were they buried here, in the Withers graveyard?

Pa stood by, silent, but there could have been the slightest hint of sadness, the tiniest suggestion of returning memories, on his face.

Keech glared at the outlaw. "You killed them, you snake. You killed my parents."

Bad Whiskey cast his one good eye up at the growing swarm of crows. "Start diggin', pilgrim, or I'll raise 'em to join the *Tsi'noo*," he said.

"I'll unearth your blasted Stone if you just confess," Keech said.

Bad Whiskey gave a rattling sigh. "I did know yer parents, boy. I rode with Screamin' Bill. We followed the Reverend in search of eternal life. But after we all uncovered the Char Stone, Screamin' Bill turned against Rose. He led Raines and the other backstabbers against the Reverend."

Keech stared off in wonder. His father had led the revolt.

"And so you killed him."

Bad Whiskey tossed back his head and laughed.

"Pilgrim, I never killed yer pa. Screamin' Bill was the one who killed *me*. Got me straight in the eye with an arrow. Now get to diggin'."

His mind reeling with a thousand baffled thoughts, Keech hacked at the hard earth with the pickax. The young riders struggled in the clutches of the *Tsi'noo*, but Keech paid them little attention. Only Pa Abner captured his eye. Pa's face had taken on the expression of someone trying to wake from a terrible dream.

Bad Whiskey grew impatient. He commanded the *Tsi'noo* to thrust Nat, Duck, and Cutter into the hole Keech had started. Three shovels tumbled in after them. "Hurry!" Bad Whiskey ordered, and together the four of them dug.

Bad Whiskey looked around, confused. "Where's the other

pup? The chubby one?" The attendant thralls shrugged. He closed his eye and stilled for a moment. When he opened it again, he screamed at a trio of skeletal creatures, "Go find him!"

After what seemed like an eternity, Keech's pickax struck something. He frowned with worry. Next to him, Duck's shovel clacked on a second hard surface, and she tossed Keech a nervous glance.

"Good!" Bad Whiskey said.

"Whiskey, you're a fool," Nat said, wiping his brow. "If the Stone is so powerful, you won't be able to control it."

"If we're lucky," Cutter added, "it'll turn him to dust."

"Ignorant pup, the Char Stone is *life*," Bad Whiskey said. "It'll restore me. I'll finally be whole again. Free."

Suddenly, the outlaw's true intentions came clear. Keech saw that all the grand talk of loyalty to the *Gita-Skog*, the high banter about devotion to the Reverend, was nothing more than hot air.

"You plan to betray Rose!" Keech said. "You want this thing for yourself!"

Something like terror dropped over Bad Whiskey's face. His eye drifted up to the circling crows, and when he looked back at Keech, the eye was full of desperation. "You don't understand, boy. The Reverend took my *soul*. He brought me back, but left me empty. The Char Stone's the only thing that can save me."

He muttered under his breath for a moment, then turned and screeched at his *Tsi-noo*. "Get 'em out of the grave!"

The mumbling corpses hauled the young riders out of the hole. As soon as the gang had cleared the pit, Whiskey leaped inside. His boots thudded on the lid of a coffin. With his one remaining hand he scooped aside the ancient dirt. Wood splintered as Whiskey broke open the lid of a pine casket. Inside rested the skeletal remains of a man—Keech's father.

"Howdy, old friend," Bad Whiskey muttered to the corpse. "Remember me?"

The sight in the box made Keech's heart stutter. The long years had corrupted most of Screamin' Bill's burial clothes, but Keech could still make out the traces of a breechcloth and buckskin tunic, secured around the old bones with frayed cords. Upon the Enforcer's chest lay a lone tomahawk, the cracked wooden handle studded with brass and animal teeth, the iron blade degraded to black rust.

Bad Whiskey hunkered over the corpse and peered at the tomahawk. "Where's your trusty bow, Bill?" he asked the dead man. After a malicious chuckle, he knocked the tomahawk from the corpse's chest and began to search the box in earnest. Keech gritted his teeth till they hurt, wanting to shout at Whiskey to halt this desecration, but the words stuck in his throat.

After a minute more of digging, the outlaw stood and brushed off his tainted fingers. "Nothin'." He turned his attention to the matching box beside Screamin' Bill. "Maybe this one, eh?" His ragged nails clawed at the wood.

"Don't you touch her!" Keech yelled.

Bad Whiskey ignored him and continued his prying. He ripped open the coffin.

Keech prayed he would see something other than the remains of his mother—a trick of the eye, a counterfeit body—but the corpse of Erin Blackwood, the mother he couldn't remember, lay inside the box. Her skeletal hands were folded over each other like the angel's and reposing upon her chest. She wore a plum-colored, ankle-length dress, the ragged frills of a petticoat peeking through the frayed, moldy fabric. The ornate neck of the dress was high, blooming out like a flower and reaching just below his mother's chin. Keech had thought he would feel trepidation when he looked upon her, the fear of seeing his own mother, perhaps a mirror of himself, lying in the coffin, forever still. Instead, the feeling was that of peaceful sorrow.

Then he noticed that his mother's hands were folded over a small object and his breath stopped.

Bad Whiskey noticed the object as well, and gave a triumphant cry.

"*At last!*" he said. "I am no longer yer dog, Rose!"

A terrible silence filled the air of Bone Ridge. Even the legion of crows had stopped their cawing and cackling to watch, to see what lay inside Erin Blackwood's hands.

Bad Whiskey leaned over the corpse to retrieve the object. Keech expected something frightful—the blast of a horrid curse or a lightning bolt that would strike their very hearts. Nat and Duck held on to each other, and Cutter clutched his bandana.

But nothing happened.

Bad Whiskey held the object up to the torchlight.

"No," he breathed. "It can't be."

CHAPTER 27
DESTRUCTION COMETH

The outlaw clutched a child's doll, the small figurine of a lady, its body stuffed with cotton and garbed in a tattered plaid dress. The doll's head was wooden, crudely carved the way Robby might have carved a toy for Patrick, the face painted on and badly chipped, the crown topped by a tiny red bonnet.

Bad Whiskey's face quivered. "A doll?"

"I got a feeling that ain't the Char Stone," said Duck.

"*A doll!*" Bad Whiskey wailed. He threw the figurine to the ground.

The outlaw's cry was so furious it seemed to kick a fierce wind across Bone Ridge. Then suddenly he hunched over, his arm clutched to his chest, his face cast down in darkness. His hat tumbled off his head.

Bad Whiskey's body was racked with spasms.

"Um, fellas, what's happening to him?" asked Duck.

"No clue, but I don't like it," said Nat.

A second gale ripped across the graveyard. Granite tombstones and wooden crosses shook; fieldstones along the wall crumbled. The black locust trees beyond the wall moaned and crackled. Cutter's hand fell to his scabbard as if to draw his knife; Keech heard him curse under his breath when he realized the blade was gone.

The thralls' makeshift torches flickered and many blew out. The muttering thralls chomped and gabbled nervously.

Bad Whiskey lifted his head. Keech was shocked to see that his eyes had changed. The clouded dead eye had cleared, and both of the eyes now brimmed a brilliant shade of green.

Both eyes could also *see*.

Bad Whiskey stood upon Erin Blackwood's coffin. His stance was different, his chest thrust out, his boots planted wide on the edges of the wooden box. Keech wondered if the doll had been the Char Stone after all, and had somehow revitalized Whiskey's crumbling body. But then the outlaw spoke.

"*Jeffreys.*"

The hissing voice crawled over Keech's skin like a nest of hairy spiders. It was the worst voice he had ever heard, a voice capable of conjuring nightmares—and it did not belong to Bad Whiskey Nelson.

"*He has been here. He took my Stone!*"

There was no doubt the voice Keech heard belonged to the Reverend Rose. He was speaking through Bad Whiskey's mouth, looking through his eyes.

Rose noticed Keech standing at the foot of the grave. A single word crawled from the thing's lips: "*Blackwood.*"

Keech froze in terror.

"You're worse than your double-crossing father."

Before Keech's paralysis could break, Rose leaped from the grave and landed in front of him. The figure loomed, its impossible eyes blazing down upon him.

"Without the amulet, you're no more dangerous than a horsefly."

The Reverend Rose pulled the outlaw's Dragoon. Whiskey's thumb moved to the hammer.

This is it, Sam, Keech thought. *I'll see you soon.*

Before the trigger finger could pull, the head of a shovel slammed into the back of the thrall's head. There was a loud *Chok!* and Rose careened forward. The Dragoon flew from his hand and landed with a dull crash down in the gravesite of Keech's parents.

Gripping the shovel, a bloodied John Wesley shouted, "Eat dirt, you mush-head!"

"John!" Cutter called.

Dropping low, John Wesley kicked at a thrall that lurched in front of him. Two rotten creatures rattled after Duck, but Nat put them on the ground with two mighty punches. Keech tried to join the Embrys, but a pair of hands seized his throat. He threw a glance at his attacker. It was Pa Abner.

"Pa, no," Keech said, his airway choked. "Turn me loose."

The sound of two dozen crows cackling in fury pierced the night. Writhing in Pa's grip, Keech saw the Reverend Rose push to his knees and slide over Erin Blackwood's edge of the grave.

A spark of humanity flickered in Pa Abner's eyes. His thick fingers relaxed around Keech's neck, letting him pull free and gulp air. Pa gritted his teeth in pain.

Keech realized he should run. The others had already broken

for the gate. He took a step after them, but his eyes remained on Pa. Waves of hope flooded his thoughts. If Bad Whiskey's claim was true, that the Char Stone could restore his life and soul, then perhaps the Stone could return life—*true* life, not this obscene shambling imitation—to Pa Abner.

"Pa, come with me," Keech panted.

Deep down, he knew this impossible hope was beyond foolish. Pa Abner had been explicit about the perils of the Stone. *Forget you ever heard of it*, the man had said. There could be no wielding it. There could be no touching it. Not without damnation to follow.

Perhaps there could be other ways. If Keech couldn't use the Char Stone, perhaps there were other energies, other forms of magic.

"We'll find a way to save you," he told Pa. "Just come."

The thrall shook his head. Crimson tears streamed from his eyes. He made a pair of fists and slammed them into his temples. He tried to speak, but the only sound he made was a tormented grunt.

"Keech, come on!" Nat called. He and the others were fighting through the *Tsi'noo*, but the sheer numbers threatened to overwhelm them all over again. Only John Wesley swinging his shovel cleared room for the group to advance.

A bullet zipped past Keech, slamming into a shambling corpse nearby. He glanced back and saw that the Reverend Rose had pulled himself over the lip of the gravesite and was firing Bad Whiskey's Dragoon.

The Reverend's voice slithered after him. "*This ends now, Blackwood!*"

His eyes hot with tears, Keech abandoned Pa Abner and ran after the others.

A snarling corpse jumped from behind a tombstone and blocked Keech's path. He plowed into the creature shoulder-first. Black nails scratched at his face, scoring hot cuts across his cheek. He shoved the walking nightmare into an empty grave. "Back to your hole!" Keech screamed.

Another gunshot roared across the graveyard. This time the slug crashed into a nearby tombstone, showering Keech with granite. Glancing back, he saw that the Reverend Rose had gained a surprising amount of ground.

When Keech looked ahead, he noticed the other young riders had scattered from sight—except for John Wesley, who stood his ground and spun in slow circles, his shovel cutting through thralls with concentrated force.

"Back, you monsters," the large boy cried. The shovel's edge tore through a blackened corpse in a buckskin jacket. The buckskin snagged the iron spade head, throwing John Wesley off his feet. Within seconds, Bad Whiskey's horde surrounded him.

"Hang on!" Keech yelled.

He barreled through the wave of bodies. He found John Wesley on his hands and knees, curled into a ball. "Get up!" He tugged at the boy's arm.

John Wesley struggled to his feet. Through bleeding lips, he grinned and said to Keech, "I think I upset Bad Whiskey when I beaned him on the head."

"That wasn't Bad Whiskey," Keech wheezed. "That was the Reverend Rose."

"*In the flesh*," a terrible voice hissed.

The horde of *Tsi'noo* parted, leaving Keech and John Wesley exposed. The Reverend Rose appeared in front of them. He held the Dragoon, cocked and ready. His voice burrowed like a worm into Keech's ears.

"*The sins of the fathers shall be visited on the heads of the children.*"

"Now that's hardly fair," another voice called.

Nat Embry galloped up, astride Bad Whiskey's stallion. When the animal saw the face of its longtime master, it reared like a mustang. The horse screamed in a way Keech had never heard from any animal before, but the anger of the steed couldn't shake Nat. The horse kicked and spun, smashing into the thrall army. The rancher kept to the saddle.

"*Filthy creature,*" the Reverend Rose said, and turned Bad Whiskey's Dragoon on the stallion. A crack of thunder smashed through Keech's ears. The horse snorted with surprise. The stallion stumbled on one hoof and toppled forward, sending Nat flying.

"Nat!" Duck had followed her brother through a slew of thralls. Running beside her was Cutter, looking bruised and exhausted.

Keech released a howl and charged at the man wearing Bad Whiskey's body. He expected to strike a figure of power. Instead, he felt like he was tackling a bag of pine straw. The dark exertions the Reverend Rose had wielded upon Whiskey's body must have turned the outlaw into a desiccated husk. Keech dropped one knee on the figure's chest.

"*One day, Blackwood, we'll meet, and then you'll know true fear,*" the monster inside Bad Whiskey promised.

"Looking forward to it," Keech said. He raised his fist to crack it against the fiend's rotten nose, but he paused the blow when he noticed the creature's awful face changing. The left eye once again became a dead yellow; the right eye reeled about inside his skull. The Reverend Rose had withdrawn, leaving behind the mealy-mouthed rogue.

"Hello, Bad. I'm glad you're back," Keech growled. The outlaw struggled to raise the Dragoon, but Keech grabbed the barrel, twisted the gun from the thrall's grip, and tossed it behind him. From the corner of his eye he saw John Wesley struggle to yank frantic thralls off Nat and Duck, but there was nothing Keech could do now but let them finish their battles. Bad Whiskey was at last where he wanted him.

The cursed outlaw kicked out and pain exploded in Keech's back, allowing Whiskey to topple away. He fumbled on his knees to retrieve the Dragoon. Keech grabbed for him, but his fingers found only his tattered overcoat. He took hold of the skirt and tugged Whiskey back before he could seize the gun.

Screeching curses, the desperado dug his fingers into the earth. "Let me go!"

A glimmer of bright orange caught Keech's eye. The amulets. They were peeking from a pocket in Bad Whiskey's overcoat. Keech pulled with all his might.

The coat's skirt tore loose with a loud rip, leaving Keech nothing but oilcloth in his hands. The outlaw's fingers scrabbled forward and fell upon the Dragoon.

"Yer done for, pilgrim."

"Think again."

Cutter stood over Bad Whiskey, his eyes teeming with rage.

"This is for Bishop." The boy slammed his boot against Bad Whiskey's hand. With his other foot, he kicked the Dragoon out of reach.

Under the clouds, the Reverend's crows flew closer and closer.

"In his coat!" Keech shouted at Cutter. "Let's end this."

Bad Whiskey bellowed as the boys dog-piled him and tore at his overcoat's frail cloth. The outlaw struggled on his back. Around him, his thralls lingered, as if unsure of what to do. He released a woeful sound of frustration and defeat.

"Have mercy!" Bad Whiskey shrieked. "I just wanted peace!"

Keech put a hand on Cutter, pausing their attack. The words he spoke next were from Ezekiel 7:25. He spoke them calmly.

"Destruction cometh, Whiskey Nelson. 'They shall seek peace, and there shall be none.'"

Then, with two strong tugs, Keech and Cutter ripped the remains of the overcoat off Bad Whiskey's body.

The amulets tumbled from the outlaw's pocket as the garment split into pieces, landing feet away from the outlaw. No sooner did they land than the Reverend's crows released a mind-shredding noise, as if dozens of frantic clocks had suddenly bellowed a nightmarish hour. They descended upon Bad Whiskey like mad vultures.

"Boss, no!" Bad Whiskey screamed. He held up his single arm, a desperate attempt to ward off the giant birds. The crows feasted on their prey, attacking every inch of him, stripping away Whiskey's flesh with their scythelike talons.

"The amulets!" Cutter shouted, as the mayhem of crows churned around them. "If we don't get them, we'll be torn apart!"

The boys dived under the cackling cloud. A pair of warped talons scrabbled for Keech's neck. He rolled sideways, barely escaping them. When he looked up, he was face-to-face with a howling Bad Whiskey, engulfed by a whirlwind of black feathers.

The outlaw no longer resembled a human being. The crows had picked him down to nothing but bone. For Keech, time seemed to halt. The monster's black skull gazed at him and grinned.

"*With a row de dow*," the outlaw skeleton sang, "*he pays all his debts with a roll of his drum*." And then Bad Whiskey's song was buried by the cackling of the crows.

A bright orange illumination filled Keech's vision. The amulets lay nearby. He reached and wrapped his hand around a freezing charm. A few feet away, Cutter had done the same and was retreating back to safety.

The boys held the charms aloft, two fists against the onslaught.

The baleful flock flapped wildly away from the charms, an explosion of fleeing birds.

Across Bone Ridge Cemetery, the *Tsi'noo* crumbled.

The rotted sinew and muscle Bad Whiskey's dark magic had woven together turned to dust and blew away. Bones cracked and fell apart, bodies collapsed. The victims of the Withers returned to their eternal slumber.

Nearby, John Wesley and the Embrys staggered to their feet. They gazed around, surprised. Keech looked up and saw the Reverend's birds continue their retreat into the dark October sky. In the place where the crows had descended, nothing remained of Bad Whiskey Nelson.

The young riders reunited, bleeding and bruised, at the center of the graveyard. The murder of crows continued to circle above them, but they kept their distance, watching.

"Why did they back off?" Duck asked, gazing at the sky.

Keech and Cutter held out their hands and showed her the shards. They were still glowing, but only faintly.

"The crows won't come near them," Keech said.

"But the crows tore Bad Whiskey apart. Why would Rose kill his own man?" John Wesley asked.

"I'm not so sure Whiskey was Rose's man," Keech replied. "He used to be a loyal member of the *Gita-Skog*. At least till the day he died. Till Screamin' Bill—my real pa—killed him. But something changed. When Bad thought he'd found the Stone, he boasted he was gonna use its power to regain his life and soul and free himself from the Reverend."

Nat shook his head. "So Bad Whiskey had planned to betray Rose?"

Keech shrugged. "I'm not sure he planned to use the Stone for his own purpose. Not till he realized he could use it to restore his own life."

"That must have been the final straw," Duck said.

Cutter scurried to the place where Bad Whiskey had perished. "My knife!" He picked up his lost blade and slipped it back into its sheath. "I thought it was gone for good."

John Wesley frowned. "Now what?" Small cuts covered his

face and neck from battling thralls, but all his normal color had returned.

Before Keech could answer, a lonely voice drifted across Bone Ridge.

"Keech."

He couldn't believe his ears. He spun around, in search of the voice.

With Bad Whiskey's defeat, every thrall had keeled over, lifeless. The idea that one might somehow still be alive had never occurred to him.

The weakened voice called again. "My boy, I'm here."

CHAPTER 28

CUT FROM THE REINS

K eech found Pa Abner kneeling between two graves, his head lowered, his arms draped over a pair of crumbling headstones. Whatever second life Bad Whiskey had bestowed on him was quickly draining.

"Pa," Keech panted. He hooked his arm around Pa Abner's waist and tried to lift him to his boots.

Pa sank back to his knees. "Lean me against one of these tombstones."

Moving the man was a struggle. The other young riders ran up. Nat took one of Pa's arms and helped prop him against one of the stones. Pa looked at Nat and smiled. "I know your eyes. You must be Bennett's son."

"I am," Nat said, his face slightly troubled at the use of his father's real name. He shuffled back. Keech noticed that all four of his trailmates had taken off their hats.

"Keech, listen to me," Pa Abner said. "There are things I must tell you. My memories have returned, but you must listen before this false life slips away."

Keech stooped to one knee. "Go ahead, Pa."

"It is vital you find the Char Stone before the Reverend Rose. As we speak, his *Gita-Skog* are closing in. For years they've been scattered across the Territories, hunting down the Enforcers, hunting down the sacred objects we hid, the dark objects Rose had stolen from ancient grounds. But what happened here tonight has focused the Reverend's eye. His sights are set."

"On what?" Keech asked.

"On the path of a man named Red Jeffreys."

Keech glanced back at the others, but none of the young riders had apparently heard the name.

"He was one of the other Enforcers who knew the whereabouts of the Stone," Pa said. "Like myself, he took the Oath of Memory. Or, at least I thought he did."

"What's the Oath of Memory?" Keech asked.

The question made Pa Abner sigh. "I knew this day would come. The day that events would force me to impart my very last lesson, the most important lesson of all.

"There is a place you must go, Keech. It's called Bonfire Crossing. I've taught you about the Osage clans who dwell in the riverlands. The Crossing is one of their best-kept secrets. Not for its size, but for the kind of knowledge that dwells within. At Bonfire Crossing I took the Oath of Memory, the ritual that cleansed my mind and obscured the Stone's burial place from the Reverend's eyes."

"The Osage taught you to forget?"

Pa Abner's breathing was ragged. "That's right. The Reverend, and many of his disciples, can reach into minds and take what they wish. The Oath of Memory veiled the whereabouts of the Stone. As well as other sacred objects."

"My pa performed this ritual, too?" Nat asked.

"He did. He also had the idea of leaving clues before our memories of Bone Ridge were gone."

A strange notion occurred to Keech. "The cursed Floodwood. It was part of that protection?"

Pa Abner hesitated, as if buried under a mountain of returning memories. "Floodwood, yes, Floodwood was a precaution," he said. "There's so much to tell you, Keech." His body slouched farther down the stone, as though he wanted to fall asleep.

"It's all right, Pa." He spoke a different question now, this time more urgently. "Who were my parents, really? And why are they buried here?"

Pa smiled feebly.

"Your mother, Erin, was a strong woman, Keech. She met your father while the Enforcers were riding through the plains, seeking shelter. Your father was a fierce fighter. Terror of the West. The Osage didn't call him Bill, though. They called him *Zha Sape*, 'Black Wood,' on account of the way no enemy could find him while hunting him in the forest. You bear his name to preserve his honor."

"He knew the Osage?" Keech asked.

Pa Abner managed another smile. "My boy, he *was* Osage.

Half, at least. His father—your grandfather—was a tribesman in the village known as Naniompa, the Village of the Pipe. Your grandmother was a trader's daughter from St. Louis."

Keech sighed, feeling a lonely kind of warmth.

Pa drew another tattered breath and continued. "When your folks died, I feared the Reverend Rose would raise them for his wicked schemes. So I carried them here to Missouri along with you and the Stone. I found refuge in the village of Snow, up the ridge. The place was long abandoned, a perfect hideout. But you were hungry, frightened. I knew I couldn't linger. I decided to hide them in Bone Ridge Cemetery."

Keech remembered the feelings of déjà vu when he had glimpsed the ruins of Snow. He had, in fact, been there before. As a toddler.

"I brought you to their graves, Keech. Just before we left for Big Timber. You were afraid of this place. You cried so hard, till I showed you the angel. You touched her robes and your tears dried."

Keech imagined standing there all those years ago, gazing at the sculpture. "Is that when you met up with the other Enforcers?" he asked.

"Soon after. We traveled to Big Timber, you and I. Then Bennett found me, and not long after, Red Jeffreys and Milos Horner. We formed our plan to hide the Char Stone. We scattered the clues that led back to this place. Then we turned to the Osage at Bonfire Crossing to take the Oath of Memory."

Pa Abner took a short breath. His eyelids began to slip. "There's something else," he said, and pointed to the silver pendant. "The amulets are sacred. They can hold the Reverend's power at bay. I shattered the original piece into five. The other Enforcers have the other fragments. Find the shards, Keech, and unite them."

Pa Abner closed his eyes.

"No, Pa, wake up!" Keech pleaded.

But Pa Abner didn't seem to hear. "I am a wild horse cut from the reins," he murmured. "Let me run to the mountains."

A tear filled Keech's eye. "Pa, don't go. You have to tell me how to get to Bonfire Crossing."

Pa Abner's eyes fluttered open, but only a hair. "Ride west, my boy. The Crossing moves, so follow the rivers, the bending trees. Beware of the crows, and hold the amulets close. The People of the Middle Waters await."

He closed his eyes again. "Remember, my young warrior. Remember who you are."

As he spoke, he lifted his hand and pointed a shaking finger to the hunter's moon.

"You are the *Wolf*," Pa whispered in Keech's ear.

Then Abner Carson stirred no more.

CHAPTER 29

THE LAWMAN'S BLESSING

Keech stood in silence over Pa Abner's body. A freezing wind raised goose bumps on his neck, but like the pain that racked him, he ignored the chill.

After a time the young riders approached. Keech asked them for help burying Pa. They collected shovels and spades, and dug a large hole beneath the angelic statue, beside Bill and Erin Blackwood's grave.

Keech spotted a small object in the dirt. It was the doll that his mother had been holding. He picked it up, gave the doll a long study, and then stowed it inside his coat pocket.

When the digging was done, the young riders lowered Pa Abner into the hole, packed the earth, and helped Keech refill the gravesite. Afterward he stood over all three graves and pondered what to say.

At first he could think of nothing. But then, as the night wind swirled the broomsedge, Keech's eyes floated up to the towering angel. Though her praying hands had been severed, she was still the most beautiful thing he'd ever seen. As he gazed at her, the tears dried in his eyes.

He realized he had words to say after all.

"I never knew who you were," he said to the three graves. "You've been a mystery to me. But you're all my family. You'll always be with me."

Cutter walked over and put a hand on his shoulder. "Nice words," he said. Then a curious expression came over his face. "So, you're Osage."

He smiled at the boy. "I'm Keech. And you're Cutter."

Cutter returned the smile. "It's Miguel," he said. "Miguel Herrera." He looked as if he wanted to add something else, but John Wesley spoke first.

"Look!"

Beyond Bone Ridge's iron gate, a trio of lights crossed the narrow footpath, one behind the other. The lights seem to float in the air as they approached the graveyard.

Duck frowned nervously. "What are they?"

"Spirits!" Cutter said. He crossed himself, and Keech wondered if the boy could be right. Maybe the lights were the spirits of his folks and Pa Abner, wandering the edges of Bone Ridge, fulfilling Keech's desire that they would stay with him forever.

"It ain't spirits," Nat said. "It's three riders." He seized one of the pickaxes. "Could be more of Rose's men. Stand ready."

As the lights passed through the gate, Duck said, "It's travelers, all right. There's a team of horses behind them."

Details of the horsemen were scarcely visible, but Duck was right. Following close behind the ghostly trio was a pack of horses attached to lead ropes.

A booming voice rumbled across the graveyard.

"This is the Big Timber sheriff! If you're armed, drop your weapons! If you're peaceful, state your names!"

Sheriff Bose Turner cantered through the graveyard, flanked by two young men escorting five horses in single file.

The past two days had nearly destroyed his body, but Keech took off running anyway, hurtling toward the lawman. The other young riders followed, limping and laughing.

"Sheriff!" Keech yelled, then noticed Felix, his pony, standing among the five escorted horses. The other ponies belonged to the rest of the gang—Nat and Duck's Fox Trotters, John Wesley's fat gelding, and Cutter's palomino mare. When the other young riders caught up to Keech, they hooted for joy.

Turner and his two companions clucked and whistled for the team to stop. The men were holding farm lanterns in one hand, percussion revolvers in the other. The sheriff's left arm was folded in a white sling—dressing for the wound he'd suffered back at Whistler.

At the sight of the desecrated graves and piles of lifeless thralls, a look of horror crossed Turner's face. "Dear heaven, what happened here?" he said.

Petting Felix's muzzle, Keech said, "Bad Whiskey kept us busy, Sheriff."

"I can see that. What happened to him?"

"Long story."

Turner scratched his face. "Why don't we start from the beginning."

———⁓———

Turner's companions were two German brothers from Whistler. They didn't know a lick of English, so they held their lanterns and remained silent as Turner explained his half of the story. Keech noticed one of the brothers wore a brown holster that contained Deputy Ballard's Colt.

"It took these fellas a whole day to round up your horses," the sheriff said. The group had moved back to the gate, and as Turner spoke, the young riders kept busy patching cuts and tending bruises. "They were scattered all over the countryside. When we found your horse, Nat, we were sure happy to see this." Turner reached into a long leather bag and pulled out Nat's Hawken rifle.

"You found it!" Nat grabbed the rifle and checked its sights.

Turner went on to explain that after the kind Whistler family had patched his shoulder, he and the German brothers had set out through Floodwood to find everyone.

"Did the forest trap you?" John Wesley asked.

Turner frowned. "Trap us? No, we were able to ride straight through. We found the town of Snow a couple hours after we set out."

The young riders looked at each other with fascination. Apparently the curse had been lifted by the time Turner and the Germans had entered.

"My friends, it sounds as if your path was much more

treacherous than mine," Sheriff Turner said. "I do apologize I couldn't be there to help."

After recounting their part of the journey and how Bad Whiskey had met his end, Keech told Turner about Pa's final instructions to seek a place called Bonfire Crossing.

"There hasn't been an Osage village near our parts for decades," Turner said. "If such a place does exist, it would be farther south in Kansas Territory, along the Neosho River."

"Pa said we'd have to go west."

Turner rubbed his mustache. "So you intend to keep going? Even though you almost got yourselves killed?"

"Big Ben is still out there," Nat said. "That monster killed our folks."

"And we intend to hunt him down," Duck finished.

Turner looked at Cutter. "What about you? You have no more vengeance to seek, now that Whiskey's dead."

Cutter sneered, though Keech could tell there was so much more to his story, so much more that Miguel Herrera had not told them. "You know what they say, Sheriff. The wicked never rest."

Turner shifted his gaze to John Wesley. "And you, son?"

With a low voice, John Wesley said, "My mother's killer is still out there, too. If I don't hunt him down, she'll never rest in peace."

Turner gave each youth a long, serious look. At last he said, "I can't allow you to run off wild and act like a bunch of vigilantes."

Each of the young riders groaned.

"But," Turner said, "if you were *deputized*, you wouldn't be vigilantes, now, would you?"

He called the young riders into a huddle. At the southern edge of Bone Ridge, under the light of three farm lanterns and a full moon, he ordered them to raise their right hands. They didn't have a Bible to swear on, but the sheriff said extreme cases called for extreme measures. After a few momentous words about duty and honor, he pronounced the words that made them official deputies of the Law.

"Apologies that I don't have stars to give you," he said. "Maybe when you all come back, I'll do it proper. Till then, consider yourselves appointed officers."

"Wonders never cease," Cutter said. "I'm a lawdog now."

The German brothers offered the gang a supply of spare tack and blankets and rations they'd brought along. Turner helped them pack the provisions and check their saddles. Meanwhile, Keech stowed Pa Abner's charm back around his neck, while Noah Embry's amulet piece went back to Duck. As long as they held the shards, the Reverend's crows would let them be. The birds would always be up there somewhere, watching from a distance, but they knew better than to attack.

Once the preparations were done, Nat called the group into a circle.

"Listen up. The wind is hard and the clouds are heavy. Best we get some miles under us before we make camp. I want this rotten graveyard as far away as we can get it."

"But where do we go next?" John Wesley asked.

"There is a town in Kansas Territory, southwest of here," Turner said. "Wisdom, it's called. It's a free settlement like Big Timber, no slavers, no hooligans. The sheriff there, Strahan, is a good man. He'll feed you, provide weapons, put you up. He knows the Osage and how they travel. Maybe he'll know a thing or two about Bonfire Crossing."

Keech said, "To Wisdom, then."

"To Wisdom," Nat replied.

Sheriff Turner and the German brothers mounted their steeds. Before reining their horses back toward Whistler, Turner offered the young riders one final word of caution.

"If you ever need to send a message, never use your real names. Your identities are precious, so you should pick a name for your group."

"The Lost Causes," Keech said at once, and looked at his trailmates.

Turner pondered the words. "It's a good name," he said. Before riding out, the sheriff shifted back on his saddle. He gazed at each of them and told them, smiling, "Go, Lost Causes. Go be legends."

Once Turner and his companions had ridden back into the forest, the gang mounted their horses and sat in silence, and the sheriff's words settled around them. Keech looked to the east. Hues of purple and gold began to dawn over the distant trees. The long, terrible night was at last surrendering to a new day.

"So," Nat said. "The Lost Causes."

Keech nodded. An image appeared in his mind. An image of a sign, hanging strong and proud against the wild of the wilderness. A symbol of family. A symbol of strength. *Protect us, St. Jude, from harm.*

They were five strong now, they were a team. This was their

new calling. Their new home was the trail. They would learn by it. They would study it.

And once they were strong enough, they would face the Reverend Rose.

For now, they were cold and a little scared.

So Keech Blackwood decided to do for his Lost Causes what he used to do for Sam, on the nights when Sam needed comfort, on the nights when Sam needed his friend.

He sang "Ol' Lonesome Joe" to comfort their souls.

> *Ol' Lonesome Joe, come ride next to me.*
> *Let's roll, ol' Joe, to the Alamo Tree.*
> *Lonesome in the heart, lonesome as can be.*
> *You won't be so lonesome at the Alamo Tree,*
> *When you sit next to me, when you sit next to me.*

THE END

ACKNOWLEDGMENTS

Because authors never ride the trail alone, we'd like to round up a passel of good people and give them a grand ol' thank-you from the bottom of our hearts. We'll start with:

Our folks, Peggy and Lou and Barbara, who always made sure to keep great books on the shelves and stirred a continual passion for literature. They kept the home fires burning in the night, and encouraged us to find exceptional:

Friends and colleagues, who keep inspiring two weary cowboys to push on. Trailmates like Jim Patterson, Michael Armstrong, Lori Raborg, Alex Abrams, Brandon Hobson, AJ Tierney, Gloria Bankler, Brad Christy, Dustin Bass, Sean Easley, Kyle Sanders, Matt Knight, the amazing folks at Lewis-Clark State College, and so many more loyal pards that we couldn't stuff all their names in a hundred saddlebags. All except for:

Shawn Chiusano, who wrote a fella's name down one day and said, "By golly, send this man a query letter!" and so we did, and that fella turned out to be:

Brooks Sherman, our rough-ridin', sharp-eyed Agent Extraordinaire, who never stopped cheering us on to perfection, so he could lasso a fine publisher and introduce us to:

Lauren Bisom, our novel's first champion. She opened all the doors at Henry Holt, so we could meet:

Christian Trimmer, our head honcho and the finest editor this side of the Mississippi. Mr. Trimmer, you surely do a bang-up job. And without your wonderful bunch at Henry Holt, our novel never would've crossed paths with:

Alexandria Neonakis, our cover illustrator and all-around swell artist. Her remarkable work puts a true grandeur on the book, as do the humbling, heart-stirring reviews we received from:

Authors Emma Trevayne, Stefan Bachmann, and Heidi Schulz, who offered us powerful good blurbs. And since we're gabbin' about kind assistance, we just can't thank enough:

All the magnificent folks of the Osage Nation and the *Wah-Zha-Zhi* Cultural Center. Director Addie Hudgins and cultural specialist Jennifer Tiger and Harrison Hudgins and Rebecca Brave and Vann Bighorse—everyone who contributed their time and energy to double-checking our historical and cultural accuracy and giving us incredible notes. We hope we've done ya proud.

Don't scurry off yet! We ain't quite done. We'd be scoundrels and outlaws if we didn't holler to the world how much we love:

Our wives, Alisha and Kimberly, who stand by us every day and lift us up. And Chloe, too, the greatest stepdaughter that Brad ever did see, who shines a light from her very soul. She reminds us of another great kid, someone we couldn't possibly forget to thank before this here book closes:

YOU, amazing reader. You're the one this whole shebang is for. We hope you've enjoyed Keech's adventure, and we'll see ya again soon for the next leg of the journey.

A NOTE FROM THE AUTHORS

The book you hold in your hands is more than the solitary endeavor of two authors. Since 2015, we've been fortunate enough to work closely with the Wah-Zha-Zhi Cultural Center and Language Department—two organizations that help comprise the Osage Heritage Center in Pawhuska, Oklahoma.

Back when we started planning the Legends of the Lost Causes series, we knew right away we wanted to tell a magical Old West story that included a diverse cast of characters, a group of resourceful kids who could join forces to fight the Reverend Rose's evil. For us, this meant examining the cultures of 1855 Missouri and Kansas. Our research led us to the Wah-Zha-Zhi Cultural Center, where we met the wonderful directors and specialists who would become readers of our story and close reviewers of our cultural content.

All of the Osage language and names seen in our series have been directly provided by the Cultural Center and its partner, the Language Department. Though we consulted some written sources in early drafts, such as Francis La Flesche's *A Dictionary of the Osage Language*, the final approval of all words, phrases, and names came from these language and cultural experts who so graciously agreed to help us.

The same holds true for all Osage customs or practices found within this series. After extensive conversations with our cultural partners, we learned a great deal about the traditional clothing, weapons, and traits of Osage warriors in 1855. In addition, the Center's consultants worked closely with us on creating the Osage characters that will be included in future installments of the series, not only providing names but also guiding their dialogue and interactions. Naturally, any mistakes or inaccuracies in these details are the fault of the authors, and no one else.

In the end, *Legends of the Lost Causes* and its accompanying stories are meant to be enjoyed as magical fantasies full of adventure. But it is also our hope that this series grants young readers a larger awareness of the remarkable cultures of 1850s America, as well as a deeper recognition of the country's darker histories of slavery, cruelty, and violence. When we understand where we came from, we can steer the course of our lives into better harmony with one another.

To learn more about the Osage Nation, please visit osagenation -nsn.gov.

GOFISH

BRAD McLELLAND

What did you want to be when you grew up?
Believe it or not, I always wanted to be a writer. There was a brief occasion when I wanted to be a baseball legend, but I found I was much better at telling stories than hitting homers.

When did you realize you wanted to be a writer?
I was about ten years old when I officially figured it out. I would find a hideaway and spend hours writing spooky stories in notebooks. I haven't quit since!

What's your most embarrassing childhood memory?
One time I tipped over a tall endcap display at a department store and shattered glass all over the floor. Not my finest moment.

What's your favorite childhood memory?
My family and I had a big trampoline in our backyard. My favorite memory is lying on the trampoline at night with my mom, looking at the stars, and telling scary ghost stories to each other.

As a young person, who did you look up to most?
Elliott from *E.T. the Extra-Terrestrial*. I loved that he was just a kid, but he took a stand to help his alien friend survive and get home.

What was your favorite thing about school?
Getting to read awesome literature in English class (and playing freeze-tag at recess).

What were your hobbies as a kid? What are your hobbies now?
When I was eleven, I started playing the drums. I loved it so much I continued into adulthood and still play to this day.

Did you play sports as a kid?
I played a little baseball, but I couldn't hit the ball very well, so I switched to tae kwon do—and was actually pretty good.

What was your first job, and what was your worst job?
My first job was helping my brother-in-law in his carpentry business. I would fetch him tools, help paint houses, and run shingles up to rooftops. That was tough work, but it wasn't my worst job. The worst was picking blueberries at a blueberry farm when I was a college student. I was terrible at that.

What book is on your nightstand now?
Right now I'm reading *The Serpent's Secret* by Sayantani Das-Gupta, and it's incredible.

How did you celebrate publishing your first book?
My family bought me a giant chocolate sheet cake with the cover of *Legends* and plastic horses on top.

Where do you write your books?
I tend to skip around between coffee shops, my home office, and my favorite local restaurant, where they let me sit in a corner booth for hours and drink coffee.

What sparked your imagination for *Legends of the Lost Causes*?
When I was a kid, I used to watch old Western movies with my dad. I also used to read the Louis L'Amour novels that I would find in my grandmother's house. My love for those Western stories and my passion for spooky tales and fantasy quests eventually inspired *Legends.*

What challenges do you face in the writing process, and how do you overcome them?
The biggest challenge I face while writing is getting stuck in a difficult section. To overcome that, I pick up a great book and start reading.

What is your favorite word?
I've always loved the word *epiphany*, which means a moment of sudden revelation. Not only is it a beautiful word to speak, but getting an epiphany as a writer is an awesome occasion.

If you could live in any fictional world, what would it be?
I would love to live in Narnia. I think I could find a lot to write about there.

Who is your favorite fictional character?
Spider-Man. Even though he's incredibly powerful, he's also super funny and kind.

What was your favorite book when you were a kid? Do you have a favorite book now?

My favorite book when I was a kid was *The Secret of Terror Castle*, the first book in the Three Investigators junior detective series by Robert Arthur, Jr. My favorite book today is *The Book Thief* by Markus Zusak.

If you could travel in time, where would you go and what would you do?

I would travel back to the Mesozoic Era, so I could see all the dinosaurs for myself (though I probably would be too scared to stick around very long).

What's the best advice you have ever received about writing?

A teacher once told me to read as broadly as I can, and as many books as I can, if I wanted to be a writer. She was absolutely right.

What advice do you wish someone had given you when you were younger?

Be patient when you're pursuing your dreams and goals. Most times what you want doesn't happen overnight; you have to earn it slowly but surely, and that's okay. Earning your dream makes it that much more fulfilling when it happens.

Do you ever get writer's block? What do you do to get back on track?

Absolutely, I get writer's block all the time. It's a natural part of the writing process. Though it can be frustrating, I find that taking long walks is super helpful. But most of the time I can get rid of writer's block by picking up a good book and reading. I keep a notepad and pencil nearby, so that when I get an idea I jot it down immediately. After that, I can usually return to the story.

What do you want readers to remember about your books?
I want my readers to remember the emotion and heart I've worked hard to put into my stories. Sure, I want them to remember the adventure and magic and fun settings, but most importantly, I want them to look back on my characters and think, "Wow, that person felt *real* to me."

What would you do if you ever stopped writing?
I can't imagine my life without writing, but if I did have to stop, I would probably work with my wife to open a coffee shop or a sanctuary for cats. Or maybe a coffee shop for cats?

If you were a superhero, what would your superpower be?
My power would be the ability to analyze all possible outcomes of a choice, like Dr. Strange can do. I could examine every possibility and then choose the one with the best outcome for me and everyone.

Do you have any strange or funny habits? Did you when you were a kid?
When I was a kid, I had a habit of hiding from people for fun, and then leaping out and scaring them (actually, I still do that today). My strange habit now is drumming on everything. I tap-tap-tap on every surface around me. It kinda gets on my family's nerves, but I can't stop.

What do you consider to be your greatest accomplishment?
I'm tempted to say getting my first book published, because it took a long time, but that seems tiny compared to the accomplishment of being a good stepdad. I'm extremely proud of that.

What would your readers be most surprised to learn about you?
That I have a bunch of tattoos—like, a *bunch*. Also, that I'm really goofy and don't mind embarrassing myself to get a laugh.

GOFISH

LOUIS SYLVESTER

What did you want to be when you grew up?
I wanted to be a reader. I would hurry to get my homework done so that I could get back to my books. I didn't think there were any jobs in the world that would just let me read, though, so I told people that I didn't know what I wanted to do. Now I'm a college professor and reading is a big part of my occupation, so I finally figured it out.

When did you realize you wanted to be a writer?
As a kid, I tried to write short stories, but I never seemed to be able to finish what I started. Then when I was a teenager, I saw a terrible movie. The story was ridiculous, the dialogue was silly. I hated every aspect of the movie. I complained about it the whole way home until one of my friends said, "Why don't you just write your own story?" His words really shook me. If I had a better story, there was nothing stopping me from creating it. So I started writing a screenplay and I finished it. Once I realized that I could finish a story, I started writing all the time.

What's your most embarrassing childhood memory?
When I was seven, my mother told me to clean up my room before I went to school. Instead of obeying, I shoved all of my

toys into the closet and told her that I had finished. Later that day, I was in homeroom and my mother walked into my second-grade class. She loudly announced that I had lied about cleaning my room and had to go home and do it right. She hauled me out of school and sent me to my room, explaining that I could not go back to school until I put my toys away properly. I cried for about an hour, then I cleaned up my room better than ever before. To this day I keep a pretty clean home. I also learned that it takes less time to just do the job correctly the first time.

What's your favorite childhood memory?
When I was a kid, a new game called *Dungeons & Dragons* had been released. My friend introduced me to the game. I asked my mother if she would buy me a copy. I knew that we did not have any extra money for games, but my mother saw how excited I was and took me straight to the game store to buy the basic set box for *Dungeons & Dragons*.

As a young person, who did you look up to most?
Han Solo.

What was your favorite thing about school?
Reading books. I loved whenever teachers allowed free reading.

What were your hobbies as a kid? What are your hobbies now?
Reading, of course. I am also a huge gamer. I started with *Dungeons & Dragons* (and still play today.) In addition to role-playing games, I also play board games and card games. My wife and I have turned our basement into a game room,

and we have over a thousand games. Walking into our basement is like walking into a game store. We go to a couple of tabletop gaming conventions each year including BoardGameGeek Con, where we play board games for five days straight.

Did you play sports as a kid?
I tried soccer when I was eight. I was terrible. The coach told me to stay out of the way of the other kids.

What was your first job, and what was your worst job?
My first job was making pizza at a place called Crusty's Pizza. I worked for three weeks and then they went out of business. I've never had a "worst" job, but I've worked for a couple different places as an accountant, and I never felt like those jobs were fulfilling. That is why I went back to school to get my PhD in English, so that I could focus on a job that allowed me to read and write and be creative.

What book is on your nightstand now?
Each year I try to read the Hugo nominations for best sci-fi novel. Currently I'm reading John Scalzi's excellent *The Collapsing Empire*. I also am reading a role-playing game rulebook for one-on-one playing called *Cthulhu Confidential*. I hope to play this game with my wife soon.

How did you celebrate publishing your first book?
Dinner with my wife.

Where do you write your books?
I sit on my couch with my laptop. I have a can of Pepsi nearby.

What sparked your imagination for *Legends of the Lost Causes*?
Working with my partner, Brad, is an exercise in sparking imagination. We build off each other. Brad will throw an idea at me and it will inspire something new, and I'll toss my new idea back and he'll be inspired with another cool idea. We go back and forth like this throughout the plotting and writing process.

What challenges do you face in the writing process, and how do you overcome them?
Sometimes I will have an idea that I think would be cool in the book series and Brad will not like it. On other occasions, he'll have an idea that doesn't work for me. The challenge we both deal with is learning how to be open to criticism without getting our feelings hurt.

What is your favorite word?
I'm a reader. I engage with wonderful words every single day. Today the word I'm enjoying is *fib*, which I define as a lie that hasn't fully grown up yet.

If you could live in any fictional world, what would it be?
The Star Trek universe.

Who is your favorite fictional character?
I'm partial to the insane ivory trader, Kurtz, in Joseph Conrad's *Heart of Darkness*.

What was your favorite book when you were a kid? Do you have a favorite book now?
My favorite when I was a kid was *The Book of Three* (part one of the Chronicles of Prydain) by Lloyd Alexander. It was my

first introduction to the world of fantasy. The greatest book I've ever read is *Heart of Darkness* by Joseph Conrad. My current favorite book is *The First Fifteen Lives of Harry August* by the utterly brilliant Claire North.

If you could travel in time, where would you go and what would you do?
I would go to the future in hopes that we have turned the world into a Star Trek paradise. Once there, I would play on the holodeck.

What's the best advice you have ever received about writing?
I had a teacher tell me that I have to pay attention to every single word I write. I heard this advice from every writing teacher I ever had, but it took about nine creative writing classes for me to really believe it.

The lesson that took me so long to learn is that writing is mostly editing. I thought that writing was about getting words on the page, but really that is only the first step. Writing is actually about writing, then rewriting, and then rewriting some more. I thought good writers were just brilliant and that awesome stories flowed out of their fingertips. But the truth is that good writers write terrible first drafts, but they keep editing and rewriting until the story is perfect.

What advice do you wish someone had given you when you were younger?
It's okay to fail. My whole childhood was spent trying not to make a mistake or get something wrong. I wish I had understood that it was okay to mess up. I often refused to try new things because I was afraid I would fail. But how can you learn if you aren't willing to fail? The best way to learn is to try something and fail and then try again.

Do you ever get writer's block? What do you do to get back on track?

Sure. Writer's block is normal. If I'm stuck on how a scene should play out, I'll think about the problem right before I go to bed and when I wake up, I'll have an interesting idea. I let my subconscious do the thinking. If I know what is supposed to happen in the story but I can't seem to get myself to write, that is usually because my mind is being lazy. To kick it into gear, I'll start writing the worst thing ever and after a few sentences, my lazy mind will say, "This is terrible." And then my brain will open up and start allowing me to write again just so I'll stop writing terrible nonsense.

What do you want readers to remember about your books?

I hope my readers will remember the characters with fondness. I hope they even remember the villains with a smile.

What would you do if you ever stopped writing?

I'm a college professor, so I have another job. But if I wasn't writing, then I'd work with my wife designing board games.

If you were a superhero, what would your superpower be?

My power would be luck. I think that everything working out would be the best power ever.

Do you have any strange or funny habits? Did you when you were a kid?

My strange habit is that I read all the time. I'll read while waiting in line at the supermarket. I also have a gross habit. I nibble on my fingernails and my wife hates that I do this.

What do you consider to be your greatest accomplishment?
Earning a PhD in English was a lot of work.

What would your readers be most surprised to learn about you?
I don't like coffee. When I'm trying to wake up in the morning, I'll drink Pepsi.

Their next mission? Find the mysterious land of Bonfire Crossing and defeat a powerful sorcerer who is one step away from being unstoppable. If it sounds like a lost cause, they're the best vigilante orphans for the job.

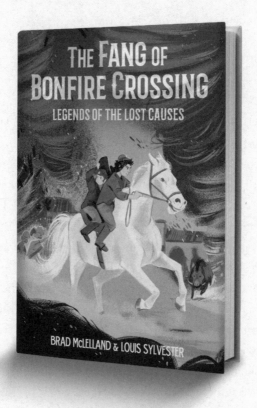

KEEP READING FOR AN EXCERPT.

CHAPTER 1

THE TRACKER

Keech Blackwood knelt beside a plump cottonwood tree, inspecting two small dips in the frozen soil. They were shaped like bowls and sat a few inches apart, each covered in leaves and brittle twigs. One hollow was larger than the other, and when Keech ran his palm over the dirt cavities, he realized a short tunnel connected the two dips below the ground.

He grinned in admiration.

The November day was standoffish with cold. Pockets of light snow and ice dappled the Kansas forest—a decline in the weather that felt too early for these parts. A heavy mist clung to the hills, turning the region ghost-pale.

Tethered to the cottonwood, Keech's pony, Felix, blustered at the cold. Keech pointed to the ground with a smile. "Felix, do you know what these holes make? A Dakota pit."

The pony gazed off into the woods, unimpressed.

"I haven't seen one of these in a long time."

Keech poked his finger down into the dirt and felt the void of the little tunnel. *Read the earth*, his foster father, Pa Abner, used to say. *Let it tell you its story*. The history here was blurry, but one tell-tale sign was clear: Whoever had filled these holes had done it willy-nilly, sliding the dirt back in with the side of one foot.

"Something interrupted you," Keech murmured, envisioning the traveler standing here. "You didn't want to leave your camp, but you had no choice."

He peered around the campsite for signs of quick passage. There were none, not even horse tracks. Disappointed, he returned his scrutiny to the indentations.

"You were sloppy to fill the holes too quick, but smart enough to erase your prints. And crafty enough to build a Dakota pit in the first place."

Those who knew of Dakota fire pits understood they had two purposes. They concealed the traveler's firelight below the ground, and their tunnel-and-vent design left no rising smoke for enemies to see. Keech had learned to build one five years ago, when he was only eight. His orphan brother Sam had been seven. Pa Abner had taken them on a two-week hunting trip up to Nodaway country. The first week, Pa had taught them how to build the fire pit and how to cook small game. The following Sunday, he instructed them to leave no sign of their camps, then left them alone for five days in the wilderness to practice. The excursion had pushed Keech and Sam to their limits, but after the week was done, Pa rewarded them with a sackful of Granny's homemade peanut brittle and a special campfire recitation of Edgar Allan Poe's "The Raven," one of Sam's favorite poems.

The memory warmed Keech's heart. It was nice to see Sam's face in his mind again. The past few days he'd been trying to remember every little tidbit about Sam—as well as Granny Nell and the others,

Robby, Little Eugena, Patrick. He'd also been trying to cherish all the memories he could of Pa Abner, whose real name, whose Enforcer name, had been Isaiah Raines. Forgetting the family that Bad Whiskey Nelson had murdered would be easier than suffering alone in their haunting memories, but Keech knew he could no more forget their faces than stop breathing.

A fierce breeze rustled around the cottonwood, fluttering Keech's dark bangs. He tucked the hair back into his bowler hat and returned his focus to the buried camp.

"Could be the Kickapoo," he said to Felix. The Kickapoo tribe resided on lands not far from here, and they would be careful not to build fires that the harsh Kansas winds could sweep across the hills and plains.

Widening his sweep of the ground, Keech realized it wasn't the Kickapoo. Whoever had built this fire pit had slipped up, leaving a clue: a heel print at the base of the cottonwood. The heel was from a large boot, not a moccasin.

"Maybe this print belongs to Red Jeffreys," Keech said.

Red Jeffreys was the Enforcer who had apparently stolen the Char Stone from the grave of his mother, Erin Blackwood, in Bone Ridge Cemetery. In the Stone's place, the thief had left a peculiar trinket in Keech's mother's hands—a child's figurine with a carved wooden head, a doll Keech now carried in his coat pocket.

Before dying, Pa Abner had told Keech that a devilish fiend known as the Reverend Rose had now set his dark sights on this Jeffreys and that Rose wouldn't stop hunting till his gang of killers found the man and retrieved the Stone.

What Rose wanted with the Char Stone was still a mystery, but Bad Whiskey had claimed it would thwart damnation itself.